THE EYE OF MINDS

www.totallyrandombooks.co.uk

JAMES DASHNER

THE EYE OF MINDS

DOUBLEDAY

THE EYE OF MINDS
A DOUBLEDAY BOOK 978 0 857 53313 5
TRADE PAPERBACK 978 0 857 53314 2

Published in the United States by Delacorte Press,
an imprint of Random House Children's Books,
a division of Random House, Inc., New York.

Published in Great Britain by Doubleday,
an imprint of Random House Children's Publishers UK
A Random House Group Company

This edition published 2013

1 3 5 7 9 10 8 6 4 2

The Random House Group Limited supports the Forest Stewardship Council® (FSC®),
the leading international forest-certification organisation. Our books carrying the
FSC label are printed on FSC®-certified paper. FSC is the only forest-certification scheme
supported by the leading environmental organisations, including Greenpeace.
Our paper procurement policy can be found at www.randomhouse.co.uk/environment

Set in Adobe Garamond

RANDOM HOUSE CHILDREN'S PUBLISHERS UK
61–63 Uxbridge Road, London W5 5SA

www.randomhousechildrens.co.uk
www.totallyrandombooks.co.uk
www.randomhouse.co.uk

Addresses for companies within The Random House Group Limited
can be found at: www.randomhouse.co.uk/offices.htm

THE RANDOM HOUSE GROUP Limited Reg. No. 954009

A CIP catalogue record for this book is available from the British Library.

Printed and bound in the UK by Clays Ltd, St Ives plc

*This book is dedicated
to Michael Bourret and Krista Marino,
for making my career,
and for being good friends.*

CHAPTER 1

THE COFFIN

1

Michael spoke against the wind, to a girl named Tanya.

"I know it's water down there, but it might as well be concrete. You'll be flat as a pancake the second you hit."

Not the most comforting choice of words when talking to someone who wanted to end her life, but it was certainly the truth. Tanya had just climbed over the railing of the Golden Gate Bridge, cars zooming by on the road, and was leaning back toward the open air, her twitchy hands holding on to a pole wet with mist. Even if somehow Michael could talk her out of jumping, those slippery fingers might get the job done anyway. And then it'd be lights-out. He pictured some poor sap of a fisherman thinking he'd finally caught the big one, only to reel in a nasty surprise.

"Stop joking," the trembling girl responded. "It's not a game—not anymore."

Michael was inside the VirtNet—the Sleep, to people

who went in as often as he did. He was used to seeing scared people there. A lot of them. Yet underneath the fear was usually the *knowing*. Knowing deep down that no matter what was happening in the Sleep, it wasn't real.

Not with Tanya. Tanya was different. At least, her Aura, her computer-simulated counterpart, was. Her Aura had this bat-crazy look of pure terror on her face, and it suddenly gave Michael chills—made him feel like *he* was the one hovering over that long drop to death. And Michael wasn't a big fan of death, fake or not.

"It *is* a game, and you know it," he said louder than he'd wanted to—he didn't want to startle her. But a cold wind had sprung up, and it seemed to grab his words and whisk them down to the bay. "Get back over here and let's talk. We'll both get our Experience Points, and we can go explore the city, get to know each other. Find some crazies to spy on. Maybe even hack some free food from the shops. It'll be good times. And when we're done, we'll find you a Portal, and you can Lift back home. Take a break from the game for a while."

"This has nothing to do with *Lifeblood*!" Tanya screamed at him. The wind pulled at her clothes, and her dark hair fanned out behind her like laundry on a line. "Just go away and leave me alone. I don't want your pretty-boy face to be the last thing I see."

Michael thought of *Lifeblood Deep,* the next level, the goal of all goals. Where everything was a thousand times more real, more advanced, more intense. He was three years away from earning his way inside. Maybe two. But right then he needed to talk this dopey girl out of jumping to her date with the fishes or he'd be sent back to the Suburbs for a week, making *Lifeblood Deep* that much further away.

"Okay, look . . ." He was trying to choose his words carefully, but he'd already made a pretty big mistake and knew it. Going out of character and using the game itself as a reason for her to stop what she was doing meant he'd be docked points big-time. And it was all about the points. But this girl was legitimately starting to scare him. It was that face—pale and sunken, as if she'd already died.

"Just go away!" she yelled. "You don't get it. I'm trapped here. Portals or no Portals. I'm trapped! He won't let me Lift!"

Michael wanted to scream right back at her—she was talking nonsense. A dark part of him wanted to say forget it, tell her she was a loser, let her nosedive. She was being so stubborn—it wasn't like any of it was really happening. *It's just a game.* He had to remind himself of that all the time.

But he couldn't mess this up. He needed the points. "All right. Listen." He took a step back, held his hands up like he was trying to calm a scared animal. "We just met—give it some time. I promise I won't do anything nutty. You wanna jump, I'll let you jump. But at least talk to me. Tell me why."

Tears lined her cheeks; her eyes had gone red and puffy. "Just go away. Please." Her voice had taken on the softness of defeat. "I'm not messing around here. I'm done with this—all of this!"

"Done? Okay, that's fine to be done. But you don't have

to screw it up for me, too, right?" Michael figured maybe it was okay to talk about the game after all, since she was using it as her reason to end it—to check out of the Virtual-Flesh-and-Bones Hotel and never come back. "Seriously. Walk back to the Portal with me, Lift yourself, do it the right way. You're done with the game, you're safe, I get my points. Ain't that the happiest ending you ever heard of?"

"I hate you," she spat. Literally. A spray of misty saliva. "I don't even know you and I hate you. This has nothing to do with *Lifeblood*!"

"Then tell me what it *does* have to do with." He said it kindly, trying to keep his composure. "You've got all day to jump. Just give me a few minutes. Talk to me, Tanya."

She buried her head in the crook of her right arm. "I just can't do it anymore." She whimpered and her shoulders shook, making Michael worry about her grip again. "I can't."

Some people are just weak, he thought, though he wasn't stupid enough to say it.

Lifeblood was by *far* the most popular game in the Virt-Net. Yeah, you could go off to some nasty battlefield in the Civil War or fight dragons with a magic sword, fly space-ships, explore the freaky love shacks. But that stuff got old quick. In the end, nothing was more fascinating than bare-bones, dirt-in-your-face, gritty, get-me-out-of-here real life. Nothing. And there were some, like Tanya, who obviously couldn't handle it. Michael sure could. He'd risen up its ranks almost as quickly as legendary gamer Gunner Skale.

"Come on, Tanya," he said. "How can it hurt to talk to me? And if you're going to quit, why would you want to end your last game by killing yourself so violently?"

Her head snapped up and she looked at him with eyes so hard he shivered again.

"Kaine's haunted me for the last time," she said. "He can't just trap me here and use me for an experiment—sic the KillSims on me. I'm gonna rip my Core out."

Those last words changed everything. Michael watched in horror as Tanya tightened her grip on the pole with one hand, then reached up with the other and started digging into her own flesh.

2

Michael forgot the game, forgot the points. The situation had gone from annoying to actual life-and-death. In all his years of playing, he'd never seen someone code out their Core, destroying the barrier device within the Coffin that kept the virtual world and the real world separate in their mind.

"Stop that!" he yelled, one foot already on the railing. "Stop!"

He jumped down onto the catwalk on the outer edge of the bridge and froze. He was just a few feet from her now, and he wanted to avoid any quick movements that might cause her to panic. Holding his hands out, he took a small step toward her.

"Don't do that," Michael said as softly as he could in the biting wind.

Tanya kept digging into her right temple. She'd peeled back pieces of her skin; a stream of blood from the wound quickly covered her hands and the side of her face in red gore. A look of terrifying calmness had come over her, as if she had no concept of what she was doing to herself, though Michael knew well enough that she was busy hacking the code.

"Stop coding for one second!" Michael shouted. "Would you just talk about this before you rip your freaking *Core* out? You know what that means."

"Why do you care so much?" she responded, so quietly that Michael had to read her lips to understand. But at least she'd stopped digging.

Michael just stared. Because she *had* stopped digging and was now reaching inside the torn mass of flesh with her thumb and forefinger. "You just want your Experience Points," she said. Slowly, she pulled out a small metallic chip slick with blood.

"I'll forfeit my points," Michael said, trying to hide his fear and disgust. "I swear. You can't mess around anymore, Tanya. Code that thing back in and come talk to me. It's not too late."

She held up the visual manifestation of the Core, gazed at it with fascination. "Don't you see the irony in all this?" she asked. "If it weren't for my coding skills, I probably wouldn't even know who Kaine was. About his KillSims and his plans for me. But I'm good at it, and because of that . . . *monster*, I just programmed the Core right out of my own head."

"Not your real head. It's still just a simulation, Tanya. It's not too late." Michael couldn't remember a time in his entire life when he'd felt that ill.

She looked at him so sharply that he took a step backward. "I can't take it anymore. I can't take . . . *him* anymore. He can't use me if I'm dead. I'm done."

She curled the Core onto her thumb, then flicked it toward Michael. It flew over his shoulder—he saw flashes of sunlight glint off it as it spun through the air, almost like it was winking at him, saying, *Hey, buddy, you suck at suicide negotiations.* It landed with a *plink* somewhere out in the traffic, where it would be crushed in seconds.

He couldn't believe what he was witnessing. Someone so sophisticated at manipulating code that she could destroy her Core—the device that essentially protected players' brains while they were in the Sleep. Without your Core, your brain wouldn't be able to filter the stimulation of the VirtNet properly. If your Core died in the Sleep, you'd die in the Wake. He didn't know *anyone* who'd seen this before. Two hours earlier he'd been eating stolen bleu chips at the Dan the Man Deli with his best friends. All he wanted now was to be back there, eating turkey on rye, enduring Bryson's jokes about old ladies' underwear and listening to Sarah tell him how awful his latest Sleep haircut was.

"If Kaine comes for *you*," Tanya said, "tell him that I won in the end. Tell him how brave I was. He can trap people here and steal all the bodies he wants. But not mine."

Michael was done talking. He couldn't take one more word out of this girl's blood-smeared mouth. As quickly as anything he'd ever done in his life, as any character in any game, he jumped toward the pole she clung to.

She screamed, momentarily frozen by his sudden action, but then she let go, actually pushed herself away from the bridge. Michael grabbed for the railing to his left with one hand and reached for her with the other but missed both. His feet hit something solid, then slipped. Arms flailing, he felt nothing but air, and he fell, almost in sync with her.

An incredible shriek escaped his mouth, something he would've been embarrassed about if his only companion wasn't about to lose her life. With her Core coded out, her death would be real.

Michael and Tanya fell toward the harsh gray waters of the bay. Wind tore at their clothes, and Michael's heart felt like it was creeping along the inside of his chest, up his throat. He screamed again. On some level he knew he would hit the water, feel the pain; then he'd be Lifted and wake up back home, safe and sound in his Coffin. But the VirtNet's power was feigned reality, and right now the reality was terror.

Somehow Michael's and Tanya's Auras found each other on that long fall, chest to chest, like tandem skydivers. As the churning surface below rushed toward them, they wrapped their arms around each other, pulling closer together. Michael wanted to scream again but clamped his jaw shut when he saw the complete calmness on her face.

Her eyes bored into Michael's, searched him, and found him, and he broke somewhere on the inside.

They hit the water as hard as he thought they would. Hard as concrete. Hard as death.

3

The moment of pain was short but intense. Everywhere, all at once, bursting and exploding through Michael's every nerve. He didn't even have time to make a sound before it ended; neither did Tanya, because he heard nothing but the distinct and horrific crash of hitting the water's surface. And then it all dissipated and his mind went blank.

Michael was alive, back in the NerveBox—what most people called the Coffin—Lifted from the Sleep.

The same couldn't be said for the girl. A wave of sadness, then disbelief, hit him. With his own eyes, he'd seen her change her code, rip the Core from her virtual flesh, then toss it away like nothing more than a crumb. When it ended for her, it ended for real, and being a part of it made Michael's insides feel twisted up. He'd never witnessed anything like it.

He blinked a few times, waiting for the unlinking process to be complete. Never before had he been so relieved to be done with the VirtNet, done with a game, ready to get out of his box and breathe in the polluted air of the real world.

A blue light came on, revealing the door of the Coffin just a few inches from his face. The LiquiGels and AirPuffs had already receded, leaving the only part Michael truly hated, no matter how many times he did it—which was way more than he could count. Thin, icy strands of NerveWire pulled out of his neck and back and arms, slithering like snakes along his skin until they disappeared into their little hidey-holes, where they'd be disinfected and stored for his next game. His parents were amazed that he voluntarily let those things burrow into his body so often, and he couldn't blame them. There was something downright creepy about it.

A loud click was followed by a mechanical clank and then a whooshing gust of air. The door of the Coffin began to rise, swinging up and away on its hinges like Dracula's very own resting place. Michael almost laughed at the thought. Being a vicious bloodsucking vampire loved by the ladies was only one of a billion things a person could do inside the Sleep. Only one of a billion.

He stood up carefully—he always felt a little woozy after being Lifted, especially when he'd been gone for a few hours—naked and covered in sweat. Clothing ruined the sensory stimulation of the NerveBox.

Michael stepped over the lip of the box, thankful for the soft carpet under his toes—it made him feel grounded, back in reality. He grabbed the pair of boxers he'd left on the floor, put them on. He figured a decent person probably would've opted for some pants and a T-shirt as well, but he wasn't feeling so decent at the moment. All he'd been asked to do by the *Lifeblood* game was talk a girl out of suicide for Experience Points, and not only had he failed, he'd helped drive her to do it for real. For *real*, for real.

Tanya—wherever her body might be—was dead. She'd

ripped out her Core before dying, a feat of programming, protected by passwords, that she only could've done to herself. Faking a Core removal wasn't possible in the VirtNet. It was too dangerous. Otherwise, you'd never know if someone *was* faking, and people would do it left and right for kicks or to get reactions. No, she'd changed her code, removed the safety barrier in her mind that separated the virtual and the real, and fried the actual implant back home, and she'd done it with purpose. Tanya, the pretty girl with the sad eyes and the delusions that she was being haunted. Dead.

Michael knew it'd be in the NewsBops soon. They'd report that he had been with her, and the VNS—VirtNet Security—would probably come and talk to him about it. They definitely would.

Dead. She was dead. As lifeless as the sagging mattress on his bed.

It all hit him then. Hit him like a fastball to the face.

Michael barely made it to the bathroom before throwing up everything in his stomach. And then he collapsed to the floor and pulled himself into a ball. No tears came—he wasn't the crying sort—but he stayed there for a long time.

CHAPTER 2

THE PROPOSITION

1

Michael knew that most people, when they felt as if the earth itself decided it just didn't like them anymore, when they felt like they were at the bottom of a dark pit, went to their mom or dad. Maybe a brother, maybe a sister. Those with none of the above might find themselves knocking at the door of an aunt, a grandpa, a third cousin twice removed.

But not Michael. He went to Bryson and Sarah, the two best friends a person could ever ask for. They knew him like no one else, and they didn't care what he said or did or wore or ate. And he returned the favor whenever they needed him. But there was something very strange about their friendship.

Michael had never met them.

Not literally, anyway. Not yet. They were VirtNet friends through and through, though. He'd gotten to know them first in the beginning levels of *Lifeblood,* and they'd grown closer and closer the higher up they went. The three of them had joined forces almost from the day they met to move up in the Game of all Games. They were the Terrible Trio, the Trifecta to Dissect-ya, the Burn-and-Pillage-y Trilogy. Their nicknames didn't make them many friends—they'd been branded cocky by some, idiots by others—but they had fun, so they didn't care.

The bathroom floor was hard, and Michael couldn't lie there forever, so he pulled himself together and headed straight for his favorite place on earth to sit.

The Chair.

It was just a normal piece of furniture, but it was the most comfortable thing he'd ever sat on, like sinking into a man-made cloud. He had some thinking to do, and he needed to arrange a meeting with his best friends. He plopped down and looked out the window at the sad gray exterior of the apartment complex across the street. It looked like a dreary rainstorm frozen solid.

The only thing marring the bleakness was a huge sign advertising *Lifeblood Deep*—bloodred letters on a black plaque, nothing else. As if the game designers were fully aware that the words alone were all they needed. Everyone knew them, and everyone wanted in on the action, wanted to earn the right to go there someday. Michael was like every other player—just one of the herd.

He thought of Gunner Skale, the greatest player in *Lifeblood* the VirtNet had ever known. But the man had disappeared off the grid recently—rumor had it he'd been swallowed by the Deep itself, lost in the game he'd loved so much. Skale was a legend, and gamer after gamer had gone searching for him in the darkest corners of the Sleep—fruitlessly, as it turned out. At least, so far. Michael wanted nothing more than to reach that kind of level, to become the world's new Gunner Skale. He just had to do it before the new guy on the scene. This . . . *Kaine.*

Michael squeezed his EarCuff—the small piece of metal attached to his earlobe—and his NetScreen and keyboard flashed on before him, hovering in midair. The Bulletin showed him that Bryson was already online and that Sarah had said she'd be back in a few.

Michael's fingers began to dance across the shining red keys.

> **Mikethespike:** Hey, Bryson, quit gawkin' at the Gorgozon nests and talk to me. I saw some serious business today.

His friend's response was almost instant; Bryson spent even more time than Michael online or in the Coffin—and typed like a secretary filled with three cups of coffee.

> **Brystones:** Serious, huh? A *Lifeblood* cop bust you at the Dunes again? Remember, they only come by every 13 minutes!
>
> **Mikethespike:** I told you what I was doing. Had to stop that chick from jumping off the bridge. Didn't go so hot.

Brystones: Why? She nosedive?

Mikethespike: Don't think I should talk about it here. We need to meet up in the Sleep.

Brystones: Dude, it must've been bad. We were just there a few hours ago—can we meet 2morrow?

Mikethespike: Just meet me back at the deli. One hour. Get Sarah there, too. I gotta go shower. I smell like armpits.

Brystones: Glad we're not meeting in real life, then. Not too fond of the B.O.

Mikethespike: Speaking of that—we need to just do it. Meet for real. You don't live THAT far away.

Brystones: But the Wake is so boring. What's the point?

Mikethespike: Because that's what humans do. They meet each other and shake real hands.

Brystones: I'd rather give you a hug on Mars.

Mikethespike: NO HUGS. See you in an hour. Get Sarah!

Brystones: Will do. Go scrub your nasty pits.

Mikethespike: I said I SMELL like them, not . . . Never mind. Later.

Brystones: Out.

Michael squeezed his EarCuff and watched the NetScreen and keyboard dissolve like a stiff wind had blown through. Then, after one last glance at the *Lifeblood Deep* ad—its red-on-black letters like a taunt, names like Gunner Skale and Kaine floating through his head—he headed for the shower.

2

The VirtNet was a funny thing. It was so real that sometimes Michael wished it wasn't as high-tech. Like when he was hot and sweaty or when he tripped and stubbed a toe or when a girl smacked him in the face. The Coffin made him feel every last bit of it—the only other option was to adjust for less sensory input, but then why bother playing if you didn't go all the way?

The same realism that created the pain and discomfort in the Sleep sometimes had a positive side, though. The food. Especially when you're good enough at coding to take what you want when you're a little short on cash. Eyes closed to access the raw data, manipulate a few lines of programming, and voilà—a free feast.

Michael sat with Bryson and Sarah at their usual table outside of Dan the Man's Deli, attacking a huge plate of the Groucho Nachos, while back in the real world the Coffin was feeding them pure, healthy nutrients intravenously. A person couldn't rely solely on the Coffin's nutrition function, of course—it wasn't something meant to sustain human life for months at a time—but it sure was nice during the long sessions. And the best part was that you only got fat in the Sleep if you programmed yourself that way, no matter how much you ate.

Despite the delicious food, their conversation quickly took a depressing turn.

"I read it on the NewsBops as soon as Bryson told me," Sarah said. Her appearance in the VirtNet was understated—a pretty face, long brown hair, tan skin, almost no makeup. "There's been a few Core recodings in the last week or so. Gives me the heebie-jeebies. Rumor is that this guy Kaine is somehow trapping people inside the Sleep, not letting them wake up. So some of them kill themselves. Can you believe it? A cyber-terrorist."

Bryson was nodding. He looked like a damaged football player—big, thick, and everything just a little off-kilter. He always said he was so freaking hot in the real world that he needed an escape from the ladies while hanging in the Virt-Net. "Heebie-jeebies?" he repeated. "Our good friend here saw a girl dig into her own skull and pull her Core out, toss it, then jump off a bridge. I guess heebie-jeebies is a start."

"Fine—I guess I need a stronger word," she replied. "The point is something's happening, and a gamer's being blamed for it. Who ever heard of people hacking into their own systems to commit suicide? VirtNet Security has never had this problem before."

"Unless VNS has been hiding it," Bryson added.

"Who would do what she did?" Michael murmured, more to himself than to the others. He knew his stuff, and suicides within the Sleep had always been rare. *Real* suicides, anyway. "Some people like the rush of offing themselves in the Sleep without the real consequences—but I've never seen this before. The skill and knowledge to pull it off . . . I don't even think I could do it. Now several in a week?"

"And what about this gamer—Kaine?" Bryson asked. "I've heard he's big-time, but how could someone possibly trap others inside the Sleep? It has to be all talk."

The tables around them had just grown quiet, and the name seemed to echo throughout the room. People stared at Bryson, and Michael understood why. Kaine was becoming infamous, and the name made people pale. Over the last few months, he'd been infiltrating everything from games to private meeting rooms, terrorizing his victims with visions and physically attacking them. Michael hadn't heard the part about trapping people until Tanya, but the very name Kaine haunted the virtual world, as if he lingered just out of sight no matter where you went. Bryson was all fake bravado.

Michael shrugged off the other customers in the café and focused on his friends. "She kept saying it was Kaine's fault. That she was trapped by him and couldn't take it anymore. Something about stealing bodies? And things called Kill-Sims. I'm telling you, even before she started on that Core, I could see it in her eyes that she was dead serious. She definitely ran across him somewhere."

"We don't even know much about the guy behind Kaine yet," Sarah offered. "I've read every story on him, and that's all there are—stories. No one has any scoop on the gamer himself. No pics, no audio or video, nothing. It's like he's not real."

"It's the *VirtNet*," Bryson countered. "Things don't have to be *real* to be real. That's the whole point."

"No." Sarah shook her head. "He's a gamer. A person. Lying in a Coffin. With all that publicity we should know more about him. The media should be all over this guy. The VNS should be able to track him, at least."

Michael felt like they were getting nowhere. "Hey, back to me, guys. I'm supposed to be traumatized, and you're supposed to be making me feel better. So far, you suck at it."

A look of genuine concern crossed Bryson's face. "No doubt, dude. Sorry, but glad it was you, not me. I know that whole suicide negotiation thing is part of the *Lifeblood* experience stuff, but who could've known yours would be a real one? I probably wouldn't sleep for a week after seeing something like that."

"Still sucking," Michael replied with a halfhearted laugh. In truth, he was better now just being with his friends, but something inside him felt like it was trying to gnaw its way out. Something dark with big teeth that didn't want him to ignore it.

Sarah leaned over and squeezed his arm. "Neither of us has a clue what it must've been like," she said softly. "And we'd be idiots to pretend. But I'm sorry it happened."

Michael just blushed and looked at the floor. Thankfully, Bryson brought them back to reality.

"I gotta use the bathroom," he announced, standing up. A person even did stuff like that inside the Sleep, while your real body took care of business back in the Coffin. Everything was meant to feel real. Everything.

"Charming," Sarah said through a sigh as she released Michael's arm and sat back in her chair. "Simply charming."

3

They talked for another hour or so, ending with their usual promise to meet in the real world soon. Bryson told them if they didn't do it by the end of the month, he'd start cutting off a finger every day until it happened. Michael's, not his own. That got a much-needed laugh.

The three of them said their goodbyes at a Portal, and Michael Lifted back to the Wake, going through the usual routine inside the Coffin until he could get out. As he walked over to the Chair, his gaze naturally landed on the big ad for *Lifeblood Deep* outside his window, followed by the usual few seconds of coveting and figurative drooling. He almost sat down but changed his mind, knowing he'd never get up, exhausted and sore head to toe. And he hated falling asleep in the Chair—he always woke up with cricks in places humans weren't meant to have cricks.

He sighed and, trying not to think of the girl named Tanya who'd killed herself right before his eyes, somehow made it over to his bed. Then he collapsed into a long night of dreamless sleep.

4

Getting himself out of bed the next morning was like breaking out of a cocoon. It took twenty minutes for the smart side of his brain to convince the stupid side that taking a sick day at school wasn't a good idea. He'd already been out seven times this semester. One or two more and they'd start cracking down.

He'd only gotten more sore in the night from his plummet into the bay with Tanya, and that strange feeling still turned in his stomach. Somehow, though, Michael made it to the breakfast table, where his nanny, Helga, had just placed a plate of eggs and bacon. A nanny, his amazing VirtNet setup, a nice apartment—he had a lot to thank his wealthy parents for. They traveled a lot, and at the moment he couldn't remember when they'd left or when they were getting back. But they made it up to him with the many things they gave him. Between school, the VirtNet, and Helga, he hardly had time to miss them.

"Good morning, Michael," Helga said with her slight but still noticeable German accent. "I trust you slept well, yes?"

He grunted, and she smiled. That's why he loved Helga. She didn't get all huffy or offended when all you wanted to do was grunt like an animal waking from hibernation. It was no skin off her back.

And her food was delicious. Almost as good as in the VirtNet. Michael finished every morsel of breakfast, then headed out the door to catch the train.

The streets were bustling—suits and skirts and coffee cups as far as the eye could see. There were so many people that

Michael could almost swear they were doubling like repro-ducing cells right before his eyes. Everyone had the usual blank, bored look that Michael knew well. Like him, they'd suffer and slog through their dreary jobs or school until they could get back home and enter the VirtNet once again.

Michael entered the flow, dodging commuters left and right, and made his way down the avenue, then turned right at his usual shortcut—a one-way alley full of trash cans and piles of garbage. He couldn't understand why the discarded trash never seemed to actually make it into the big metal containers. But on a morning like this, sharing the street with empty chip bags and discarded banana peels beat the heck out of the marching masses.

He was halfway to the other side of the alley when the screech of tires stopped him in his tracks. The surge of an engine reverberated up the street from behind and Michael spun around. The instant he saw the oncoming car—its paint gray and dull, like a dying storm—he knew. He knew that this car had something to do with him and that it wasn't going to have a happy ending.

He turned and ran, recognizing on some level that who-ever was after him had planned to trap him in that alley. The end seemed miles away now; he'd never make it. The sound of the car grew louder as it gained on him, and de-spite all the strange and crazy things he'd experienced in the Sleep, terror exploded in Michael's chest. Real terror. And he thought, *What a way to end—squashed like a bug in a trash-riddled alley.*

He didn't dare glance behind him, but he could *feel* the

approach of the vehicle. It was close, and he had no chance of outrunning it. He gave up on trying to flee and dove behind the next garbage pile. The car screeched to a halt as he rolled and jumped back to his feet, ready to sprint in the other direction. The rear door of the sedan popped open and out stepped a sharply dressed man with a black ski mask pulled over his head, eyes fixed on Michael through slits in the fabric. Michael froze, just for an instant, but it was long enough. The man tackled him, slamming his body to the ground.

Michael opened his mouth to scream, but a cold hand clamped over his face, silencing him. Panic cut through his body like a hot sword, and adrenaline flooded his system as he twisted and shoved his attacker. But the man was too strong and flipped Michael over onto his stomach, pinning his arms behind him.

"Stop fighting," the stranger said. "No one's gonna hurt you, but we don't have time to mess around. I need you to get in the car."

Michael's face was pressed against the cement. "Oh really? I'll be perfectly safe? I was just thinking that."

"Shut your smart-aleck mouth, kid. We just can't let anybody know who we are. Now get in the car."

The man got to his feet, dragging Michael up with him.

"Your butt," the stranger said, pausing for effect. "In the car."

Michael made one last pathetic attempt to break free, but it was useless. The man's grip was iron-strong. Michael had no choice but to do what he was told. The fight drained out of him, and he let the man guide him to the backseat of the car, where he squeezed in next to another masked man. The door slammed shut and the car lurched forward, the screech of the tires echoing up the walls of the concrete canyon.

6

As the car tore out of the alley and onto the main road, Michael's mind spun—who were these people, and where were they taking him? Another wave of panic washed over him, and he acted. He slammed his elbow into the crotch of the guy to his left, then lunged for the door as the man doubled over in agony, cursing things that would've made even Bryson blush. Michael's fingers had just curled around the door handle when the original thug yanked him backward, his arm encircling Michael's neck. The man squeezed until Michael was gasping for air.

"Stop it, boy," he said far too calmly. For some reason those were the last words Michael wanted to hear. Anger surged in his chest, and he struggled to break free from the grip.

"Stop it!" the stranger screamed this time. "Stop acting like a child and calm yourself. We're *not* going to hurt you."

"You're actually hurting me right now," Michael coughed out.

The man loosened his grip. "Behave, and that's the worst of it. Do we have a deal, kid?"

"Fine," Michael grunted, because what else could he do? Ask for time to think about it?

The man seemed to relax at that. "Good. Now sit back and shut up," he directed. "Wait, no, first apologize to my friend—that was totally uncalled for."

Michael looked over at the guy to his left and shrugged. "Sorry. Hope you can still have babies."

The man didn't respond, but his glare through the ski mask was fierce. Humbled by the man's anger, Michael looked away. The adrenaline had faded, his strength was exhausted, and he was being driven through the city by four men in black masks.

Things didn't look so bright.

7

The rest of the ride went by in complete silence. Michael's heart, however, continued to thump away like a heavy-metal drumbeat. He thought he'd known fear before. He'd been thrown into countless horrific situations in the Virt-Net that had felt perfectly real. But this *was* real. And the fear was beyond anything he'd experienced. He wondered if he would drop dead of cardiac arrest at the ripe old age of sixteen.

As if in mockery, every glance outside seemed to land on those red-on-black *Lifeblood Deep* posters. Even though the tiny optimistic side of his brain kept trying to tell him that somehow he'd get out of this alive, he knew that being kidnapped by masked men usually didn't end well. The signs only reminded him that his dream of reaching the Deep probably wouldn't happen after all.

Finally, they reached the outskirts of the city and turned into the huge parking lot of the stadium where the Falcons played. It was completely empty, and the driver pulled to the very front row, where he stopped and set the emergency brake, the massive structure looming above them. A sign in the front of the parking space read RESERVED. VIOLATORS WILL BE TOWED.

A beep sounded from somewhere in the car, followed by a crack from outside, then the whir of machinery. Immediately afterward the vehicle started to sink into the ground, and Michael's heart leaped. As they descended, the brightness of day quickly melted into fluorescent interior lighting.

Finally, the car came to rest with a soft bump, and Michael looked around to see that they were in a huge underground garage with at least a dozen cars parked along one wall. The driver released the emergency brake and pulled into an empty spot, then cut the engine.

"We're here," the driver announced. Rather needlessly, Michael thought.

8

They offered Michael two options: they could drag him by the feet, facedown, for a close-up view of the cement, or he could walk with them under his own power without trying anything. He chose the second option. As they marched next to him, his heart kept trying to break through his rib cage with its relentless pounding.

The four men escorted him through a door, down a hallway, then through another door into a large conference room. At least, he assumed that was what it was, based on the long cherrywood table, plush leather chairs, and lit bar in the corner. He was surprised to see only one person waiting for them: a woman. She was tall with long black hair and wide-set, exotic-looking eyes—somehow she was gorgeous and terrifying at the same time.

"Leave him with me," she said. Four words, softly spoken, but the men practically dove out the door, closing it behind them, as if they feared her beyond anything else.

Those striking eyes focused on Michael's face. "My name is Diane Weber, but you'll refer to me as Agent Weber. Please, have a seat." She gestured toward the chair closest to Michael, and it took every ounce of his willpower to hesitate before he sat. He forced himself to count to five, staring at her, trying not to look away. Then he did as she asked.

She came over and sat next to him, then crossed her long, pretty legs. "Sorry for the roughhousing to get you here. What we're about to discuss is extremely urgent and confidential, and I didn't want to waste any time . . . *asking*."

"I'm missing school. Asking would've worked just fine." Somehow she'd put him at ease, which made him angry. It was clear that she was manipulative, that she used her beauty to melt men's hearts. "What could you possibly want me for, anyway?"

Her smile revealed perfect teeth. "You're a gamer, Michael. With serious coding skills."

"Is that a question?"

"No, it's a statement. I'm telling you why you're here because you asked. I know more about you than *you* do. Understand?"

Michael coughed—had all his hacking finally caught up to him? "I'm here because I'm a gamer?" he asked, struggling to keep his voice steady. "Because I like to dink around in the Sleep and code a little? What'd I do, knock you out of first place somewhere? Steal from your virtual restaurant?"

"You're here because we need you."

The words brought with them a sudden shot of bravery. "Look, I don't think my mom would approve of me dating an older woman. Have you tried the love shacks? I'm sure a good-lookin' gal like yourself could find—"

A look of such quick and sudden anger burned across her face that Michael shut his mouth, then apologized before he had time to think.

"I work for the VNS," she said, calm and cool once again. "We have a serious problem inside the VirtNet and we need help. We're also very aware of your hacking skills, and those of your friends. But if you don't think you can bring yourself to stop acting like a ten-year-old, I'll move on to the next person in line."

Somehow in only three sentences she'd made Michael feel like a complete idiot. And now all he wanted in the world was to know what she was talking about. "Fine, I'm sorry. Getting kidnapped kind of shakes up a dude. From here on out I'll be good."

"That's more like it." She paused, uncrossed and re-crossed her legs. "Now, I'm about to tell you three words, and if you ever repeat these three words to another human being without our explicit direction, the most optimistic outcome for you will be lifetime in a prison that, as far as the general population is concerned, doesn't exist."

Curiosity hummed through Michael, but her words made him pause. "So you won't kill me?"

"There are worse things than death, Michael," she said with a frown.

He stared at her, half wanting to beg her to let him go without saying another word. But his curiosity won out. "Okay. No repeating . . . Hit me."

Her lower lip trembled slightly when she said it, as if the phrase shook her somewhere deep inside: "The Mortality Doctrine."

9

The room sank into silence—complete and absolute—and Agent Weber stared at him.

What could those three words possibly mean that they could cost him his freedom? "Am I missing something?" he asked. "The Mortality Doctrine? What is *that*?"

Agent Weber leaned forward, her face somehow growing even more intense than before. "Hearing the words has committed you to joining us."

Michael shrugged—it was the only thing he felt safe doing.

"But I need to hear you say it," she said. "I need to *hear* your commitment. We need your skills in the VirtNet."

That little boost of pride brought Michael back to himself a bit. "I want to know what it is."

"That's more like it." She leaned back and the tension in the room seemed to lift. "The Mortality Doctrine. At this moment we know very little. It's something hidden in the VirtNet—somewhere off the known grid. A file or program of some sort that could seriously damage not just the Virt-Net, but the real world as well."

"Sounds promising," Michael muttered, immediately regretting it. Luckily, she let it pass. The truth was that he'd perked up at the notion of a secret part of the VirtNet. He wanted to know where it was.

"This . . . *doctrine* could devastate humanity and the world as we know it. Tell me, Michael, have you heard of the gamer who calls himself Kaine?"

The name made Michael's heart lurch. The girl, Tanya. Her face came back to him, as well as her words. How Kaine was tormenting her. Michael gripped the sides of his chair because it suddenly felt like he was falling off the bridge all over again. How did all these things relate?

"I know of Kaine," he said. "I saw a girl kill herself. . . . She mentioned him. . . ."

"Yes, we know," Agent Weber acknowledged. "That's a small part of the reason you're here. You're a witness to how bad things are getting. We've been able to tie Kaine to this Mortality Doctrine, and it's all linked to cases like what you saw happen. People trapped in the VirtNet and driven to decoding their own Cores. It's the worst cyber-terrorism we've ever come across."

"Why am I here?" Michael asked in a dry croak, feeling an embarrassing lack of confidence. "How can I help?"

She was silent for a beat. "We've found people comatose inside their Coffins. CAT scans reveal brain damage—as if they were the victims of some sick experiment. They are complete vegetables." She paused again. "We have evidence that Kaine's involved. And somehow it's all related to this Mortality Doctrine program hidden somewhere inside the VirtNet. We need to find both the man and the Mortality Doctrine. Will you help us?"

She asked it so simply, as if she was asking him to make a quick trip to the store for some milk and bread. Michael wanted to run. Actually, he wanted a lot of things just then—time travel would've been great, he thought—but more realistically, he wanted his room and his bed, his Coffin, escape to some brainless sports game, beginner level, Dan the Man Deli, bleu chips, hanging out with Bryson and Sarah, a movie, a book, his mom and dad back from traveling, and to never hear about this again.

But one word popped out of his mouth, and he didn't know he meant it until he heard himself say it.

"Yes."

CHAPTER 3

A DARK PLACE

1

Michael had barely closed his mouth when Agent Weber stood up so abruptly that her chair flipped backward.

Michael jumped, surprised at her reaction. "Was I supposed to say no?"

But she wasn't looking at him. She was looking at the door, her hand held to her ear as if she was listening to some kind of device planted there. "Something's wrong," she said. "You were followed."

Michael got to his feet, shaken by how quickly this woman had gone from terrifying to terrified. "Followed? By who?" he asked.

"*You don't want to know,* Michael. Come on."

She didn't wait for his response. Without another word she charged for the door. Michael went after her, and soon they were out in the hall, surrounded by several armed guards. This time without the ridiculous black masks.

"Get him back home," Agent Weber directed, in charge again. "And make sure no one sees you do it."

A man and a woman appeared, took Michael by the arm, and started leading him down the hallway.

"Wait!" he yelled, struggling to put together the sudden turn of events. "Wait! You barely told me anything!"

Heels clicking along the tile floor, Agent Weber approached him. "Tell your friends what I just told you. Bryson and Sarah. No one else. No one. Do you understand me? Tell anyone—even your parents—and we'll erase them."

That last bit shifted everything inside of him to anger. "*Erase* them?"

"I need the three of you to dig, Michael," she said, ignoring him. "I suggest you start in the darkest, seediest places inside the VirtNet. Ask around, follow the rumors. I need you to find where Kaine's hiding out—it's the only way we can learn the complete truth behind the Mortality Doctrine and how he plans to use it. Do whatever it takes. You have the skills. We'll have tracers on you and we'll follow you in once you've discovered where he's hiding it. Help us solve this problem and you'll be set for life, whatever you want. We have others searching, too. Get there first and you'll be rewarded."

His mouth opened—to say *what*, he had no idea—but she'd already turned and was making her way back down the hall.

"Let's go," one of the guards said.

They pulled Michael along in the opposite direction.

2

They didn't go back to the car. The guards—they didn't say one word to Michael the entire time—escorted him down countless hallways until they came out of an old abandoned building next to a subway station, where they left him. People milled about, the sun shone down through a break in the clouds, and a candy wrapper floated through the air on the breeze. The world had gone along exactly as before, while his life had just changed forever.

Going to school was furthest thing from his mind. Dazed and scared, Michael wandered to a coffee shop and got the biggest cup they had. Then to the train station and home. The first thing he did there was arrange a meeting for the next day with Bryson and Sarah. He gave them just enough information to get them interested—he knew if he told them too much, they wouldn't sleep, and he had a feeling they were going to need all the rest they could get.

3

Michael made the mistake of watching the NewsBops that night.

He was all alone, curled up in the Chair—his parents weren't home, and he still couldn't remember when they'd be back. Helga usually went to bed when the sun set. His NetScreen shot out of his EarCuff and hovered before him, revealing all the dreary news of the day. Murders, bank failures, natural disasters. *Nothing like a pick-me-up right before going to bed,* he thought sadly. Usually such things seemed far away—things that happened to others. But for some reason it all felt a little closer to home after his talk with Agent Weber.

He was just about to turn the news off when a story flashed open that made him stop. An older news anchor was talking about the latest buzz lighting up the VirtNet: the cyber-terrorist known as Kaine.

With a flick of his finger, Michael turned up the volume and leaned forward, focusing as if the next couple of minutes were the most important of his life.

". . . the cause of several suicides, according to witnesses and messages sent by victims before their deaths," the lady said. "Kaine has been known to infiltrate almost every popular game and social site in the VirtNet, not to mention countless reports of individual harassment. Not since the disappearance of the legendary Gunner Skale has an individual's story lit up the VirtNet quite like this. What Kaine's purpose might be, no one can guess. The VNS has given its word in an official statement that they are doing everything within their vast resources to locate the man and shut his access down permanently."

She continued speaking, and Michael stared and listened, half fascinated and half terrified. Virtual kidnappings that ended in virtual torture and incarceration from which people were unable to Lift themselves back to the Wake. Entire games or networks shut down or erased, nothing left but a line of code stating that "Kaine was here." Brain-dead players found in their NerveBoxes.

Michael had now heard all too much about the horrors

committed by Kaine. What could be the man's purpose? Was he doing it all just for kicks?

Kaine.

The Mortality Doctrine.

People trapped in the Sleep. People showing up brain-dead. Others killing themselves just to escape the guy.

Michael sighed. *Happy thoughts, all.*

On that note, he crawled into bed and went to sleep. For some reason he dreamed about his parents and a vacation to the beach they'd taken together long, long ago.

4

Michael was thankful the next day was Saturday. Helga made some mean waffles and topped them with all the things that make a person fat—butter, whipped cream, syrup. She threw in a few strawberries to lessen the guilt factor. Neither of them spoke, and Michael wondered if she'd been watching the same NewsBops as he had. Cheerful stuff. At least he was going to see his friends later.

A couple of hours after breakfast, Michael's real body was snug inside the Coffin, while his liberated VirtNet body sat down on an out-of-the-way bench in New York's Central Park, another one of his favorite meeting spots. The second-best thing to virtual food was to be surrounded by nature. A sight he didn't see too often in the smoggy concrete jungle he called home.

Bryson and Sarah were waiting impatiently when he arrived.

"This better be good," Bryson announced. "Like, wet-my-pants good."

"Why were you so cryptic, anyway?" Sarah added.

Michael wasn't so much scared anymore as excited to spill everything that had happened since he'd been nabbed in the alley. A little worried that someone could be eavesdropping, he started his story in a whisper but soon was speeding through the details so fast he was barely coherent.

Sarah and Bryson just stared at him in confusion.

"Um, maybe you should start over," Bryson said.

Sarah nodded. "From the beginning. And talk like a normal person."

"Okay, yeah." Michael inhaled a long pull of fresh—but fake—air and started over. "So, I was walking to catch the train for school yesterday when this car pulls up and practically runs me down. Then these psycho dudes in black masks jump out and drag me into the backseat."

Bryson interrupted. "Wait. Michael, did you eat something funny today?"

Michael rolled his eyes. "No, just . . . listen." He couldn't blame them for having doubts, but he was starting to get frustrated that he couldn't get his story out.

He took another breath and kept going, and by the time he got to Agent Weber discovering he'd been followed and having her guards whisk him away, he could see that his friends believed he was dead serious. He finished up by relaying the horrible things from the NewsBops—most of which they'd heard themselves.

They sat in silence for at least a minute, stealing glances

at the trees and bushes around them to see if anyone might be spying.

Bryson broke the silence. "Wow. Why would they ask three teenagers to solve their problems?"

"I've been thinking about that," Michael said. "Agent Weber said others would be searching, too. Maybe they're finding the best gamers and coders around and giving them an opportunity to crack whatever secret location Kaine has created. She knew we could hack and code. I'm telling you, it wasn't a joke."

"But how can we do anything the VNS people can't do?" Sarah asked. "That's their whole job, and frankly it scares me that they're trying to pawn it off on kids."

Bryson scoffed. "Old geezers always know that the next generation is smarter than they'll ever be at this stuff. I mean, we hang out in this place. We *do* know it better than anyone. We can do it because it's *not* our job. It's our hobby."

"And it has to do with more than programming," Michael added, glad that Bryson was making it sound legitimate. "They need users, not just makers. Who's better than us?"

"You sure that's it?" Sarah asked. "Or do you just want an excuse to play?"

"Don't you?" Michael asked.

"Yeah, well." She shrugged and smiled.

"And what was that little part about being set for life if we find it?" Bryson asked. "That lady better have meant all three of us, not just you."

"I'm sure she did," Michael answered, even though he

didn't know for sure. "We'll be rich, work for the VNS, whatever. But we absolutely can't tell anyone about this." For some reason he couldn't bring himself to mention the less-than-veiled threats Agent Weber had also doled out. But then, maybe they didn't apply to his friends.

"I admit, it sounds fun—it'd be a good challenge," Sarah said.

Michael agreed. A game that wasn't a game anymore—it was more important than a game. In that second he got so excited to start that he almost stood up, ready to move.

Bryson must've read the expression on his face. "Hold on to your pants, there, brother. We've gotta be sure about this."

"I know," Michael replied. "I am." And he meant it fully.

Something happened then. An uncomfortable oddness suddenly permeated their surroundings, flooding Michael with fear. Everything in the park around them slowed to a crawl, like a fly trapped in syrup.

Sarah's hand was moving to tuck her hair behind her ear. Bryson's mouth was stretching into a smile—his mischievous one, his way of letting everyone know he agreed and was committed. The tree branches above them swayed lazily. A bird flew past, and Michael could see its wing move up, then down. The air thickened, filled with a stifling humidity.

And then it all disappeared in a flash of light, replaced by spinning stars and a maniac's laughter.

5

Michael's body had been subjected to everything imaginable in terms of motion within the VirtNet, the Coffin always doing its trick to make things as realistic as possible. Roller coasters, diving airplanes, rockets being shot to other universes at light speed, more falls than he could ever count. But whatever happened to them in that moment felt like it was going to rip his body into a hundred pieces. His stomach turned and his brain split into ten kinds of pain. All the while, stars spun, and he couldn't tell if his eyes were open or closed. He lost all awareness of his surroundings, and he suddenly wondered if the Coffin would be able to handle the stress.

Abruptly, the craziness stopped. Michael's insides clenched and he heaved, but nothing came out. He slowly regained his breath and looked around. All was frozen in darkness except for small lights winking in the distance.

There were two bodies next to him. He could barely see them—they weren't much more than shadows—but he knew it was Bryson and Sarah. It had to be.

The lights began to swirl, then coalesce, moving more rapidly with each passing second—collecting immediately in front of them into a ball that grew larger and brighter, until Michael could barely look at it. It spun like a celestial body, pulsing with brilliance.

Michael and his friends—floating, frozen, silent—waited. Michael tried to speak but couldn't. Tried to move but was paralyzed. Fear surged through every last inch of him. And then a voice spoke from the blinding ball of light, throbbing with each word. And it was terrifying.

"My name is Kaine," it said. "And I see all."

6

Whatever had paralyzed Michael didn't release its hold on him.

The chilling voice continued, "Do you really think I'm not aware of VNS and their efforts to stop me? Can you imagine that I'd let anything happen within the VirtNet that doesn't serve *my* interests? This is *my* domain now, and only the boldest, the strongest, and the smartest will be allowed to serve me in the end. VNS and players like you will be rendered utterly insignificant."

Michael strained to break free from the force that held him.

"You have no idea the power I have," Kaine's voice said. "I'm warning all who try to stop me. You will not be warned twice." The voice paused. "See what awaits if you don't heed my words."

The ball of spinning light vanished, replaced by a huge rectangle that looked like one of the screens on which they used to watch movies decades ago. Images flashed across the screen as it grew wider and taller, until it almost filled Michael's entire vision.

It was as if he'd been inserted into the mind of a lunatic: A city of rubble, devoid of color, people huddling in the gutters.

Several slack-jawed men in a smoky room, seemingly waiting to be burned alive as flames licked at the edges of a door.

An old woman in a rocking chair, slowly raising a gun.

Two teenagers, laughing, pushing little kids off a high cliff and watching them fall.

A hospital full of frail, sickly patients, its door chained and locked from the outside. Several haggard-looking people splashing gasoline on its walls, one of them pulling out a lighter.

The horrifying scenes continued, flashing one after another, growing more unspeakable. Michael's body trembled with the effort to break free. It was worse than any nightmare from which he'd ever struggled to wake.

Kaine's voice spoke again, coming from everywhere at once.

"You know so little about what's *really* going on. You are children in every sense of the word. All this and more awaits your mind if you continue."

And then it ended. Everything vanished, and Michael found himself back inside his Coffin. But his throat hurt, and he realized he must've been screaming for quite some time.

CHAPTER 4

NO CHOICE IN THE MATTER

1

Michael thought Tanya's suicide had been bad, but this time he was barely able to pull himself out of the Coffin. He didn't even bother putting on shorts. Trembling, sweating, he stumbled to his bed. A part of him still floated in Kaine's version of a deep-space theater, surrounded by the horrors he'd predicted for Michael's future. For his *mind*, whatever that meant.

It made his skin crawl. After a lifetime of seeking out wilder and wilder experiences, he'd had two run-ins inside the VirtNet that made him long for the days when everything had been fun—and not quite so wild. He didn't care what the VNS was offering, what they'd threatened if he didn't try to help. Seeing someone rip their Core out before his eyes, and Kaine's vision of punishment should Michael seek him out, had made up Michael's mind. What if the man could somehow reach him even in the Wake? Michael had never had that paralyzed, helpless feeling before, inside the VirtNet or out.

He didn't know how he could possibly fulfill the challenge the VNS had given him. Shooting aliens, rescuing princesses from goblins, dealing with *Lifeblood*'s day-to-day drama, then Lifting out of it all to do homework seemed just fine—and Bryson and Sarah would always be there in the Sleep to do it with him. He'd just go back to his normal, boring life. He never wanted to cross paths with Kaine again.

Firmly believing that, Michael was finally able to fall asleep.

2

The next morning, a dull and dreary Sunday to match Michael's mood, Helga made him eat cornflakes for breakfast, claiming she had a headache. He wanted to tell her she had no idea what a headache was. To tell her every little detail of the fun time he'd had with Kaine the day before, ask her if she thought maybe that kind of experience sounded a little worse than a few hours of brooms, dusters, and laundry baskets.

But he liked Helga too much, and he was ashamed for even thinking it.

So instead he told her how sorry he was and ate three bowls of the cereal she'd set on the counter. Then he took a very long and very hot shower. Afterward, he felt a little better; the memory of his encounter with the cyber-terrorist started to fade, almost as if it'd all been a nasty nightmare.

The rest of the day was spent trying to forget it all. He jogged a few miles, took a long nap, ate a perfect lunch: sandwiches, chips, and pickles. He finally settled down in the Chair to have his inevitable conversation with Bryson and Sarah about the Kaine extravaganza. When the EarCuff flashed its screen in front of him, there were already messages from both of his friends on the Bulletin.

It looked like they were all in agreement. Games were games, but dealing with some psychotic man who was terrorizing people and couldn't be handled by an organization as powerful as the VNS—well, Michael thought, that was a different story. His friends agreed that it'd been a nice offer, but . . . no thanks. Kaine was too dangerous, and he made the threats from the VNS seem cute. The programming feat he'd done to trap them was unimaginable.

When the question arose of whether Michael should let the VNS know about his and his friends' decision, he figured *not*. He didn't want to talk to those people. Hopefully they'd been bluffing. Maybe they really had offered the challenge to a slew of gamers, betting that some of them would continue. Michael didn't plan to find out—he was a little scared to go back into the Sleep but figured Kaine would leave them alone as long as they didn't start snooping. As long as they heeded his warning.

Michael and his friends ended their conversation by saying they'd hang out later in *Lifeblood*, go gaming, leave the whole affair behind.

But things didn't quite go as planned when Michael hooked into the Coffin later that afternoon. Instead of Sinking into the VirtNet, all he saw were big block letters:

ACCESS DENIED BY VNS

3

They'd cut him off.

Michael got out of his Coffin and ran to the Chair, tried his EarCuff. It didn't work. He ran to the couch in front of the WallScreen and clicked the TV controls. Nothing. He could hear Helga walking around the apartment, huffing and puffing, trying to make calls. But cell service had been disconnected, too. Michael went back to his Chair and attempted to hack his way into the NetScreen for an hour, to no avail.

Cut off. Completely.

All he could do was go to his bed, lie there, and stare at the ceiling, feeling sicker by the minute. How in the world had he gotten into such a mess? In a matter of a day or two, his life had been hijacked by the VNS and threatened by a madman. He missed the days when school and an occasional stomachache were the only things he had to complain about.

But anyone who'd known him for more than five minutes could have guessed where his thoughts headed next. Yes, he'd been shown a vision worse than anything he'd ever laid real or virtual eyes upon, and he'd been promised it would be his future if he did what the VNS wanted. He had no doubt that the VirtNet could be programmed that way for him. Kaine was exactly right: when you had the power to make someone see and experience *anything,* there were definitely things worse than death. And that bottomless trench had been dug in front of Michael.

Then someone has taken his access away, and there was no chance he could live with *that.*

More important, Agent Weber's words now haunted him more vividly. She'd threatened him and his family, and cutting off his access was definitely only the beginning of worse to come. Michael had to get things square. Maybe he'd been too quick to give up.

He got out of bed and decided to stop feeling sorry for himself. He knew the VNS would give him another chance—he'd seen firsthand what they were dealing with. And if they'd come to him for help, they needed it desperately. The horrors of the Kaine vision had faded a bit; Michael's calmer, more rational side had begun to think that this was no different from any other VirtNet experience. None of it was real, and as long as he was careful, he could do this. In all his years of dinking around in the VirtNet, he'd never met anyone better than he was at coding or hacking, or who'd gotten closer to *Lifeblood Deep* so quickly. Kaine was good, but he was just another gamer after all.

Michael was ready for the challenge, and kind of ashamed that he'd cowered in the first place. How could he ignore threats against his family?

Mrs. Perkins next door just about had a heart attack when Michael pounded on her door. She opened it up with wide eyes and half of her face covered in some kind of greasy cream, her hand on her chest.

"Why, Michael," she said, her eyes rolling in relief. "Goodness gracious heaven and earth. What's wrong? You almost—"

"Gave you a heart attack, I know. Listen, I need you to do me a favor."

She put her hands on her hips. "Well, I'd expect a little more politeness if that's the case."

Michael loved Mrs. Perkins. Really, he did. She smelled like baby powder and mentholated gel, and she was the nicest lady on the planet. But right then it was all he could do not to push the woman out of the way to get to her phone.

Forcing himself to be calm, he said, "I'm really sorry. It's urgent."

"Apology accepted, dear. What can I do for you?"

For some reason, a smile broke out on his face. "Will you call the local VNS office? Tell them that your neighbor Michael says he's back in. Tell them I'll find what they're looking for."

4

His access was reinstated immediately. He knew from his message board that Bryson and Sarah had gone through the same thing and that they'd taken it just as seriously as he had. School on Monday was the most agonizing thing Michael had ever sat through, but by that evening he'd reconnected with his friends and they decided to begin their investigation the next afternoon.

They were determined to be more careful and less open this time. They'd use their coding and hacking skills like never before. There was a reason the VNS had chosen him and his friends, Michael thought, and he was glad for the reminder of the lengths they'd need to go.

We can do this, he told himself. Over and over.

CHAPTER 5

THE OLD MAN

1

"While you guys were wigging out," Bryson said, "I was putting a Tracer on Kaine's Aura. We'll know next time he gets close."

Michael was sitting with him and Sarah in a tree house on the outskirts of the outskirts of *Lifeblood,* a place they'd coded—or *built*—in secret. It was in a small forest that Michael was pretty sure even the programmers of the game didn't know about.

"Did you upload the Tracer to us yet?" Sarah asked him. She was so good at keeping them focused.

"Yeah."

"Good. And I think if we use my Hide-and-Seek program and Michael's Cloak-and-Dagger, we should be able to avoid that snake for a while."

"Or at least stay two steps ahead of him," Michael added. He and Sarah had worked together to create the two masking programs, which had come in handy more than once.

They went silent for a moment, closing their eyes and concentrating to access the raw data of the world around them. Michael pulled up screens and connected with his friends; then they shared codes and installed programs and made sure everything was linked and good to go. No one needed to say that they should've been smarter the first time around, but at the time it had almost seemed like a harmless game. Which, Michael told himself, had been really stupid.

When finished coding, he opened his eyes and rubbed them—they were always a little bleary after linking to the code. He got onto his knees and looked out the window that faced the side of the forest leading back into the main sections of *Lifeblood*. It was foggy this far out, since the programming was weaker, but Michael liked it. The tree house they'd constructed through their own programming tricks was warm and well hidden, so it felt cozy and safe. Just add some knitted socks and a stocking cap and he'd be an official grandma, he thought with an embarrassed grin. But there was still a part of him that feared the things they were about to get into. A huge part.

"So?" Bryson began. His question was obvious.

"The old-timers," Sarah answered. "That's where we start."

Michael snapped out of his funk and let his adventurous side take over again. "Definitely," he said as he turned and sat back down. "Those geezers outside the Old Towne shopping district will know something, if anybody does. Throw 'em a few credits to Casino and we won't be able to shut them up."

Sarah was nodding, but her eyes were focused on the

same window Michael had been gazing through. She never looked at you when she was deep in thought. "I'm trying to remember the barber's name. He must be a thousand years old."

"I know that dinosaur," Bryson said. "We used him when we needed to get the passwords for the Pluto mission. You'd think the guy would buy a breath-mint program. I had to keep sucking air through my mouth, he smelled so bad."

Michael laughed. "If you had every gamer in town knocking on your door for advice, you wouldn't do anything to make it easier on them, either. His name's Cutter, by the way."

"That's where we go," Sarah said. "We'll just plug our noses."

2

Old Towne was the most visited place in the VirtNet, the New York City of the simulated world. And the shopping district within it was always packed with people. At first Michael worried about being so much in the open, but once he was there, he realized it would be even easier to blend in and be lost by a searching eye. Especially with their Hider programs doubled up and working at full capacity.

Two malls, each with thousands of stores, arcades, restaurants, upload huts, entertainment bars, and anything else you could think of, bordered a huge plaza that stretched for miles. Along it were amazing fountains and air dancers and roller coasters, and Michael had always been just as much of a sucker for it all as anyone else. The whole place was designed for two things: to provide good times and to drain people's life savings. Things often cost as much in the Sleep as they did in the Wake; the possibilities were just more vast. Especially if you could code.

Sarah had to yank Bryson away—by the ear—about five times before they made it to the long, narrow alleyway they were looking for. It branched off from the broad plaza and led to a section called Shady Towne, where less mainstream affairs like digital-tattoo parlors and pawnshops lined a cobblestone road that made Michael feel like he'd traveled hundreds of years into the past. He even saw a horse trot by.

"His place is right up here," Sarah said, pointing.

No one had said much since exiting the plaza, and Michael knew exactly why. There were a lot fewer people, which meant if someone was looking, Michael and his friends would be easier to spot. Michael put his faith in Bryson's Tracer, trusting that they'd know if Kaine slipped past their Hider programs and got close again. Then they could find a Portal and Lift to the Wake before being dumped into that black abyss.

Cutter's place was aptly named the Old Man's Barbershop. It didn't take a genius to know that in a simulated world a person didn't need haircuts, but that wasn't how most people rolled. The more lifelike, the better. And eighty percent of those in the Sleep had themselves programmed to grow hair. If you were skilled at coding and really wanted a ponytail, you could just access the code and quickly program it.

"What do we do?" Bryson asked when they stopped a

few feet from the front door. "Just barge in there and start throwing questions at the dude?"

Michael shrugged. "I bet he gambles every chance he gets. We'll program him a buy-in for the next poker tournament, and just like I said, he won't shut up till we walk away."

"And whose head is he shaving?"

Sarah pulled her hair back protectively. "Not mine. I'm thinking he's not the type to cut girls' hair, anyway."

"Make yourself shaggy," Michael said to Bryson. "We're wasting time."

It had been at least a year since Michael had last pried information out of Cutter—something about a cheat in a martial arts game—so he'd forgotten how odd-looking the man was. If ever someone had shaped their VirtNet Aura after a storybook troll, there he stood, snipping away at a stranger's hair. Michael and his friends waited patiently until it was Bryson's turn for the scissors.

Cutter's own mane was nothing but a tuft of gray combed over his spotted red scalp. He had more hairs coming out of his ears than he had up top. He was short and squat and ancient, and every word that came out of his mouth made Michael think the man would drop dead at any moment from old age. Surprisingly, the majority of people liked their VirtNet self to mirror their real self, so Michael could only imagine meeting Cutter in the Wake. A real pleasure to live with, he was sure.

"Why are you damn kids standin' there gawking at us like vultures at a dying rat?" His fingers worked faster than Michael would have thought possible for a man his age, snip-snipping away. Evidently, he wasn't used to people watching him so closely.

"Because we're here for more than donating hair to your floor," Sarah said, her voice as firm as Michael had ever heard it.

"Oh really?" he rasped. Michael guessed the man had more phlegm in his throat than a sinus-infected toddler. "Well, why don't you enlighten me, young lady."

Sarah looked at Michael, which was his cue. Leaning close to Cutter, he whispered, "We want information on the gamer named Kaine. Word is that he's up to something big." He paused, thinking too late that he should've shown a little more respect. "Um, sir. Please."

"Save your fancy talk for someone else," Cutter replied. His breath caught Michael this time, and he had to step away before he gagged.

He half expected Cutter to keep talking, start telling what he knew, but the old man didn't say another word. He hadn't slowed in the slightest with his clipping, and Bryson was starting to look downright handsome as a result.

Sarah gave it a try. "Come on. We know every rumor in the Sleep slides its way through here at some point. Tell us what you know about Kaine and where he's hiding his secrets."

"Or where we can find out," Bryson added.

Cutter barked a laugh. "If you're so damn smart, then you know what it takes to get information around here. All I've gotten so far is a headache and a handful of virtual hair cluttering up my floor."

For some reason the guy's last sentence made something in Michael snap, and he let out a small laugh before he could cut it off.

Cutter glared. "Laugh all ya want. I'm not the one who needs something. Last I remember, that was you."

Sarah gave Michael her special look of reprimand—the one that only girls seemed to be able to manage. "We're sorry, sir. Really. We obviously don't have the slightest clue how to go about this. We've never done anything like this before."

Michael winced at that—the man might've been old, but surely he remembered them. Michael jumped in to make up for the lie. "We can give you something for the information. Full buy-in for the Casino poker tournament this weekend." He just had to hope his parents wouldn't notice the money missing from their bank account.

Cutter's eyes locked on his; there was a depth of clarity in the old man's gaze that Michael had never seen, and he knew they'd won.

"Plus drinks," the old man said. "Bottomless cup, mind you."

"Fine," Michael answered. "Now spill the beans."

"You may not like what I got, but it's the best I got. And you're gonna have to trust me that I'm setting them feet of yours on the right road to findin' what you're seekin'."

"Okay," Sarah responded. "Let's hear it."

Cutter had stopped cutting Bryson's hair, though Michael couldn't recall when he'd done so. He wiped the back of the cape his friend was wearing, then took it off him. Bryson said a quick thanks and stood to join his friends, looking as excited as Michael to hear what the barber had to say.

"I've heard a lot of gossip come through this joint over the years," the old man said. "But you're asking about the scariest information I've heard yet in my eight decades."

This only got Michael more excited. "And?"

"Plenty of news about this Kaine chap goin' round, that's for sure. He's up to no good. Kidnappings, lobotomies . . . Word is that there's a place he's hiding something, too. Don't know what he's hiding or where. Just that it's big."

"We already know all that," Sarah pointed out. "How can we find him or this place? Where do we start?"

Cutter's mouth curled in what might've been a smile, but Michael wasn't sure. It looked more like a grimace. "That poker night better pay off, kids, 'cause I've told less people about the place I'm about to reveal to you than I've got toes on my right foot. And I lost one of those to a rabid canine in Des Moines."

"Where do we go?" Michael pressed, impatience straining his every muscle.

Cutter leaned in toward them, the foul stench of his breath wafting out even before he began talking again. "You need to go to the Black and Blue Club. Find Ronika. That old witch is the only one who can tell you how to find . . . *it*."

"Find *what*?" all three of them replied in unison.

"The thing that'll lead you to Kaine." Cutter made that mysterious smile-grimace again, then spoke in a harsh whisper. *"The Path."*

Michael frowned. Two simple words—but the way the man said them turned his insides cold.

CHAPTER 6

THROUGH THE FLOOR

1

Michael had heard of the club. *Everybody* inside the VirtNet had heard of the Black and Blue. But he'd never met anyone who'd actually been there, because it was impossible to get into—unless you were extremely rich, famous, or high up on the criminal chain. Or, of course, a politician, which would make you all of the above.

Michael and his friends were none of those, and to make matters worse, they were teenagers. Their coding skills were advanced enough that they could make themselves look older, and they could conjure up fake ID docs quicker than Helga could make waffles. But everyone tried to fool the Black and Blue, and the club was far too good at seeing through the trickery.

Michael, Bryson, and Sarah stood across the street from the entrance, gawking at the people waiting in line. Michael figured more money had been spent on their jewelry and designer clothing than most people made in a year. *Lifeblood* was the one place in the VirtNet where not just anyone could look however they wanted. To have fancy things, you had to be rich enough to *afford* fancy things in the real world or know how to schmooze, flirt, or con your way into getting what you desired. Or be really good at coding and hacking.

"What's the plan?" Bryson asked. "I can barely sneak my way into Jackie Suede's Shake-Your-Booty Bar, much less the Black and Blue."

Michael was racking his brain. "This Ronika person can't live in there twenty-four hours a day. What if we just wait for her to come out and then follow her home?"

Sarah responded with something like a groan. "Sounds slightly creepy—not to mention we don't know what she looks like. Plus, you're forgetting this isn't the real world. That could very well be the only place she ever goes in the Sleep—she may Sink and Lift directly to a Portal in the back room for all we know. Especially if she's as famous as Cutter made her out to be. And I doubt she's a Tangent, being in that kind of position. Managerial types are always human."

Bryson let out an exaggerated sigh. "If only I could have five minutes with her. She'd be so bamboozled by the charm, we'd have our info before she knew what hit her."

"Um, no comment on that one," Michael said.

Sarah really groaned this time. "How did I become friends with you two, again?"

Michael quickly moved on. "Listen, I hate to say it, but we've only got one choice."

Bryson and Sarah gave him a puzzled look, but he knew very well that they were thinking the same thing. Doing something blatantly illegal is always the last resort.

With a mischievous smile, he said, "We have to cut our way in."

2

Michael had always thought of hacking into a simulated location within the VirtNet as much like breaking into a building in the Wake. It took planning and smarts. And like in the real world, if you made one wrong move, your butt could end up in jail if the VNS caught you.

"Everyone put on your I'm-not-suspicious face," he said. "And follow me."

"Dude, why'd you say that?" Bryson complained. "Now I'm gonna look guiltier than ever."

They took an indirect route to get to the back side of the club. They went several blocks out of their way, hoping that anyone watching wouldn't guess what they were up to. As they walked, they grew quiet, and Michael tried to start a new conversation; the goal was to look like a normal group of friends out for a stroll.

"No offense, but I'm kinda sick of talking about your nanny's cooking," Bryson finally said as they turned the last corner, the club just a hundred feet ahead. "Especially since I've never met her and probably never will."

Sarah had taken the lead as they moved along, and Michael hoped that meant she was feeling confident about the job they were about to do. "Maybe we should meet up on the outside, at Michael's place," Sarah said. "Then Helga can whip up one of these things you keep bragging about."

"Is Helga hot?" Bryson asked.

Michael shivered at the thought. "She's at least sixty, man. Maybe seventy."

"So? You didn't answer my question."

Sarah stopped and Michael almost ran into her. It was just a couple of buildings away now. A small black door was the only thing marking the back of the club. Even without a sign, there was a reason Michael had no doubt it was the Black and Blue: two enormous men, heads as big as their chests—and no necks in between—stood outside of it, eyeing every passerby as if they hadn't eaten in days and loved the smell of raw human meat. Every club had bouncers, but these guys looked monstrous.

"This should be easy," Bryson murmured.

Sarah spun around and whispered that they should stop looking in the direction of the club.

Something on her face told Michael to listen. "What are you scheming?"

"I can't imagine what kind of firewalls this place has built around it. Could we hack them? Sure. But something hit me when we turned onto this street." She risked a quick glance at the guards. "I think we can get inside without cutting our way in."

Bryson's expression showed exactly what Michael felt: total bewilderment. "Really?" he asked. "And how do you plan on walking past those nice serial killers down there?"

Sarah just rolled her eyes. "I'm serious about this. We don't have to hack into the club, we just need to hack into the *bouncers*. Into their personal files. And then we waltz right through those doors."

She went on to explain the specifics, and Michael remembered why he liked her so much. She had to be the smartest girl ever born.

3

It took forty-three minutes.

The three of them sat with their backs against the wall and linked up to examine the programming. Michael loved the process: closing his eyes and focusing his consciousness back to the Coffin and accessing the crude elements of the VirtNet itself, the core code of what he'd been seeing all around him. It took instinct and a lot of experience to work on it with others, but he and his friends were really good at it. It was another reason they got along so well.

Once they'd isolated the coding for the two bouncers, they broke in and downloaded a few of the men's personal files into their own systems, then Sank back fully into their own VirtNet Auras. What they had planned was a huge bluff—but bluffing seemed a quicker option than trying to break through all the club's firewalls, of which there had to be many. When Michael opened his eyes again, he could feel the sweat trickling down his simulated face. They had stepped well past the legal limits of manipulating code, and they were about to get in deeper. With such little planning, he knew the risk of getting caught was way too high for comfort.

Sarah jumped to her feet. "Let's hurry before they notice we did anything."

Michael and Bryson scrambled to follow her, and as they approached the behemoths guarding the back door of the Black and Blue Club, Michael had a small but comforting thought: The VNS had *asked* them to do this. Maybe they'd be given some leeway on things that were "technically" against the law.

The bouncer on the left noticed them first, and he looked at the three approaching teenagers with pure amusement. He could tell they had their sights on him, and he probably relished the prospect of denying another lame attempt at getting inside. He cracked his knuckles and let out a low rumble of boorish laughter, nudging his partner.

"You do it," Michael whispered to Sarah, suddenly losing his nerve. "It was your idea."

"Amen," Bryson added.

They stopped just a few feet in front of the bouncers. The one on the right had joined his companion in staring them down.

"Let me guess," the one on the left said. Michael realized that the two men were practically twins. "You wanna offer us a lollipop so we'll let you in to play? Maybe some sugar bunnies?"

His partner chuckled, the sound like cracks of thunder. "Don't waste our time, kids. Go to the arcade and kill some aliens. Or go to that teenybopper club up the street. Just get out of our faces."

Michael couldn't believe how nervous he was. They'd done millions of crazy stunts, but now that so much was on the line, his knees were a little weak. Sarah, however, seemed in her element.

"We stole your code," she said, her voice so calm it scared Michael a little. "I'm sending over proof now." She closed her eyes for the briefest of moments as she sent the few files they'd stolen, then gave the bouncers a nasty glare. The bluff was on.

The man on the left froze and his eyes shot wide; his partner reeled back, as if he'd been punched in the stomach. "They'll throw your butts in jail for this," he growled. "I bet someone's breaking down your door as we speak."

"I guess that's our problem to worry about," Sarah said. "Now, I'm going to start counting. When I get to five, I'm sending out some little . . . tidbits we dug up in the filth that's your memory bank to all the people on your contact list. If I reach ten, we start . . . erasing things you wouldn't want erased."

"You're lying," the man on the right countered. "And I think I just might start counting myself. When I reach two, I start pounding you senseless. Or maybe do some of my own hacking."

"One," Sarah said softly. "Two."

The bouncer on the left was getting more and more agitated. "You wouldn't dare. You can't mess with our personal information!"

"Three. Four." She turned to Michael—he was quiet, actually enjoying the show. "Get the distribution list ready."

"Got it," he said, trying hard not to smile.

Sarah faced the giants again. "Fi—"

"Wait!" the man on the right yelled. "Just stop!"

"We'll let you in," his partner said. "Who gives a crap? Just make yourselves look a little older so we don't get in trouble."

"Fair enough," Sarah replied. "Come on, guys."

"Dude," Bryson said to one of the men as they passed him. "After what I just saw in your files, I hope you never have kids."

4

The Black and Blue Club was mostly how Michael imagined it would be, just a little louder, a little more sweaty, and filled with so much human beauty he knew he'd never see it replicated back in the real world. Skull-pounding music thumped and bellowed from the massive speakers hung on the ceiling, and strobe lights flashed and dazzled. A red glow permeated everything else, cast over the people dancing and gyrating and jumping out on the floor. Body heat filled the space, warm and sultry. Everywhere Michael looked, he saw perfection. Perfect hair, perfect clothes, perfect muscles, perfect legs.

Not my cup of tea, he thought with a smile. He preferred dorky girls with messy hair and potato chip crumbs on their shirts.

"Let's walk around, find that woman!" he yelled at the other two. He wondered if lipreading was a popular download of those who frequented the place—he couldn't even hear himself speak.

Bryson and Sarah just nodded. They started winding their way through the herds of beautiful patrons.

The pounding beat of the bass felt like a blacksmith's anvil in Michael's head, hammer blow after hammer blow. He couldn't remember if he'd had a headache before they weaseled their way past the bouncers, but he sure had one now. It was impossible to move without bumping into people, sweaty arms slicking against his. He found himself involuntarily dancing as he walked, and Sarah looked mortified at his lack of talent.

She mouthed the words *You're cute,* but she rolled her eyes as she said it.

A sea of people. Pure, unbreakable noise. Disorienting lights. And that unending beat. Michael was already sick of it. But they needed to find a person named Ronika, who supposedly knew everything about everything. How were you supposed to find anyone in a place like this?

Michael looked around and realized Bryson and Sarah were no longer beside him. With a jolt of panic, he spun in a circle searching for them, pointlessly calling out their names. He was on edge—they'd gotten in illegally, and it made him nervous—but his friends' disappearing so fast felt wrong. Michael stopped, and someone pushed him from behind; an elbow struck him in the side of the neck. Over the deafeningly loud music, he heard a woman's laugh.

Then he fell through the floor.

5

It wasn't like a trapdoor. And the floor didn't collapse. Instead, as everything around him continued on, his body became immaterial and transparent, and he sank as the dancing people around him seemed to rise toward the sky. Michael quickly looked down and saw his legs and torso slip through the shiny black tile like a ghost.

He instinctively closed his eyes when his head went through, and when he opened them again he'd emerged in a dimly lit room filled with formal furniture. Tufted couches, mahogany paneling, and ornately carved lamps surrounded him, and his feet landed softly on a lush Oriental rug. Bryson and Sarah were standing nearby, looking at Michael as if he was late for a party. But no one else was in the room.

"Um, what just happened?" Michael asked. Seeing his friends made him feel better, despite the fact that he'd sunk through the floor.

"Something pulled us in here is what happened," Bryson answered. "Which means we probably didn't get into the club quite as stealthily as we thought."

"Hello?" Sarah called out. "Who brought us here?"

A door in the back swung open, spilling a fan of light across the floor. A woman walked in, and the only word Michael could think of to describe her was *whoa*. Not beautiful, not sexy, not old or young or anything else. He found it impossible to guess her age or even say if she was ugly or pretty. But her elegant black dress, her gray hair, her wise face, everything about her screamed authority.

Michael prayed that Bryson wouldn't say something stupid.

"Have a seat," the woman said as she walked toward them. "I have to say I'm impressed with your little trick outside, though the two idiots who fell for it have already been fired." She sat down in a plush leather chair and crossed her legs. "I told you to take a seat."

Michael realized that all three of them had been staring at her with their mouths slightly open. Embarrassed, he quickly made his way to the couch on her right and sat down just as Bryson and Sarah took the one on the left.

"I assume you know who I am," she said. Michael couldn't tell if the lady was angry or upset. He'd never heard such indifference in a voice before.

"Ronika," Sarah replied in a reverent whisper.

"Yes, my name is Ronika." She turned her cold gaze on each of them in turn, and Michael was mesmerized. "You're sitting in this room for only one reason: I'm curious. Your age and background give me no clue as to why you might be here. Judging by the time you spent stumbling around upstairs, it wasn't to dance."

"How did you . . ." Michael stopped himself before asking the dumbest question of his life. Of course this lady knew how to find their information. Her hacking skills were probably ten times his own. You didn't become a club owner—much less the owner of the Black and Blue—without talent and loads of money.

She merely raised her eyebrows at him, which was answer enough. She continued.

"I want to make this clear: the Black and Blue didn't get its reputation in the VirtNet by chance. People who've tried what you did today have ended up in places ranging from hospitals to mental wards. Answer my questions. Be up-front and you'll be fine. But be warned—I despise sarcasm."

Michael exchanged a look with Sarah. She'd been the one to get them inside; he knew that now it was his turn. It seemed like Bryson always got off easy.

"Why are you here?" Ronika asked.

Michael cleared his throat and swore to himself that he wouldn't let the lady see how badly she intimidated him. "We were told to come here because we're looking for information."

"Who sent you?"

"An old barber over in Shady Towne."

"Cutter."

"Yeah, he's the one." Michael almost made a joke about his bad breath but stopped himself.

Ronika paused for a second. "I think I already know the answer to this question, but what are you looking for?"

"We're looking for Kaine. The gamer." He assumed that would be enough, but he continued. "Cutter said something about 'the Path.'"

Bryson suddenly stood up, his hands flying to his temples, his eyes squeezed tight. "Oh, crap. Oh, crap."

Michael's heart sank. This couldn't be good.

"What?" Sarah asked.

Bryson dropped his arms and opened his eyes. He looked over at Ronika. "My Tracer just lit up. Kaine knows we're here. He's close."

Ronika seemed completely unfazed.

"Well, of course he is," she said.

CHAPTER 7

BLACK AND BLUE

1

They all looked at the woman, waiting for her explanation. Michael wanted to get up and run, but he knew they might never get another chance to learn anything if he did.

"He's been here before," she said. "I assure you my firewalls are solid. That man wouldn't dare cross me, considering I saved . . . one of his most cherished . . . Tangents from Decay."

Her odd pauses almost made Michael forget they were in danger. He knew that all Tangents eventually went through Decay—an artificial-intelligence program *that* complex and *that* lifelike, with such realistic intelligence, couldn't last forever before its very existence began to contradict its instincts. The research showed that it always started with essential elements in the Tangent's life disappearing for no reason—its artificial memory lost its ability to "fill in the blanks." Then weird things started happening to its "physical" body. The manifestations supposedly varied from Tangent to Tangent. But once the signs got too bad, became obvious to players, the programmers would shut them down. Kill them.

Ronika's voice pulled him back to the present.

". . . wouldn't be around this long if I hadn't cleaned out its coding and basically rebirthed Kaine's prized Tangent. That's not easy to do without erasing its memory, not to mention that the whole thing is illegal. Kaine owes me. He supposedly spent years developing that specific program. I didn't know then what I do now about him, but I will say, I probably still would have done it. It's always good to have friends—and enemies—in your debt."

"He doesn't seem the type to care if he betrays an old friend," Michael pointed out. "Also, he's been trapping people inside the Sleep. He's ruthless, and I don't think we should stick around to see what he does."

Ronika eyed Michael carefully. "Then you are most welcome to leave."

"She won't help us anyway if they're friends," Bryson said.

"Friends?" Ronika repeated, saying the word as if the concept was foreign. "He paid me a ridiculous amount of money. I'm no friend of any gamer. Only an associate. All I'm saying is that what I did for him involved a rare talent of mine, and he wouldn't dare risk jeopardizing its availability in case he needs it in the future."

Michael didn't feel much safer, but they had to start prying. Sarah seemed to have the same idea.

"Look," she said. "We don't have that kind of money. Is there a way we can earn information from you?"

A small wry grin appeared on Ronika's face. "There are a lot of things more valuable than money. The fact that you're sitting here tells me a lot about you. All I want in return for the answers to your questions is one simple favor."

That seemed way too good to be true. Michael had been gaming for long enough to know there were a million terrible things she could ask them to do.

"What favor?" he asked hesitantly.

The smile hadn't left her face. "Oh, I couldn't say now. I will tell you when I need it."

Michael had no clue how the woman could say such innocent things and make them sound so menacing. And yet at the same time he found himself liking her.

"Deal," Bryson said, not bothering to consult with his friends first. But Michael had no heart to complain; they didn't really have much choice but to accept.

"And you two?" Ronika said, looking at Sarah, then Michael.

They both nodded.

"But we have to hurry," Bryson said. "My Tracer is thumping and I wanna get out of here."

Michael didn't need to weigh the options.

"Fine," Ronika said, seemingly satisfied with their arrangement. "Ask your questions."

2

Michael had gotten his friends into this mess, so he conducted the interview, despite his instinct to run. They couldn't come this far and get nothing. He decided to just be quick and to the point. And even though they'd come specifically to ask about the Path, he was going to find out as much as he could.

"Kaine," he began. "Have you heard of something linked to him—something secret, hidden deep inside the Virt-Net?"

"Yes."

Michael held back his excitement. "Any details?"

Ronika remained straight-faced. "Almost nothing. But I think there's definitely something major happening." Her calm was maddening to Michael—he couldn't tell if she knew more than she was letting on.

"Cutter said something about a path."

She nodded. "Yes. The Path. With a capital *P*. How that man finds out about these things, I have no idea."

"What is the Path?" Sarah asked.

Ronika didn't hesitate, which gave Michael confidence she was telling the truth. "It's the only way to get to the Hallowed Ravine, a place hidden deep within the Sleep—just like Kaine and the Path itself. Again, that's a capital *H* and a capital *R*. The word is, that's where Kaine's doing his business. It's nearly impossible to get to—and they say it has several layers of infallible security measures surrounding it. As you seem to know, however, there's always a way through. Always."

"The Path," Michael repeated.

Ronika nodded. "The Path."

Michael noticed that Bryson's knee was bouncing up and down.

"Closer?" Michael asked him.

"He's practically right outside this room, man." Bryson looked at the ceiling, his eyes lit with worry. "We need to go."

"You'll be fine," Ronika said. But for the first time since they'd arrived, Michael sensed the slightest doubt in her voice. "I can only tell you where to start. I've never been on the Path, and I have no interest in doing so."

Michael leaned forward, so excited to finally have some hard information. "Okay, where do we go?"

"Have you ever played *Devils of Destruction*?"

Michael shook his head. *Devils of Destruction* was a lame war game that only old people played. "Never wanted to."

"Because that game sucks," Bryson threw in. "No wonder it starts there—no one would ever notice it. You'd have to be desperate and bored to play that game."

Ronika's expression seemed to have become a little more tense. She was nervous, and they could hear it in her voice. "There's a trench somewhere in the hot zone of the battlefield that has a weak spot in the code. If you can hack your way through that weak spot, there's a Portal to the Path. That's all I know." She stood up. "Now our business is done, and please don't forget your debt. I *will* collect at some point."

"What's wrong?" Michael asked her, standing up himself.

The woman's eyes narrowed. "Maybe I was a little over-confident about our safety."

Even as she said it, Michael heard one of the worst sounds he'd heard in his life.

3

It was unearthly, something between a high-pitched screech and a howl. A scream that was impossibly grating, discordant and harsh. He clamped his hands over his ears and squeezed his eyes shut. All he wanted was for it to stop.

For what had to be a full minute, the sound tore through his body. Then it ended.

Michael opened his eyes and tentatively lowered his hands. Sarah and Bryson were both pale, as if they might throw up. Even Ronika was no longer the picture of calmness she'd been earlier.

"What was *that*?" Bryson breathed.

"It's not Kaine your Tracer picked up," Ronika answered. "He sent . . . something else."

A low rumbling noise started, which somehow seemed to come from everywhere at once, shaking the room around them, then passing into a long moment of silence. All four of them were frozen in place. Michael was embarrassed to admit it, but he was waiting for Ronika to tell them what to do.

The screech exploded through the air again, piercing and raw. Michael fell back on the couch, clamping his hands back over his ears. The noise cut off sooner than before, and he scrambled to his feet, no longer willing to rely on their host.

"Come on," he said, pointing at the door Ronika had come through earlier. "Let's get out of—"

Another eruption of the awful scream sliced off his words, but Bryson and Sarah got the point. They started moving toward the exit, but a sound like a breaking tree branch sent Michael stumbling. He turned to look just as a shadowy hand twice the size of a human's crashed through the wall, sending huge pieces of wood flying through the air. Michael ducked to avoid the debris before he got a good look. The huge fingers lit up with a flash of yellowish light from within.

Michael hit the rug on his knees, arms curled over his head to protect himself. He heard the *click-click-click* of what had to be nails or claws scratching the wood on the other side of the wall, a few huffs of monstrous breath.

Ronika jumped into action. "Quick, follow me!"

Michael didn't waste a second. Ronika started running toward the door, but something thumped against it from the other side, then thumped again. The door trembled in its frame. Ronika changed direction and suddenly fell to the floor in the corner of the room. Michael reached down to help her before he realized she was swinging a hidden panel away from the wall. She crawled into a long compartment, and he got down on his hands and knees and followed her into the darkness. Bryson and Sarah squeezed through the small opening behind him, pushing him against Ronika.

"Close it up," she whispered. "Hurry."

Bryson did as she said, pulling the hidden door back into position.

There was just enough room inside for them to shift until they sat, backs against the wall, four in a line. Michael's head brushed the ceiling. Before any of them had a chance to speak, Ronika closed her eyes tightly and a screen appeared in the air, hovering above her lap before floating over to the wall in front of them. The screen showed the room from which they'd just escaped.

As Michael watched, something exploded out of the hole the strange hand had torn through the wall. A dark, wolfish shape with blurred features leaped past splintered wood and landed on the tile floor, yellow eyes gleaming in its gray head. Three more shadowy creatures jumped through the wall after it, and they each ran to a different corner of the room. The edges of the room were dim, and Michael watched with growing horror as the creatures seemed to vanish into the shadows, melding with the darkness until there was nothing but those two pinpoints of bright yellow light in each corner.

Since they didn't have a Portal to Lift themselves back to the Wake, Michael had no idea what to do. What were those things out there? He'd never seen anything like them in the Sleep before. And why were they just waiting?

Ronika turned to face Michael and his friends, and they waited for her to speak. She'd said that Kaine had sent "something else" to the Black and Blue, so Michael hoped she knew what it was.

"Well?" Bryson finally said in a low whisper.

Ronika gave him a sharp look; then she answered the obvious but unspoken question.

"Those are KillSims. And we're in some serious trouble."

4

Michael had never heard of a KillSim before Tanya had used the term what now seemed like eons ago—but he knew enough that those two words together sent goose bumps across his arms. "What are they?"

"Kaine's creation—stories have been surfacing recently." Ronika looked at the screen. There was still no movement in the room, only dark shadows and yellow eyes. "They're a version of antimatter for the VirtNet. *Antiprogramming* would be a more apt description. If they can bite you and latch on, they'll literally suck the virtual life into some digital abyss that's God knows where. You'd Lift back into your Coffin in the Wake and be ruined, have to start all over. It could even damage your brain in the real world, which might be what happened to some of those people you mentioned earlier."

More chills for Michael. He flinched when a low growl came from the other side of the secret door, but there was no movement on the screen. The noise wasn't like that of any kind of animal in the natural world. There was something staticky and digital about it. Michael braced himself, wondering if that awful screech would come next, but it didn't happen.

"Why aren't they attacking us?" Sarah whispered. "They have to know we came in here."

"I'm not complaining," Bryson murmured.

Ronika spoke so quietly that Michael had to lean in to hear her. "My guess is Kaine wanted to trap us. And now we're cornered better than he even imagined. Maybe he's coming himself, trying to break through my firewalls."

"How do we fight those things off?" Bryson asked. "Do you know anything about them?"

The last word had barely come out of his mouth when the ear-piercing howl tore through the air again.

As soon as it stopped, Ronika answered. "I have no idea," she said, her voice empty of any sense of hope.

The only thing left was for Michael to take charge. "Listen, Ronika, they're obviously here for us. But we can't sit here all day—we're just waiting for Kaine to stroll right in, and he'll find us eventually. You stay while we make a break for the door."

"No," she said. "I'm not leaving you until we're all safe."

Her protectiveness surprised him. "All right, but you know as well as we do, it can only get worse. Especially if Kaine shows up."

"And how do you expect to fight those things off when they pounce on us?" Bryson asked.

"Don't let them bite you," Sarah answered.

Ronika pointed to the screen. "We just have to make it up those stairs outside the door. Somehow Kaine's blocked me from contacting my security detail. But once we're to the top and into the main section of the club, my bouncers will swarm and be too much even for the KillSims."

"Okay. To the door, then," Michael said. "And up the stairs. No problem." But the truth was, terror raced through his body, making it hard for him to breathe.

"We need to stick together," Sarah added. "Stay in a pack."

Michael got onto his hands and knees, ready to crawl through the secret door. "Bryson, you're closest, so you'll have to go first."

"Figures," he replied.

Michael knew Bryson was kidding, but he was right. It shouldn't be him at the front. Michael pushed his way past Sarah and then Bryson to get to the exit. "No—I got us into this mess," he said. "I'll go first."

"But now if *you* die I'll feel bad," Bryson whined.

Michael liked that his friend was at least trying to keep his sense of humor. "You'll just have to live with it."

5

As soon as everyone was lined up behind Michael, he slowly pushed the small wood panel open. Something like candle glow filled the dimly lit room, making everything ethereal and warm. It felt peaceful, but Michael knew the truth: violence hid in every shadow.

He studied the wall directly ahead of them. He couldn't make out any distinct shapes; aside from those yellow eyes, it was just shadow on top of shadow. Michael tried to focus to get a count of how many creatures there were, but an odd thing happened—the yellow eyes vanished when Michael looked directly at them. He turned his head and they came back into view in his peripheral vision. So far nothing had moved. Maybe they *were* waiting for Kaine to give further orders.

Michael kept his gaze averted and carefully inched forward, moving out of the hidden compartment, then edging along the wall, heading for the door. The rug under the furniture gave way to tile, which hurt Michael's knees as he crawled. The digital growl started up again, and he saw a flash of yellow in the gaping hole the creatures had torn in the wall—only about twenty feet away. Michael stopped.

Bryson bumped into him. "Keep going!" he whispered, so loudly he might as well have said it in a normal voice.

Michael stole a glance at his friend. "They might attack if we move too fast."

"They might kill us if we don't!"

Silence settled on the room for a few seconds; then the growling began again. The rumbling static rolled through Michael's body. It was impossible to tell where it was coming from. He sucked in a huge breath and started forward.

When the door was only ten feet away, Michael pulled himself up into a crouch, ready to make a run for it. Movement caught his eye to the right. He turned to look, and it was as if the darkness had melted and splashed onto the floor. Then it coalesced into the same wolf shape he'd seen earlier, yellow eyes blazing like pinpricks of fire. Michael looked directly into the glowing gaze and the eyes seemed to disappear; then a shattering scream erupted from the creature. Michael's hands had barely flown up to cover his ears when the sound stopped, replaced by the strange growling, like an old-school computer buzzing its last moments of life.

He now had no doubt that what they'd guessed was correct. These things just wanted to guard them, make sure they didn't leave. Kaine was coming.

And Michael didn't plan on being there when he showed up.

6

Michael averted his gaze, and the creature's eyes came back into focus; then he slowly stood from his crouch, sliding up against the wall behind him. On instinct, he put his hands out as if to pacify the beast, but he knew it meant nothing to the antiprogram.

"I'll open the door," he whispered to the others. "You guys run for it." The words came out before he realized that the plan meant he'd be the last one to leave the room. And most likely the first to get attacked.

"Let's do it," Bryson replied.

Michael nodded. "Now."

He ran to the door, reaching for the knob just as he noticed the KillSim's head jerk back. Something told him Kaine was watching through those yellow eyes and was shocked to see that Michael and his friends weren't waiting around, cowering in fear. Michael's fingers curled around the cool metal of the handle and he twisted it, swung the door open just in time for Bryson to flash through the opening. Terrible piercing screams tore through the air, and a blur of movement caught the corner of Michael's vision as Sarah ran through, then Ronika.

He was right on her heels. He reached back and grabbed the handle, started to pull the door closed behind him. It was five or six inches from slamming shut when something ripped the whole thing from his grasp, tearing the door from its hinges.

He bolted forward just as Bryson got halfway up the stairs.

"Go! Go! Go!" Michael yelled.

Then something was on his right shoulder. Heavy and sharp. It slammed him to the floor, knocked the air out of his lungs. Gasping for breath, he twisted onto his back, kicked and punched at the huge thing pinning him to the ground. Two yellow lights stared down at him, but everything else was darkness and shadow, seeming to alternate in form between solid and vapor. Michael heard footsteps on the stairs, heard Sarah call his name. Other dark shadows leaped over the one attacking Michael, barking their awful noises. Human screams followed almost immediately. It was an ambush.

The KillSim started battering Michael with four massive fists, as if it had changed its shape from canine to human. For a brief moment Michael pictured his real body back in the Coffin, thrashing as the different elements of AirPuffs and LiquiGels and NerveWire made him feel every last pounding of the creature. It was his own fault for choosing the most realistic Coffin on the market.

Adrenaline burned inside him. He gathered all of his strength and kicked out with both legs, connecting with the KillSim's middle. It flew off him and slammed into the wall of the short hallway between the door and the stairs.

Even as the creature crouched for another attack, Michael was scrambling backward. He hit the opposite wall, then climbed to his feet. The thing jumped, its yellow eyes flashing as it flew toward him. Michael dove to his left to avoid it, leaping back to the ground toward the stairs, and heard its body crash behind him. On his feet again quickly, he turned to see that the thing seemed dazed, slowly trying to right itself on wobbly legs of shadow.

Madness surrounded Michael. The other KillSims had attacked his friends and Ronika, all of whom were fighting to get free. He watched Sarah get loose from her monster, kicking it in the face so that it tumbled down the stairs. Bryson was almost to the door at the top, punching and clawing. Ronika was in the worst shape, just a few feet away from Michael. The KillSim on top of her had pinned each of her limbs to the ground. Its mouth was yawning open above her, the jaws stretching impossibly wide as if it planned to swallow her entire head with one bite.

Michael moved forward to help, but just as he did, a creature pounced on him from behind. It threw him to the right, cutting a gash in his left shoulder. His head slammed into the wall and he collapsed, stunned. He'd barely recovered when the KillSim landed on him and knocked him onto his back, pinning his arms to the ground. Michael still couldn't focus on its true form, but a dark wolf-shaped head leaned in closer to his face and the creature snarled its mechanical growl.

Michael couldn't move. His muscles seemed to have turned to jelly, and his mind spun as he tried to focus on the code, wondering if he could bring in some sort of weapon or skill from another game. But it was impossible to think. The KillSim opened its jaws wider and wider, and Michael saw that it had no teeth, no tongue—nothing but pure darkness hovered above him. It was as if a black hole had winked into existence, ready to suck Michael into the cosmos. Behind him he heard Ronika screaming, heard Bryson and Sarah grunting as they fought, heard the thumps of bodies falling against the ground and walls. Michael tried to free his arms, to kick out again, but nothing did what he told it to. The mouth of the creature yawned wider, coming closer and closer, filling his entire vision.

There was a sharp crash behind them, like glass shattering. Another one followed immediately, the sound clear even over Ronika's screams. All Michael could see now was blackness.

Then Bryson shouted in a strangled voice, "Its eyes! Squeeze its freaking eyes!"

The pain in Michael's head turned to something else. More like an achy buzz, as if bees swarmed between his ears. He couldn't tell anymore if his eyes were open, couldn't feel the creature's paws pinning his arms and legs. The hard floor seemed to no longer press against his body from below. He was floating. Floating in a dark void where the only thing that existed in the great abyss of the KillSim was that deep ache. The buzz increased in volume until he heard almost nothing else. Ronika screamed one last time, as if from a great distance. Sarah was yelling something, but it reached Michael's ears as gibberish.

His thoughts wandered. For some reason he pictured the advertisement outside his apartment for *Lifeblood Deep*, pictured his parents, who'd been gone on their stupid trip for ages, it seemed. He remembered being a little kid— baseball, ice cream, playgrounds.

Michael realized he was completely disoriented. Enveloped by darkness, he squeezed his eyes shut and focused, throwing all his mental effort into pooling every bit of his consciousness into one place. Bryson had told him what to do—something about its eyes. Sarah was nearby, maybe trying to help.

They'd figured something out.

He had to fight back.

This thing was going to kill him.

Michael gathered his energy and screamed, then jerked his arms away from the shadow paws that held them down. He pulled free and groped blindly above him, finding the head of the KillSim, searching with his fingers until he found the place where those yellow lights had glowed. Michael could feel that the creature was trying to pin him again, but he rolled to evade its grip. His hands found two warm orbs, almost hot. He instantly took hold, clamping his fingers into tight fists around what had to be the Kill-Sim's eyes.

With every last drop of strength left in his body, Michael

squeezed as hard as he could. The eyes felt hard and smooth as glass but gave way like gel. As his sight cleared, he watched the eyes begin to ooze between his fingers. The creature let out an anguished shriek and thrashed against Michael, struggling to get loose.

Then its eyes burst.

7

It was as if two eggs had imploded in Michael's hands. The instant it happened, he felt a charge of electricity scorch his palms and run through his arms and chest. He screamed at the pain coursing through his body and pushed until the KillSim fell off him and thumped on the floor. Light swarmed back into Michael's vision, and nausea hit him like a punch to the gut.

The room seemed a different color, duller than before, and his head ached like nothing he'd ever experienced. His thoughts were still jumbled, his mind in a haze. The KillSim lay in a heap at his feet, its outline distinguishable once again. Everything about it seemed to have shrunk; lying there on the ground, it looked like nothing more than an eyeless black dog.

"If we'd just known that from the start," Bryson said.

Michael snapped his gaze away from the creature and toward his friend. The movement sent a spike of pain through his entire skull.

Bryson and Sarah knelt next to Ronika, another dead

KillSim only inches away. Two other creatures had been killed as well—one at the bottom of the stairs and one halfway up. Both of Michael's friends were still breathing heavily, and a quick glance showed him that their hands were burned raw. He looked down at his own and saw the same thing. Only at the sight of them did the pain hit him.

Ronika. Why wasn't she moving?

Michael took a step forward and was just about to ask them what had happened when a blue light flashed from Ronika's forehead and stopped him short. A crackle filled the air, and as Michael stood there frozen he watched her body completely transform.

Blue lights sparkled along her brow, increasing in brightness and frequency until he could no longer see her skin. Then the lights started to grow and spread, moving into her hair and down across her eyebrows, into her eyes and along her nose, her cheeks. Bluish-green butterflies—sparks that looked like wings—replaced her features as the twinkling lights expanded. The wings flapped and sent out sound like a zap of electrical current.

As if she'd been infected with some horrific skin disease, Ronika's entire head submitted to the transformation, and soon there was nothing but a round ball of fluttering blue and green planes of glowing light where her skin had once been. Gradually the ball moved down her neck and spread across her shoulders, along her chest, leaving the strange butterflies in its wake. Michael stood there, helpless, no idea what to do.

Sarah finally spoke, her voice sounding odd through the

crackling electricity emanating from Ronika's disappearing body. "We must've been too late. The thing sucked her digital life out. Just like she warned us."

"That would've been you in another minute," Bryson added, giving Michael a look that said they'd probably never get over just how close it had been.

Michael returned his attention to Ronika without answering. Half her body had been devoured, and the butterflies that covered her head started fluttering away, floating several inches into the air before they suddenly lit up in a bright flash and then disappeared entirely, leaving nothing behind. Soon her entire face was gone forever.

As mesmerizing as the display was, and as badly as Michael's head hurt, it finally hit him that they couldn't waste another second. He looked to his friends, and without a word they got to their feet and ran up the stairs two at a time.

They got out of the club before anyone could ask questions, found a Portal, and Lifted themselves back to the Wake. By the time Michael stepped out of the Coffin, his head felt like a nest of scorpions had hatched inside it.

CHAPTER 8

A VERY SHORT MAN

Miserable, Michael lay in bed. Helga was nicer than ever, bringing him hot tea and soup and bananas—it was all he could stomach—whenever he dinged the little bell she'd placed on his nightstand. His parents had to extend their trip yet again, so with only him and Helga there, the apartment was quiet. He kept the blinds closed and didn't listen to music or watch any shows. The sign that something was *really* wrong with him, though, was that he barely even looked at his NetScreen.

His head just plain *hurt.* And along with that was nausea. Constant, unrelenting nausea. He felt like he was going to throw up at least once or twice an hour. Hence the strange menu requests for Helga. As he lay there in agony, there was plenty of time to think about what had happened in the basement of the Black and Blue Club.

The KillSims. What they'd done to Ronika. How far had

the creature gotten with Michael? Had some of his Aura's essence been sucked out? How close had he come to being another brain-dead victim of Kaine? Had he suffered permanent physical damage? With his eyes closed and his skull throbbing, it sure felt like it. He worried that he was growing stupider by the minute—that he'd forget everything he'd learned and experienced inside the VirtNet.

He knew these thoughts were crazy, and he tried to stay positive. Hopefully they'd stopped the thing in time and his headache would slowly go away. He couldn't imagine spending the rest of his life feeling like he did.

But surprisingly, the pain in his head didn't make him want to stop. It only made him hate Kaine and made him sure of what they were doing. He wouldn't stop until they found the place the VNS was looking for. Threats or no threats, it was simple. Like many games Michael had played before, it was kill or be killed.

Except this time it was for real. And his headache didn't let him forget it.

He didn't get out of bed for a day and a half.

Two days after their rendezvous with Ronika, Michael's head felt much better. He could get up and walk around, shower, even look out into the brightness of the morning without wanting to curl into a ball from the pain. Energized, his spirits lifted, he sat down in the Chair and called out for a private conversation with Bryson and Sarah on the Bulletin. They joined him within ten minutes.

Brystones: It's about time. That nasty headache go away? Helga kiss you, make you all better? Ooh, never mind, don't wanna picture that.

Sarahbobara: Bryson, you have free rein to say what you want because you saved us. You have about a week until I start being your mother again.

Brystones: Now, that I *really* don't wanna think about.

Mikethespike: I was so worried that thing had done permanent damage to me. Still am, but at least it's getting better. And I can speak and type without slobbering on myself.

Sarahbobara: Nice.

Brystones: So when are we gonna do this thing? Find the Path?

Sarahbobara: Sooner than later.

Michael breathed a sigh of relief—they were still in. Scared, maybe—just like him—but in. If anything, the gamer and his dogs had ignited a fire under them.

Michael and his friends went on to talk about school and how they'd manage their schedules. It didn't take long to decide that a few "sick" days wouldn't hurt anybody—at least, not as much as the VNS or Kaine would. The thought brought Ronika to mind, which gave Michael a pang of guilt. Maybe she was lying somewhere in the Wake, brain-dead, like the other victims who'd shown up. Maybe that was the whole point of the KillSims. But how was it all connected?

Sarah suggested they spend that day studying gamer reports on *Devils of Destruction,* the game in which Ronika had said they'd find the entrance to the Path. Maybe there'd be some clues about where to find this weak spot in the code. Then they'd get a good night's rest.

When morning came, it'd be time to move.

3

Michael's doorbell rang in the middle of the afternoon. He was immersed in researching *Devils of Destruction.* He knew it was a war game based on history—which was part of the reason mainly old people liked it. No one his age cared about something that happened years and years ago, but in order to get through it, Michael figured he had to know the details of the war. He'd spent the previous hour reading about the War of Greenland in 2022, where several nations fought a bloody battle over a massive vein of gold discovered there the year before. Everyone wanted it, of course, and they all had their reasons why they could claim the land. The details interested Michael more than he expected them to.

The factions in the war used guerrilla tactics and somewhat primitive weapons, because there were so many sides that using nuclear arms or big bombs was too dangerous.

Weapons with a large blast radius would wipe out some of the enemy, but chances were you'd hit a few friendlies, also. It was a nasty battle that lasted for two years before enough senseless death occurred that everyone stood down. Brilliant world leaders at their best.

The Devils of Destruction were an actual group of mercenaries who fought during the War of Greenland, hired—sometimes by more than one side—to seek out specific targets and eliminate them. And that was what Michael and his friends would be doing in the game. Dropping into the heart of battle with nothing more than machine guns, hoping to find the trench Ronika mentioned before they got killed. Then hope their hacking skills proved their worth.

He ignored the doorbell when it first chimed—the research was far more fascinating than he'd thought it would be, and he wondered why he'd never actually given the game a shot. He assumed Helga would answer the door, but when it rang again he remembered she'd gone to visit her sister for the day.

Grumbling the whole way, Michael pressed his EarCuff to shut down the NetScreen and headed for the front door. When he pulled it open, he was surprised to find no one there. A chill ran down his spine—nothing seemed like simple happenstance now that he was involved in something so heavy. He looked up and down the hall and at the stairs, but didn't see anything. He was just about to close the door and lock it tight when he noticed a note had been taped to the outside.

A short message had been handwritten on the small slip of paper:

Meet me in the alley where we picked you up. Now.

4

He didn't have to think twice about doing as he'd been ordered. He knew it might be a trap, but the odds seemed slim. Kaine didn't seem as dangerous in the real world—why not, Michael couldn't say—and how would anyone else know where the VNS had picked him up that day? Then there was Agent Weber. The last thing he could afford to do was tick her off.

It only took twenty minutes for him to get there. He turned off the main road and walked down the long, deserted alley. There wasn't a soul in sight—not even a car—but several large Dumpsters waited in the middle of the road, and something told Michael that was where he'd find the person he had to meet. It was hot outside, but there was a nice breeze that cooled the sweat on his neck. Loose pieces of trash blew past and danced in the air. The alley was gray and uninviting.

As he approached the first Dumpster, his heart picked up speed and he hesitated before finally peering around its side. He relaxed when he saw an extremely short bald man wearing a three-piece suit. The stranger wasn't threatening. He had a full beard, which made his hairless dome look even more stark, and his hands were in his pockets.

"Are you—" Michael began, but the man cut him off.

"Yes, Michael. Now get over here so people can't see you from the street." He jerked his head, indicating to Michael where to go, then backed up a couple of steps, his face as glum as a funeral director's.

Michael had to hold back a snicker as he joined him. The guy was short. Straight-out-of-a-cartoon short. "What did you want to see me for?"

"Progress report," the man answered. He avoided looking Michael in the eye. His gaze flicked left and right, as if he expected an ambush at any moment. Which didn't make Michael feel very safe. "What's happened, what have you learned, what are your plans, that sort of thing."

"Well, we—"

The stranger cut him off again. "And make it snappy. We shouldn't be seen together. I've got plenty of business to get to."

"Oh . . . kay," Michael said. *What a weird dude,* he thought. "I think we're on the right track, but we've been attacked by Kaine twice now."

"*By* Kaine?" the little man asked, taking a step forward and looking at Michael directly for the first time. "You're absolutely sure it was the . . . man himself?"

Michael searched for words, suddenly unsure. "Well, yeah, I think so. I guess we didn't know for sure the second time. They were KillSims, and Ronika assumed Kaine had sent them."

"Ronika? Who's Ronika?"

"You really don't know?"

"Like I said, we want to hear it from you. Tell me everything."

"How do I know you are who you say you are? Actually"—Michael hesitated before he spoke again—"you haven't even told me who you are."

The impish man was obviously annoyed. "My name is Agent Scott, and I work for Agent Weber. That's all you need to know. We're running out of time."

When Michael didn't answer, the stranger rolled his eyes and pressed his EarCuff. A VNS badge floated out between them and, a little embarrassed that he had to bend over to see the thing, Michael pretended to study it as if he knew what to look for. Hoping the man hadn't just called his bluff, he nodded.

"All right," Scott said. "*Now* tell me everything."

Michael did. About being trapped in a void of space and hearing—*seeing*—Kaine's terrible warning, about Cutter, about Ronika and the Black and Blue, the KillSims, the Path, the Hallowed Ravine to which it supposedly led, the plan to enter *Devils of Destruction* in the morning—all of it.

When he finished, Agent Scott scratched his bearded chin, his elbow resting on the palm of his other hand, and looked at the ground studiously. It was as if he was the world's shortest version of Sherlock Holmes. Michael waited patiently, fighting another urge to laugh.

Finally, the agent returned his attention to Michael. "Go ahead and move forward, then. But don't assume that Kaine is the only one following you or trying to stop you. Do you understand me? Assume everyone you meet is your enemy."

"That ought to be fun," Michael muttered, but his insides twisted as he spoke.

"Do you understand me?" the man asked again slowly.

Michael wanted to remind him that he was the taller one. But he just nodded.

"Michael—I need verbal confirmation."

"Yes, I understand."

"Good." Agent Scott seemed satisfied. After yet another glance up and down the vacant alley, he leaned in close to Michael. "We've still got you and your two friends' Auras tagged with Tracers. Even with your Hider codes we'll be able to find you, so don't worry. We'll know where you are, and we'll be able to send in the cavalry when you finally break into this Hallowed Ravine you've heard about. If the Mortality Doctrine program is being hidden anywhere, that'll be the place. So be sharp. And safe."

"Yes, sir." Suddenly the man didn't seem so short anymore.

"Good. Very good. I'll be off, then."

"Uh, sir?" Michael asked hesitantly. "If we get in trouble before the Hallowed Ravine, are you going to help us? Since you'll be watching?"

Agent Scott shook his head as if he'd never heard a more ridiculous question. "That's not how this works. We can't act like we know what's going on. We've got a lot of teams working on this, and we'll just have to hope one of you makes it in. Until you do, we can't help."

"And what if we get killed?" Michael asked. "Or have our Auras erased, like what happened to Ronika?"

The little man smiled for the first time since they'd met. "Be vigilant. There's something about Kaine that's . . . fishy. That's all I can say."

And with that he turned and started walking down the alley.

5

Michael stood there by the Dumpster until the agent had disappeared around the corner. *What a strange little man,* he thought again, and finally let out the snicker that'd been building inside, probably from stress more than anything. But he couldn't remember the last time he'd laughed or even felt good. The day brightened ever so slightly.

He turned to head home but had only made it halfway down the alley when a sudden pain lanced his skull. It was so powerful he grabbed his head and dropped to his knees. He was barely aware of his groans echoing off the canyon-like walls of the alley.

The pain was far worse than what he'd felt lying in bed after being attacked by the KillSims. It pulsed with every heartbeat. With his eyes squeezed tight, he crawled blindly to the side of the alley until he felt the wall, then sat with his back against it, rubbing his temples. Slowly, he tried to open his eyes, but the brightness of the day sent a fresh wave of agony through his head. And something about where he was didn't seem right. He squinted, trying to figure out what was off.

The lane before him quivered and rippled as if it had been turned into a river of gray oil. The Dumpsters to his right floated up into the air and spun in circles. Flashes and images of bodies kept appearing and disappearing all around him. The buildings that bordered the alley were askew, leaning in impossible directions, defying physics. The sky had turned a horrible purple color, bruised and splotchy with dark red clouds. Panicked, Michael squeezed his eyes shut and curled up into a ball on the pavement, begging for the episode to end.

And a few seconds later it did. The pain in his head just stopped. There was no lingering ache. It was just . . . gone, like it had never happened.

Relieved but wary, he opened his eyes to see that everything was back to normal. Still shaky, he climbed to his feet and looked up and down the alley. Nothing was out of the ordinary.

The only thing Michael could do was continue what he'd been doing moments before. Once again, he started down the alley toward home, this time with one scary thought in his mind: That KillSim had done something to him. Something terrible.

6

When Michael got home, he went straight to his room and flipped on his NetScreen. A thought had occurred to him on his walk back—even before he talked to his friends about what had just happened, he needed to find out what had become of Ronika in real life after the KillSim attack.

It took him almost two hours to put all the pieces together. And it wasn't pretty.

Ronika was obviously not the woman's real name. And being in her position, running a club like the Black and Blue inside the VirtNet, she would've done everything in her power to make sure people didn't find out who she was in the Wake. But after digging through every last NewsBop, running dates and times, and comparing them to when he and his friends had been at the club, Michael was able to build a plausible story.

There was a woman in Connecticut named Wilhelma Harris whose job was to oversee the firewall security for a gaming software development firm Michael had never heard of in New York City. Her job description, and research on her lifestyle, both pointed to the fact that she was almost always in the Sleep and had few friends or family in the real world. This same woman had been found by police wandering the streets of her local downtown area—right after Michael had seen Ronika destroyed by a KillSim at her club—with what they described as a "dazed look," and she grew hostile when they approached her. Then she fell into a coma, in which she'd remained ever since.

The police were asking for friends and family to come forward because her Coffin had short-circuited and there was absolutely zero trace of her existence in the VirtNet—it was as if she'd never once Sunk into the Sleep. They also said that her life readings weren't doing well and that she might not live much longer.

And then the kicker: she had a dog, and the tag on its collar read RONIKA.

It had to be her.

Michael shut everything down and went to lie on his bed. Staring at the ceiling, he thought of what they'd seen happen to the club owner. Her skin and hair and clothes transforming into digital ashes, then blowing away and winking out of existence. She'd been erased by a KillSim. And Michael thought about what it had done to her actual body.

A coma. Life readings not doing so well. Might not live much longer.

And whatever had happened to her, the same process had at least been started on Michael. He could be partially damaged.

Remembering the intensity of the pain that tore through his head in the alley and the wild visions that had horrified him for those few moments, he decided to put off telling his friends about it. Tomorrow was a big day, and they had big plans. Maybe they could talk about it on the way.

It took a long time for Michael's thoughts to settle down. Right before he fell asleep, he had the distant and foggy realization that Helga must've decided to stay with her sister for the night. She'd never come home.

CHAPTER 9

NONE SHALL PASS

1

Michael woke up ten minutes before his alarm went off. Though the now ever-present fear was at the back of his mind—anxiety about what awaited him in the Sleep—excitement filled his bones as well. Gaming had always been the love of his life, and here he was about to embark on a mission where the stakes couldn't be any higher. This would truly be the game of games—something the great Gunner Skale might've envied. There was a part of him that wondered if one day he'd look back and think he was naive to be so excited. But that part was tiny and easy to shut down.

It was lonely in his apartment without his parents or Helga, and he wanted out of there. After a quick shower and two big bowls of cereal, he went back to his room to get in the Coffin. The early-morning light spilled in through the window, and in an almost somber moment of tribute, he gazed at the huge advertisement for *Lifeblood Deep*. He had to catch himself before he spoke out loud to the thing. He wanted it to know that he hadn't given up, that the Deep was still his ultimate goal in life.

And finding Kaine and this Mortality Doctrine would surely punch his ticket there.

2

Michael Sank into the Sleep and met Bryson and Sarah at the Gaming Depot, a popular hub for frequent gamers. There were spots to hang out, eat, and use credits to upgrade everything from weapons to spaceships. Most important, it was a place where you could swap cheats and secrets and build alliances.

All three of them knew a ton of people there, so they met at a little-known Portal that was out of the way and behind a big display of trees and fountains. Sarah transferred over a simple disguise program for their walk to the *Devils of Destruction* entrance. They couldn't let others find out they were up to something unusual—it would be weird if anyone saw them enter the game. No one their age played *Devils*. It had always been a grandpa game.

When they started walking, Michael finally got up his nerve and told them about the meeting with the suited dwarf and the massive headache he'd had immediately afterward. As the story came pouring out, relief filled him. He'd almost decided to just keep it to himself—at least the part about the strange visions. But these were his best friends, and that just didn't seem right, especially with what he was asking them to do.

He finished by telling them he felt fine now and he hoped it was over.

"You lying sack," Bryson said. "I can tell you believe that about as much as you'd believe Sarah and I are married back in the Wake."

"Which we aren't" was Sarah's response. "Just want to make sure that's clear."

Michael shrugged as they passed a group of men dressed in full armor. "Just trying to stay positive."

"Well," Sarah chided, "if it happens again, you better not wait until the next *day* to tell us or I'll make you hurt somewhere else to take your mind off the noggin." She smiled and touched his arm gently. "You have to trust us, Michael."

All he could do was nod.

Bryson was shaking his head. "I can't believe that stuff about Ronika. Seriously. Are you sure it's her?"

"Positive," Michael replied. "That KillSim barely got started on me and look what happened. According to Ronika, the whole point of those creatures is to erase your mind, remember? Not just your Aura but your mind in real life."

Bryson stopped and looked at them. "And yet we're jumping right back into the fire. What if KillSims are just the start of it?"

Sarah and Michael shrugged at the same time. Bryson followed, but he continued shaking his head as if he knew they were making the wrong decision, but he'd do it to appease his friends.

"You want to turn back?" Michael asked him, then tried to make light of it. "Just say the word, brother. I'll buy you a pacifier and you can go home."

Bryson didn't miss a beat. "Nah, I'll just borrow one of yours."

And that was when they turned a corner and saw the sign for *Devils of Destruction*.

3

Michael loved how the VirtNet was a visual soup of archaic imagery mixed with the most advanced technology humans had ever known. This section of the Gaming Depot resembled an old boardwalk by the ocean, where arcades and restaurants and old-looking social clubs lined a walkway of wooden planks. Most of the shops here were actual games, though—a faux entrance to an entirely different world.

The sign for *Devils of Destruction* was huge and bordered with burning lightbulbs that flickered and sizzled. The letters were written in dark green—which Michael assumed was a reference to Greenland—with a red glow behind the word *Devils*. On the right side of the sign, there was a picture of a heavily clothed, helmet-wearing soldier, a machine gun pointed to the sky in one hand and a severed head, dripping with blood, hanging from his other fist. It seemed a little over-the-top.

They stopped right under the marquee, their necks craned to get a better look.

"Greenland," Bryson said. "I'm almost seventeen years old and I've never played a game set there before. Must be one happenin' place."

Sarah turned to face her friends. "Most of it's covered in snow and ice, big glaciers. We're going to freeze our butts off."

"Or something worse," Bryson muttered. Then he flashed a playful grin like he'd just told the funniest joke of his life.

"Then keep 'em warm," Sarah said with an eye roll.

He pointed to the front door, a rickety piece of wood that looked like it hadn't been painted in ages. More specifically, a door that had been *programmed* to look like it had been neglected. It was all part of the atmosphere. "Well, we've studied the maps and we've made our plan. Let's go for it."

"When you die it makes you go back to the beginning," Sarah said. "So if it happens to one of us, the other two need to die on purpose. We can't get separated if we're going to all get through."

Michael didn't necessarily agree with that. "I don't know. As long as we figure out where the Portal to the Path is, that's all that matters—we can't waste a chance if we're deep inside the battle zone. We just won't actually go *through* the Portal until we're all back together. If someone dies, the others wait for them."

"Yeah," Bryson said with a mock look of arrogance. "I'll be sure to hold off until you guys catch up. Now come on." Without waiting for a response, he walked to the door, opened it, and stepped inside.

4

It was an old-fashioned lobby with red carpet and lightbulb-bordered posters for other games covering the walls, the lights flashing around each in a clockwise loop. A concession stand stood in the middle, and the smell of popcorn filled the air. Michael noticed a teenage girl with black hair and bright red eyeliner at the register, smacking her gum like she hoped to pulverize it to nothing.

To the right was the ticket counter, behind which stood a woman, arms folded across her ample bosom, scowling at the newcomers. Everything about her was ample, actually. Large shoulders, thick neck, huge head. She wore no makeup, and her graying hair was stringy and unstyled. *A real looker,* Michael thought.

"Um, I'm scared," Bryson whispered. "Could one of you buy the tickets, please? I think that lady slaughtered half my village when I was a baby."

Sarah laughed, louder than she probably meant to. "I'll do it, you big teddy bear."

"I'll come with you," Michael whispered. "I think I'm in love."

"What do you want?" the lady asked gruffly when they stepped up to the counter. "Popcorn's over there." She nodded toward the concession stand, but the rest of her body didn't move a muscle.

"We're not here for popcorn," Sarah said coolly.

"Then what *are* you here for, smart aleck?" The woman had an unpleasant way of speaking out of the side of her mouth.

Sarah looked at Michael, half amused and half puzzled.

"Hey!" the lady barked. "I asked you, not your boyfriend."

Sarah's head whipped back to face the woman. "Well, obviously we want to play the game. *Devils of Destruction*? There's a huge sign for it right outside your door? Maybe you've heard of it."

Michael winced. Sarah was going too far.

The ticket lady laughed, a deep rumble that sounded like it should've come from a man. "Go on, kids. I'm not in the mood."

Michael tried the nice approach. "Ma'am, we really do want to play. We have the day off from school. I've been studying Greenland."

The woman unfolded her arms and put her hands on the counter, then leaned forward. Michael caught a whiff of something like cat pee. "You're serious, aren't you?"

He knew his expression showed how perplexed he was. "Um . . . yeah. Why are you acting like this? We just want three tickets to the game."

Her face actually softened a bit. "You really don't get it, do you? You aren't just being a wise guy?"

Michael shook his head in response.

"Kid, you can't play this game if you're under twenty-five. Now scram."

5

The three of them stood back outside the building a little shell-shocked and very confused.

"What in the world?" Bryson asked, glaring at the shoddy door. "All I've heard about is how crappy this game is. What could possibly be in there that makes it A.O.?"

A.O. stood for Adults Only, and Michael was just as confused. "Maybe when people say that only grandpas play it, that's literally what they mean. They're the only ones who are allowed to."

"No way," Sarah responded. "If there was really stuff in there that made it A.O., we'd know all about it, because every kid on the planet would be figuring out ways to break in. They have to be trying to stir up interest. They probably just changed it."

Again, just like with his strange attack in the alley with the headache, Michael wasn't buying any coincidences. "Or more likely a certain someone doesn't *want* us playing it. This would be an easy way to throw a roadblock at us."

Sarah scoffed. "All they've done is add another hour or two to the trip. Ratings haven't stopped us before."

"Ain't that the truth," Bryson said. Then he let out a sinister laugh. "Who could forget our adventures in the Vegas Vat of Doom?"

"Oh boy" was Sarah's response.

"Let's get to work," Michael said. They went to a bench that overlooked the ocean, closed their eyes to focus on the code, and started maneuvering.

6

Two hours later, they still had nothing.

They'd tried everything, pooling their experience from years of gaming and programming and hacking and other illicit doings. But nothing worked. It wasn't that the firewalls and shields protecting *Devils of Destruction* were impenetrable; they were just elusive. Almost like they didn't exist—and if you couldn't find a wall, you couldn't climb it. After searching and searching, they all agreed it'd be useless to even keep trying. Michael had never come across such a thing before.

"This is weird," Michael said, looking out at the endless sea. The sky was dark with clouds. "I almost wonder if the game's even real. Who knows—maybe if we had been adults, the lady would've had some other excuse to keep us out. It doesn't add up, does it?"

Sarah was staring at her shoes, concentrating hard on something. "Maybe the game is really, really awesome and super popular with older people, and they don't want us knowing about it or getting in on the action. It could use old security technology we don't even know about. Either way, what are we going to do? I don't think we can try the same trick we used at the Black and Blue."

"If we did," Bryson said, "that old lady would probably sit on us until we had to Lift out or suffocate."

Michael stood up. Determination raged like an inferno inside him. He was getting into that game, no matter what.

"Come on," he said. "We're doing this the old-fashioned way."

"We are?" Bryson asked, surprised.

"Yes, we are. I'm going back inside." Michael stomped off, not knowing where his sudden bravery had come from and not caring. His friends hurried to catch up.

7

Michael didn't really have a plan. And he knew there'd be more waiting for them than that gum-smacking girl and the lady he thought of as Stonewall. The game people had to have other ways to keep them out. But Michael was ready to get past them all. He was fired up and ready for a fight.

Bryson grabbed his shoulder and spun him around just as they reached the shabby door.

"What?" Michael asked. "If you try to stop me, I might chicken out."

"Call me crazy, but shouldn't we talk this through a little? I don't know, come up with a plan, maybe?"

Michael knew he should calm down, but he didn't want to. "Think of all the crap you've dragged me into over the years. It's my turn now. Just follow my lead. It can't be too bad in there—they know people won't just try to break in. The visual evidence would be too strong, and they'd end up in jail. But we're desperate enough to try, so let's go."

Sarah was smiling at him with her eyebrows slightly raised, as if she was impressed. "I like this side of you."

"Yeah, I know. Come on." He turned away from them and opened the door.

8

As soon as they entered, Michael could tell that the huge lady behind the ticket counter knew they were going to start trouble.

She shook her finger at them. "No, no, no you don't. I can see it in your eyes, boy. I already told you—there's no way I'm letting you game today. Just turn your butts around and scoot on back out the door."

Michael hadn't stopped walking, hadn't slowed a bit. He stayed on course for the back of the room, with Bryson and Sarah right behind him. When he reached the concession stand he noticed that the black-haired girl had momentarily stopped chewing her gum. She just stood there staring at them with a shocked look on her face as they passed by.

"Why'd they let you work in a place like this, anyway?" Michael asked her, but she didn't answer.

Stonewall was moving out from behind her counter, flabby flesh swaying on her arm as she waved at them to stop. "Stop right there, mister. Stop. Right. There." She took a path to cut them off, but they were walking too fast for her.

Michael didn't know the layout of the place, but from what he could tell, aside from where they came in, there was only one exit from the lobby, which had to be the entrance to *Devils of Destruction*. It was a shadowy hallway that branched off the back right corner of the room. And that was where he headed.

Suddenly a booming voice filled the air. A deep voice

with a thick Southern accent. "How'd you like your pretty faces filled with holes?"

Michael stopped in his tracks, then turned around just as he heard two heavy metallic clicks—the sound of a shotgun being cocked. When he saw the source of the voice, his breath caught in his throat like the air had turned into balls of cotton. That same girl who'd been smacking her gum and acting like she didn't care one whit about the world was standing on top of the concession stand holding two sawed-off shotguns, their barrels pointed at Michael and his friends.

"The name's Ryker," the girl said. "And I ain't letting punks like you three steal entry on my watch. Ain't, can't, won't. Now get your runty little butts out of here before I start shooting."

Michael had frozen in place, eyes glued to the strange person with the guns named Ryker.

"Y'all think I'm just some clown at a rodeo?" Ryker asked, holding her weapons up a little higher. "It'll be some awful mess to clean you all up, but y'all better believe I'll do it. I'll lose every last penny of my pay this month if you get in. Now get lost!"

At some point during her rant, Michael decided that he wasn't leaving. If he had to go through the horror of being shot, so be it. He'd wake up in his Coffin and come marching right back. This girl wasn't going to kick him out without a fight.

"Fine," he called. "We'll just mosey right on out the door."

Holding his hands up, he slowly made his way toward

her. He knew he'd only get one chance at this, and he hoped his friends didn't end up being the ones who got shot.

"Careful, there," Ryker said. "Make one more move and you'll be hurting good before Lifting back to the Wake. How's that sound?"

Michael took another slow step toward the girl. She was only a few feet away now. "Look, I swear we didn't mean any harm. We just have some questions."

"I said *careful*!" She aimed both shotguns at his face. It should have relieved him that Bryson and Sarah were no longer in immediate danger, but he found himself wishing she'd go right ahead and aim the stupid things back at them.

Another step. Then another. Hands up, his eyes wide and innocent, steady pace with no sudden movements. So close now.

"Stop!" Ryker screamed.

Michael froze. "Okay. Okay." He put his hands down and pretended he was going to turn away and head for the door again. "I'm sorry we—"

He spun and leaped into the air, swinging his arms up as he did. He swatted at the barrels of the two guns, tipping them toward the ceiling just as the girl pulled the triggers. Twin booms thundered in the air. Pellets riddled the ceiling and walls, breaking glass and splintering wood. Michael slammed into Ryker, and both of them tumbled over the edge of the concession stand and crashed to the floor. She struggled to get free, but he was on top of her and he was bigger. He wrestled the two guns out of her hands and pointed one of them at her face.

"Tables . . . are turned," he said through heavy breaths. "Don't tempt me."

Ryker squirmed beneath him but with less effort than before. "Such a brute, pointing that thing at a girl's face. Your daddy beat up your momma, too?"

"Oh, shut up. You were the one threatening to kill us." He lightly tapped the tip of the gun on her nose, then got up.

"Ow!" she yelled. Michael had never seen such a look of ferocity on a girl's face before.

"That was dangerous," Sarah said dryly. He looked over to see her and Bryson exactly where he'd left them.

"It worked, didn't it?" Michael realized something then. "Hey, where'd that lady go?"

Bryson pointed over at the ticket stand. "She ran over there and disappeared under the counter."

Michael knew immediately that something was wrong. He climbed over the concession stand and joined his friends, handing one of the shotguns to Bryson. "Let's get out of here."

That was when Stonewall popped up from behind the counter, huge arms folded across her chest, just like the first time they'd seen her. "You picked the wrong day to mess with me. Did you really think I'd let you waltz in here and play a game you're restricted from? Huh? Did you?"

A hissing sound suddenly came from all directions at once. Michael spun in a circle to find its source, and it took him a moment to realize that several holes had appeared along the walls and in the ceiling. Before he could warn his friends, thick lengths of black rope were shooting out, slithering through the air like flying snakes.

He turned to move, but the ropes were everywhere. A piece wound around his ankle, squeezing tightly, as if it was alive.

As he bent over to yank it off, the rope jerked him off his feet and flung him into the air.

Michael's stomach lurched as his body twisted, the rope whipping him back and forth like a dog does its prey. And just like a dog's prey, he was disoriented. But somehow he'd held on to the gun. As he flew around the room, he focused all his energy into trying to get it cocked. Lights flashed and the colors of the lobby spun until they merged into one. His head began to ache, as if another episode was coming on.

Michael gripped the shotgun with both hands, strained to double over, and aimed, making sure his foot wasn't in the way. Then he fired.

The gun recoiled and flipped him backward. The floor came into view and kept coming, rushing up until he slammed into it face-first. Through the pain, he could feel the rope around his leg break free—he'd hit his target.

Its partners closed in, coiling and twisting in the air. There were dozens of them, and Michael scanned the room to see what had happened to his friends. Bryson was pinned to a wall, one black cable around his thigh and another one clasping his arm as he struggled to break free. Sarah had avoided outright capture, but she had the loose end of one of the cords in her hands and was trying to keep it from her face, as if it was a cobra straining to strike.

A rope found Michael, snaked up his leg, and began to twist around his knee. He grabbed it and yanked, jumping over it as he did. Then he batted another one coming for his head. Sarah lost her battle—the black cord had wrapped around her neck and was now dragging her to the wall where Bryson stood, his eyes closed and no longer struggling. Terrified that Bryson had been hurt, Michael started in that direction but was cut short by ropes attacking from both sides. He dove to the ground and rolled, kicking out to fling the cables away.

A draining, hopeless feeling tried to suck the life from him. How in the world could they get out of this? He only had one more shell in his shotgun; Bryson's had slid clear across the room and landed at the foot of the ticket counter, behind which Stonewall stood like a statue, silently watching. Something about her made Michael do a double take—she *was* like stone, unnaturally still. Her eyes were glazed over and focused on some point in the distance. He'd never seen anything like it.

A cord tightened around Michael's waist, pulling him back to the fight. Too late he tried to grab it and wrench it from his body; it had a solid hold. The cable jerked him across the floor, and he struggled to free himself as he slid toward his friends, both of whom were now cinched up against the wall with several more ropes than before. The gun started to slip out of Michael's grasp, but he held on, knowing that last shell was his only chance.

Another rope began to wrap around his left ankle; he kicked it away. One came in from the right, straight at the gun, but he knocked it down with the gun's barrel, almost pulling the trigger on reflex. Both hands free for a moment, he gripped the weapon tightly and aimed it two feet down the length of cable that had him by the waist. The blast sent him slamming into the floor again, dazing him for an instant. But he was able to tear loose from the now-limp coil. He rolled, dropping the gun, as it was now useless, and scrambled to his feet, slapping ropes away. That was when it hit him: he suddenly knew what the old lady was doing. Why she was so still and focused.

She was controlling the ropes.

He'd only have one chance at this.

Stonewall was thirty feet away, behind the ticket counter. In front of it, Bryson's gun lay there for the taking. Between it and Michael, cords of black rope flew through the air like living vines, forming a spiderweb of traps. He sprinted forward.

They all attacked him at once, swarming in from every direction. He flung his arms wildly, jumped, and twisted, exploding with adrenaline. A cord tripped him up, sent him crashing to his stomach. Two ropes immediately snaked around his torso and he spun, grabbing them and pulling them off. He kicked and flailed, swatted and punched. Somehow he got back onto his feet and moved forward again, now several feet closer to his target. The ropes came again.

He pushed ahead, acting on instinct. He must've looked ridiculous, like a cracked-up dancer. He clambered toward the gun, getting closer and closer. A rope found his arm and cinched tight before he could do anything. It flung him into the air as he gripped it with his other hand and ripped his arm loose from its hold. Luckily, it had been pulling him in the right direction, and he slammed into the floor and slid forward until his head smacked the bottom of the ticket counter. The gun was right in front of his face.

He grabbed it, held it tight with both hands. Before he could get up, the ropes flew in, going for his legs and waist and chest, wrapping tightly around him. As he was fighting off those attempting to wind around his arms, the other ropes lifted him into the air.

He shot up and Stonewall came into view, her features still frozen. Michael only had an instant—the black cords were converging on his arms, trying to take the gun away. He aimed for her chest. But everything stopped before he could pull the trigger.

The ropes let go of him. As Michael crashed to the ground, the sounds of their retreat filled the room, a ringing metallic hiss as they slid back into their cubbyholes. The breath knocked out of him, Michael rolled over to look at his friends. They were free, too. He glanced back at Stonewall, saw her body slumped forward on the counter.

"What . . . ," Michael started to say, but he came up empty.

"I hacked her," Bryson said from behind, his voice trembling with exhaustion. "She's a Tangent—I shut her down. I've never been able to do that before—I got lucky, found a weak spot. Barely."

So that's why his eyes were closed, Michael thought, so relieved he wanted to laugh.

"Let's get going," Sarah said.

And Michael knew exactly what she meant. Into the game.

CHAPTER 10

THREE DEVILS

1

It took a few moments, but Michael was finally able to get the air flowing normally into his lungs. Sucking in one deep breath at a time, he walked over to Bryson and Sarah. Without speaking, they knew what to do. All three of them turned and made for the hallway in the back of the lobby.

A familiar voice rang out from behind them, and Michael turned to see Ryker standing on the concession stand again.

"Y'all are as clueless as can be," she called out. "You think you know what you're lookin' for, but you don't."

Her words felt ominous to Michael. He knew how the Sleep worked, and he wondered if they had some deeper meaning that spelled trouble. Was she talking about the Portal or something bigger? Like Kaine himself.

"Oh, go lick your mama's wounds," Bryson replied.

Before Ryker could answer, the three broke into a run. Michael hoped he never had to lay eyes on that girl again.

2

The hallway grew dark, then cold, and Michael began to shiver. Though there was no light source, they could see just enough to be able to keep moving forward, and the hall went on and on and on. Gradually, when they realized no one had followed them, they slowed to a walk, and as they pressed forward, the temperature dropped. Soon Michael could see his breath in front of him.

He guessed they'd gone well over a mile before anyone spoke.

"This is the weirdest entrance to a game I've ever seen," Bryson said, breaking the silence.

"You don't think it's a trap, do you?" Michael asked. "Maybe they dropped us into another game since we didn't have access."

"That's against the law," Bryson responded.

"So is breaking into a game," Michael said.

Bryson shrugged. "Yeah, well."

"Look up there." Sarah was pointing ahead. "The walls change. And it gets lighter."

They started running again and soon came upon a place where the walls were covered in ice that seemed to glow from within. Suddenly Michael could see better, and everything was *different*.

"Holy crap," Bryson said, looking down at himself.

Their clothes had changed from their daily wear into puffy white snowsuits littered with pockets, all kinds of gear strapped to the belts. Michael noticed straps over his shoulders and realized he and his friends wore stuffed backpacks as well. Its weight didn't hit Michael until he'd fully examined his new uniform.

He tightened the pack's straps a little and started examining his belt. He had five grenades, a canteen, a knife, and some rope. "Well, guess that answers that question," he announced. "We're in."

"And it looks like we're on the glacier front," Sarah said. The gold vein—the thing everyone was fighting over—ran mostly below Jakobshavn Glacier, one of the bigger ones in Greenland. But the battlefronts ran all the way down to the tundra as well, a messy goop of swamp and mud.

"They better have real weapons waiting for us up there," Bryson said, nodding down the tunnel. "I don't know if I can stomach fighting with a knife today, game or no game."

Michael pulled his blade out and looked at it—solid and gray and sharp. "Yeah, me neither."

"That makes three of us," Sarah said as they started walking again. "Maybe we can code something in from another game. I just hope we don't end up in jail for any of this."

Michael waved his hand, dismissing the suggestion. "We're doing all this *because* of the VNS. They're not going to throw us in jail for following orders." Though even as he said it, he wasn't sure he was right.

"Oh yeah?" she replied. "You positive about that? All

that stuff about how top secret this is? They'll look the other way when you come crawling to them for help someday, say they've never even heard of you."

Michael knew his friends could see the anxiety on his face. "All the more reason to find Kaine."

They grew silent and picked up their pace, jogging down the long, icy tunnel. The gear was heavy and started to wear on Michael—he could tell he was slowing. Then the tunnel began to slope upward, making it even harder.

"How long *is* this stupid thing?" Bryson asked.

No one answered. No one could.

3

They finally reached the end: a metal door held closed with a heavy bar anchored by two enormous iron rails. Wooden benches lined the walls, and there was a huge open locker full of machine guns and ammo. Michael took a moment to catch his breath.

"I assume that when you die out there," Sarah said, "you end up right back here."

"Probably so." Bryson started rummaging through the locker. "But I've got news for you. I don't plan on dying out there."

"Me neither," Michael said. "Let's get going."

He and Sarah followed Bryson's lead, and soon they each had a heavy gun and several spare clips of ammo. Michael loaded his and checked the weight and settings—he'd used similar weapons plenty of times. Maybe they wouldn't need to risk trying to hack into their other games after all.

"I'm just as worried about the cold," Sarah said. "Maybe that's one of the reasons this game is A.O. Most kids would run out there and think killing people was all that mattered. We need to make sure we stop and warm up now and then so we don't get frostbite."

Bryson was shaking his head. "That can't be it. There's gotta be something worse out there. A lot worse. It's hard to get rated A.O."

Michael agreed completely. They'd all seen plenty of games that *weren't* A.O., and many of those included some truly mentally scarring experiences. "At least we studied up. Nothing to do but get started. Find that gateway to the Path."

"Prepare to freeze your heinies off," Bryson said as he walked over and hefted the bar off its rails. He tossed it on the ground, where it clanged, then rolled to a stop at Sarah's feet.

"You were born to be a soldier," she said.

Bryson winked at her, then yanked open the heavy door. A burst of arctic wind and swirling ice crystals tore through the tunnel. It was the coldest thing Michael had ever felt in his life.

Bryson yelled something unintelligible, then stepped into the world of Greenland. Michael and Sarah followed.

4

The sky above was a brilliant blue, and Michael realized it wasn't actually snowing—the frost in the air was just snow and ice carved off the ground by a fierce wind. At least they didn't have a blizzard to contend with, too.

The wind ripped at Michael. It was so strong it felt like it could pull his clothes free. When he left the tunnel, he stumbled and fell onto hard-packed snow. His hands—which he'd used to break his fall—burned, then went numb with cold, and he knew he wouldn't last ten minutes without gloves. What a stupid detail to forget. There didn't seem to be anyone nearby, so Michael and the others took a moment to manipulate the code and create warm hats and gloves. Once those were on, Michael felt better, but not much. He thought the programming had seemed a little tougher to crack than normal—especially for such a simple thing—and wondered if the tougher effects of Kaine's firewall were already evident.

Michael adjusted the backpack on his shoulders and readied his gun to defend himself. It was harder to get a finger on the trigger with the gloves, but it was manageable enough. Looking around, he saw that fields of white stretched in every direction and there was no one in sight. But far in the distance, smoke floated skyward, marking it with a long black streak.

Sarah leaned in and spoke loudly. "Makes sense that the action would be in that direction." She pointed at the pillar of smoke. "The maps showed we should walk due north from the starting point in a direct line. Based on the sun . . ."

"Yeah!" Michael yelled back. "Let's get moving."

Bryson stood several feet away, watching them as if he already knew what they needed to do. Michael pointed where Sarah had indicated, and Bryson nodded. They headed off toward battle.

5

Michael thought trudging through the wind and snow had to be far worse than any fighting could possibly be. Every step was an effort, mainly because he was walking into the wind and his boots sank into the icy ground an inch or two with every step. He gripped his gun tighter as he pressed on, eager to get close and learn what was happening on the fronts. *Careful what you wish for,* he thought glumly.

When they finally topped a rise, a scene of horror opened up below them. As soon as it came into view, the three friends dropped to the ground. Michael pushed the muzzle of his gun forward and propped himself up on his elbows to get a better look through the sight on his weapon.

A huge valley stretched for miles in every direction and was covered with seemingly random trenches dug into the snow and ice. A rough path yawned down the middle of it all. Each trench looked like it had been lined with something, a dark material, probably to keep the moisture at bay. He couldn't see too deeply inside the wide ditches, but every now and then a head would appear and a soldier would lean out. On the other side of the valley, at the end of that long corridor between the trenches, tents had been set up, but it was impossible to make out what they were for.

It was the blood that upset Michael the most. Everywhere he looked, it dotted the otherwise white landscape. It was concentrated along that middle corridor. There, countless fights were going on, mostly hand-to-hand and brutal. He caught sight of a man stabbing another in the chest and then jumping on him to twist the knife in deeper. A few dozen feet from that, a woman slashed the throat of a soldier from behind. Other groups were punching and wrestling each other. A horror show, through and through.

No one seemed to have noticed the newcomers at the top of the hill.

Michael put his gun down and looked at Bryson to his left, then Sarah to his right. "What *is* this place? We haven't fought wars like this for at least a hundred years. They look like a bunch of Neanderthals fighting over who gets what cave. I know our research said it was chaotic, but this is nuts."

"And the position of the trenches doesn't make sense," Bryson said. "Or the uniforms—I see at least four different kinds, and some of them are fighting people wearing the same thing. And why do you have tents and trenches in the same area?"

Sarah crawled forward a bit so that they could all see each other. "I'm starting to understand why this game is A.O. I don't think *Devils* has much to do with the actual war of Greenland at all. Maybe the setting, but not much else."

"What do you think it's for, then?" Bryson asked. "I mean, why didn't we receive a mission as part of the game? Something. Do people really just come here to beat the tar out of each other until they're ready to come back for more?"

"Maybe that's exactly it," Michael answered. A thought had occurred to him about the tents, too. "And maybe they have rewards when you're done. Things innocent kids like us shouldn't be doing or watching." He smiled. "To the victor go the spoils—it's something my dad used to say."

"*Devils of Destruction,*" Bryson said absently. "Well, that's exactly what it looks like down there."

6

Guns pointed forward, they started making their way down the long slope to the mayhem below. The red blood against the white snow only made the scene more horrific to Michael. The sounds of battle carried on the wind, and they were as horrible as the sight of it all. Grunts and screams and bloodthirsty growls. But for some reason, Michael didn't hear much gunfire.

"Wait a second," he said, a terrible thought occurring to him. "Do these things even work?" Pointing the muzzle skyward, he gripped his machine gun and pulled the trigger. There was a clicking sound, but that was all. Disgusted, he threw it to the ground.

Bryson tried his and chucked it away when it didn't fire. "You've got to be kidding me! This is nothing but a disguised game for barbarians. Why don't these people just go back to the Dark Ages?"

"Do I even waste the strength to pull my trigger?" Sarah asked. She did, and of course nothing happened. She blithely tossed it over her shoulder and continued walking toward the battle. "We might have some serious programming ahead of us."

7

Michael didn't dare admit it to his friends, but he was beyond terrified. They'd paid a lot of money for their Coffins, making the VirtNet drastically real—which was great for the pleasures in life. Not so great for getting stabbed, beaten, and strangled. Michael had done a lot of stuff inside the Sleep, but what lay below him looked worse than any of it. He was walking into sheer brutality. And bringing in other skills or weapons through the code didn't look like the brightest prospect after the difficulty they'd had programming hats and gloves.

Scattered fights dotted the perimeter of the valley, but most of the battle was concentrated in the middle, around the trenches. The noise had steadily increased as they descended the hill, and it was so brutal that Michael was tempted to turn around and run back. Somehow hearing the sounds of pain made the sights worse. Choking gurgles and lunatic screams and hysterical cackles of glee. The laughter might've been the hardest part of it all.

And it wouldn't be long before soldiers began to notice them.

"It's not quite like we've strategized," Sarah said. "Their game descriptions were obviously a bunch of lies. Do we split up or stay together?"

Bryson drew out his knife and gripped it in a gloved hand. Michael imagined that beneath the material his friend's knuckles were turning white.

"We better stick together," Bryson said. "It'll take longer to figure out which trench has the Path Portal, but I'm guessing these players have been doing this a long time. We're going to have to gang up to survive."

"Sounds good," Michael replied, hearing the fear in his voice. He pulled out his own knife and tried to remember if he'd actually ever been in a game where he had to fight another person with just a blade, to the death. Usually players had more sophisticated weaponry. "I think we need to pull in something more than this."

"It'd just make us stand out more," Sarah countered. "They might gang up on us." She pointed to the closest trench to the left. "Let's go in a circle. Make our way along the outside and spiral in so we don't miss any of the trenches."

Michael and Bryson agreed—they adjusted their course and headed to the first trench.

"Oh, crap," Bryson said, glancing to the right.

Michael followed his line of vision and saw three soldiers sprinting full speed toward them. Two men, one woman. As he saw them, they started shouting and gesturing with their bloodied blades. The woman had a long metal pole in her hands, too. Michael's stomach turned a little when he noticed a chunk of what looked like meat stuck to the end of it.

Bryson was right. These people were animals.

8

"Fight hard," Sarah said calmly. "And remember—it's okay to die."

That part we really *don't need to remember,* Michael thought.

He and his friends dropped their backpacks and got into a battle stance, knives held at the ready. When the oncoming soldiers were about twenty feet away, Michael wondered about the grenades on his belt. He guessed those didn't work, either, but it was too late to check. The attackers were close enough to reveal the rage in their eyes, and all three of them were screaming what Michael assumed were obscenities in another language, spit flying from their mouths.

When they came to within a few feet, the soldiers split up as if they'd decided beforehand who would attack whom. The woman came after Michael, which was not good news. She looked meaner than the other two combined—her black hair wild and matted with sweat, streaks of blood across her face, several teeth missing. And that pole. That terrible pole and its trophy gummed to the end. Michael's insides sank a little.

134

With a piercing scream that reminded him of the Kill-Sims, she raised her shaft and swung it at his head as she charged. He ducked but kept his eyes on the long blade in her other hand, which she stabbed at his face with as the pole whipped past his shoulder. Deflecting it with a forearm, Michael dropped onto his back and rolled, trying to get away from her. From the corner of his eye, he saw her flip, then land squarely on her feet like an acrobat. He was in for the fight of a lifetime.

His attacker had a grin on her face, pausing as if she wanted to relish the fear that must've been obvious in Michael's expression. But he had enough experience that he wasn't completely cowed. If this lady was going to beat him, he'd make sure she limped off with a few aches and pains of her own.

He held his knife up. "We don't have to do this," he said. "All we want is to look around the place." The words sounded ridiculous, even to him.

Her brow wrinkled in confusion, and then she spoke. Michael had no idea what she was saying—he couldn't even tell the language—but she seemed angry.

He took a step back as if he was scared and about to run, then charged forward, hoping to catch her off guard. But instead of retreating, she smiled even more, seeming happy to let the attack come to her. Michael flashed his blade as if to stab her but then leaped off the ground, kicking both legs out straight toward the soldier's chest. She tried to dodge but moved too late, and his feet slammed into her. Letting out a strangled cry, she stumbled backward and fell onto her side.

Michael crashed to the cold ground, too, but was back on his feet in an instant, running at the lady, who was only just putting her hands down to push herself up. He dropped his shoulder and tackled her, the two of them tumbling over each other several times before they came to a stop, Michael on top. She'd lost her knife but had somehow held on to the metal pole. She swung it at Michael and he dropped his blade, caught the shaft in both fists, then struggled to rip it out of her grip—but she was too strong. Seesawing left and right, neither of them would let go. Finally, he squeezed the pole and slammed it downward, smashing it into her mouth.

The awful sound of teeth breaking made Michael weak, and he almost lost his grip. The woman screamed and released the pole, both of her hands shooting to her face. She wailed as she tried to struggle out from under him, but he squeezed her torso with his thighs like a man on a horse, refusing to fall. The pole now fully his, Michael raised it and slammed it back down again. There was a terrible, hard thump and the woman went still and silent.

As soon as she stopped moving, Michael jumped up and grabbed his knife, pole and blade both held firmly, ready to fight if he needed to. But she remained frozen.

He stayed that way, breaths coming ragged, the cold air burning his lungs, until someone tackled him from behind, hitting him so hard his head whipped back and smacked into the attacker's face. Together they landed on the ground, and Michael felt every last bit of air leave his lungs. The person spun him onto his back and then straddled him, pinning Michael's arms with his legs. The man's face hung over Michael's, flushed and covered with cuts, mad blue eyes drilling holes into him. The stranger was twice the size of the lady who'd attacked him first and held a knife at Michael's neck.

Michael didn't care what Sarah had said; he wanted to use the code to pull in a weapon from another game. He closed his eyes and lost himself in the sea of programming, frantically thinking through his options. But it was too late.

The man on top of him spoke in the same strange language the woman had, then calmly slid his blade across Michael's throat. Cold pain flared through his neck, followed by warmth as the blood started flowing out of his body.

A few seconds later, he died.

CHAPTER 11

IN THE TRENCHES

1

Michael hated the uncomfortable period of twenty to thirty seconds after he'd died within a self-contained game like *Devils of Destruction*. There was a disturbing dark vacuum of nothingness before you started your next life. It was done on purpose, to give people more of a real sense of death—to give them a moment to ponder what had happened and what it might be like if it had been for real. Time to think, *What if I had* really *kicked the bucket? What if this was it?*

This time, as Michael waited it out, he was just angry. They'd barely begun, and already he'd been killed. He didn't even get a chance to look in one stinking trench! How in the world would they ever search them all? Mentally tapping his fingers, he lay there in silence. Finally, a light appeared before him and grew until it pulled him back into the full world of the VirtNet.

His eyes snapped open, and he was lying in front of the

door that led into the snowy world where he'd just been murdered. The bar was back in place across the entrance. He breathed a sigh of relief, glad he hadn't been sent all the way back to the lobby. He didn't think he had it in him to get past Stonewall and Ryker-the-angry-cowgirl-child again.

Groaning from the painful aftereffects of his two fights—if he could call the doomed second tussle an actual fight—Michael sat up. He was alone in the tunnel, so he knew that Bryson and Sarah were still alive or had died and already gone back out there.

He was still dressed head to toe in warm garb, and the stuffed backpack was beside him. After a quick check of the guns in the locker—none of them worked—and a somewhat foolish test of a grenade—it didn't, either—he pulled the heavy bar off the door and slipped back out into the frigid, windy air. As he walked, he brainstormed how he could use code to help himself in this brutal war.

2

Michael saw two people off in the distance trudging up the long white slope. He was sure it was his friends—long brown hair streamed from beneath Sarah's ski cap, and Bryson's cocky gait was recognizable even from a distance. He knew he'd never catch up with them, so he decided to take a different route. Instead of marching straight down into battle like an idiot—they hadn't really known what to expect the first time, he supposed—he planned to skirt to the right and hide along the rise of the hill until he could find a more subtle place to sneak into the fray. He'd gone a couple hundred feet when he saw that Bryson and Sarah had made the same decision, though they'd moved off toward the left.

Good, Michael thought. Maybe collectively they'd at least get a few trenches inspected before some crazed mountain man or lunatic woman slit their throats again.

The wind whipped at Michael's clothes, and the ice and snow stung the exposed skin on his face. His lips were starting to feel like burnt paper, ready to crack if he dared moisten them again. He almost wanted some action just to get his blood pumping.

The sounds of battle—the screams and haunting cries they'd heard earlier—grew louder as Michael approached the top of the slope. He crouched down and started crawling, thankful for the thick gloves on his hands.

He made it to the lip of the rise and dropped to his stomach, then took a moment to take everything in. Far to his left, Bryson and Sarah were sprinting from hill to hill, pausing behind each before moving on to the next. It didn't look like they'd been spotted yet, and they were getting close to the outer trenches, where fewer people were concentrated. Most of the fighting still took place in the long, bloody corridor going down the center of the trenches.

The sounds of metal clashing against metal, animalistic grunts, and primal screams were carried on the wind to Michael. He still couldn't believe that anyone would voluntarily take part in such brutality. As he watched one of the closer fights, he saw a man stab another man, shouting at the top of his lungs the whole time. After everything Michael had seen in countless movies and experienced in games, he still had to look away. This place was hell.

Focus, he told himself. *Avoid being seen, and concentrate on the trenches.*

Staying just below the sight line of those battling in the valley, he crawled military-style across the frozen snow. Worried that his backpack would give him away, he finally took it off and chucked it, not sure why he had it in the first place. He'd be thrilled if he lived long enough to worry about needing food or extra clothing.

He made his way down to the right of the valley, so far unseen. Several rows of trenches lay between him and most of the fighting now, but it was still impossible to get a good look at how many people waited inside them. He stopped behind a small mound of packed snow and gathered his wits. The memory of that blade slicing his neck was still fresh, as if the pain still lingered there.

Closing his eyes, he focused on the surrounding code for a second. It seemed elusive and hard to read, as if the sea of numbers and letters churned in a fierce storm. It took him a few minutes, but he was finally able to latch on to a string of programming he'd used in a game called *Dungeons of Delmar*. It would give his knife a magical quality, bursts of unseen force from its tip that might go unnoticed.

It was better than nothing.

As he had to do sometimes in the Sleep, Michael gave himself a pep talk, a reminder that as bad it seemed, he wouldn't *actually* die if he was killed. Pain, yes. Terror, yes. Traumatized forever, maybe. But at least he'd still be alive at the end of the day.

Eyes closed. Deep breaths. Eyes open again. Code-enhanced knife pulled from his belt, gripped firmly in his right hand.

He got up and ran for the closest trench.

3

His heart pounded and cold air burned his lungs raw, but Michael willed himself to set it all aside and run as fast as possible. A few soldiers noticed him, but they were on the far side of the trench Michael was headed for, and no one approached him—they just kept beating on each other.

The edge of the trench was suddenly at his feet. He pulled to a stop and looked down, quickly scanning the interior—about fifteen feet deep. It was empty except for a wooden bench and a slushy path going down the middle. The walls were covered by black tarps—held in place at the top by old tires and pots and pans. There were no soldiers inside.

Because Michael didn't see a clear Portal, he almost turned and ran for the next trench, but he stopped himself. Who knew what the Portal looked like, anyway—or whether the weakness in the code would be easily spotted? It hit him then, the enormity of the task that lay ahead of them. It would take forever to search each trench from top to bottom. And they didn't even know what they were searching for, exactly.

Sighing, Michael found a ladder and climbed down to begin.

4

The black tarps that covered the walls of the trench were easy to move. Michael pulled one back and ducked underneath it, then walked along the side of the trench from one end to the other, feeling up and down the expanse of ice. But that's all it was—ice and hard-packed snow. Nothing suspicious or out of the ordinary. Every once in a while, he closed his eyes to look for anomalies in the code or anything that stood out. But it was all solid.

When he came out of the tarp on the far side, he checked to make sure the trench was still empty, then moved on to the other wall.

Nothing.

He walked once more down the center, kicking through the slush and checking the code for anything weird. Then he examined the bench. Another check of the programming.

Nothing.

As Michael climbed the ladder out of the ditch, he tried not to think of how much time he'd just wasted. There'd be no way of knowing which trench held the Portal until he and his friends searched them—one by one. He sighed again. He supposed no amount of effort was really a waste.

At least that's what he told himself. He couldn't shake the hopeless feeling that they'd never find what they were looking for. There were still at least a hundred more to go.

No one was running at him—at least not yet. And a glance around the battlefield showed no sign of his friends.

Michael headed for the next trench.

5

No one was inside that one, either.

Michael scaled down and began his search. He slipped under a wall tarp and made his way down one side, then up the other, checking the code now and then. But it all looked fine. There was nothing there.

He climbed out, discouraged but ready to check the next space. He'd let his guard down, so he was surprised when he saw a woman standing there, waiting for him. Dressed in the same winter camouflage Michael wore, she looked clean and fresh, like she'd just walked out of the tunnel. Her face would've been pretty if it wasn't screwed up into a nasty snarl.

"Micky told me I'd have an easy kill over here," she said. "Nothing like a stray kid who's tippy-toed his way in without permission. You'll be a good game-starter for me." Her expression had warmed a bit as she spoke but twisted back into a snarl when she finished.

"Easy?" Michael repeated. "What makes you think I'm gonna be easy?" He casually took a step backward, lining up the heels of his boots with the top edge of the trench. He wanted to look like someone who was scared but trying not to act like it.

"How many times have you been in here?" she asked, again relaxing that horrible face only to pull it back when she was done talking.

"This is my first time," he said innocently. "But I did have a kill already. That's not too bad, right?"

She shook her head. "I'm going to enjoy this way too much."

Michael just grinned and said, "Go for it."

He wanted her to make the first move, and it worked. She came at him, her angry face flushed a deep red.

She pulled back her fist, and right before she hit him Michael dropped to the ground, onto his side. He knew there'd be a risk of slipping over the edge and into the trench, but he was willing to take it to avoid another fight. He squeezed the handle of his knife and sent a bolt of invisible power at her torso, and she catapulted forward.

She flew over Michael and fell, screaming, to the trench floor. Before she had time to get to her feet, Michael was sprinting for the next trench. If he was lucky she'd broken a leg.

6

There was a man sleeping on the bench inside the next trench. Other than that, it was empty. Michael was ecstatic. He ran to the steps and climbed down. At first he considered doing a quick search without bothering the guy, but then thought better of it. The man might wake up while Michael was under the tarp, and Michael would be wide open for attack. He couldn't take any chances.

Michael stood near the sleeping man, watching his chest rise and fall. Not wanting to get too close, he quietly pulled out his blade and aimed, then shot a clear laser of power across the man's neck, trying not to gag as the soldier sprang awake and grabbed at his bleeding wound. He fell off the bench, and for the second time that day, Michael had to remind himself that he hadn't actually killed a person. It looked so real.

The man bled until his body was empty, then vanished.

A quick but thorough search of the trench revealed that once again Michael had struck out. Three down, dozens to go. He groaned.

"Not happy down there?"

He glanced up to see a man and a woman standing directly above him, right on the edge of the trench. The woman was bouncing a grenade from hand to hand.

"Um, no, I'm just taking a breather is all." Thankfully his clothes were now dirty and smeared with blood. He fit in much better, looked like he belonged.

"Nothing but a dumb kid," the man said to the woman.

"Think you're going to get away with using code from other games? And there's no doubt you're a rookie."

Michael narrowed his eyes. "What do you mean?"

"Because you haven't turned to run yet. You're probably pretty sure this grenade doesn't work."

Michael started to answer, but before he could get a word out the woman pulled the pin and tossed the grenade. It landed with a wet thunk in the slush at Michael's feet. He looked at the pair of soldiers with defiance. They turned and ran.

When the grenade blew, Michael felt it. This time there was a brilliant explosion of pain so acute and short he didn't even have time to scream. Then came the void of dark space that they called death.

7

He woke up back at the beginning, in the icy tunnel. Bryson was sitting there and didn't seem the least bit surprised when Michael appeared before him.

"Sucks being killed out there," Bryson said. "I hurt." He paused. "All over."

"Yeah, me too." Michael stood up and stretched, felt the lingering aches and pains from his two deaths. They weren't quite the same as real injuries—the Coffin stimulated nerves for physical reactions—but enough to ensure you wouldn't forget too quickly.

"How's Sarah doing?" he asked.

Bryson shrugged. "I don't know. We got separated."

"How many trenches have you seen?"

Bryson held up two gloved fingers. "But nothing yet."

"Man," Michael groaned. "This is gonna take years."

"Nah, we'll be fine," Bryson answered, climbing to his feet to join him. "Having fun?"

Michael looked at him for a second. "No, I hate every minute of it," he finally said, then held up his knife. "I ended up borrowing a little something from *Dungeons of Delmar.*"

"Yeah," Bryson replied absently, his face screwed up in a grimace. "It's weird how these old geezers like to kill—like they're animals. I need to program myself a little help."

Michael nodded. "Let's just find that stupid Portal."

Out the door they went.

8

The next couple of days were pure hell for Michael.

He died twenty-seven times, in every way imaginable, within the borders of that brutal, icy arena. Some deaths were worse than others, but somehow he kept going back out there. His knife trick helped a few times, and he tried other things like a special leaping ability from the *Canyon Jumpers* game and enhanced speed from *Running with Ragers.* They were hard to isolate and program, and ended up only delaying his inevitable doom.

But he pressed on.

Oddly, every day a horn blew at dusk, and the battles ceased immediately. People who'd been going at it like lions were suddenly pals, walking—often limping—toward huge dinner tables with arms around each other's shoulders, laughing.

Michael and his friends joined them to eat, then headed toward a place where warming lamps and sleeping bags had been laid out. The first night, they'd tried to sneak toward the trenches to search, but they'd come across a temporary firewall and were all too tired to hack it. The security programming in the frigid place was definitely above average.

The next morning it all started up again. Kill, kill, get killed. Pain and suffering. Kill some more, get killed some more. For the first time in his life, Michael understood why real soldiers coming back from real wars often had a hard time getting over the things they'd seen and done. And had done to them. If Michael had a soul, it was starting to leak out of his pores.

The one solace he had was that he and his friends were together. They didn't say much—or have time to—but at least they were together.

In the late afternoon of the third day, Sarah found the Portal.

CHAPTER 12

A DIRE WARNING

1

Michael had just been killed again by a working grenade. If he'd learned anything in *Devils of Destruction,* it was that no matter how many times your body exploded, it never got any easier.

Sarah was waiting for him back in the tunnel. She was sitting on the ground, back to the wall, legs folded underneath her, and she looked exhausted. Michael sat down across from her, and she told him.

"I found it," she said softly. Her voice sounded dead. Michael felt just as empty, and he thought he knew why: they'd paid too heavy a price. He knew he'd never be the same.

He did feel some sense of relief, though. "Where?" he finally asked, and the way Sarah looked at him, he knew she was just as relieved as he was.

"It's five trenches in from the tents, near the middle, on

the left side. There are five or six people inside, who knows what kinds of weapons. I barely detected the Portal before they killed me."

"We'll be fine," Michael told her. "We'll wait for Bryson, and we'll come up with a plan. Maybe we can even do it without jumping in there and going medieval on everybody."

She gave him a smile. It was weak and small, but it lifted him up a little. "At least we know where it is. I don't think I could've lasted much longer out there, running from one trench to the next, wondering what joyful way I'd die next."

"I'll take a nice trip through space killing aliens with lasers anytime over this."

Sarah's eyes met Michael's and stayed there, both of them silent, sharing the experience they'd just endured. Then pain exploded inside his head.

2

Michael collapsed to the cold floor and curled up into a ball, barely aware of Sarah by his side, leaning over his shoulder, yelling at him to tell her what was wrong. He couldn't form words. He gripped his head, rocking back and forth as the pain pounded inside his skull. He was aware enough of what had happened to him in the alley back home that he refused to open his eyes.

The visions. Those creepy, terrifying visions. He didn't know if the effects on his mind would be the same in the

VirtNet as they were back in the Wake, but he didn't want to find out. He kept his eyes squeezed shut and waited for the pain to fade.

Finally, just like before, it vanished in an instant. No slow recovery, no lingering ache. He was in agony one second, totally fine the next. Though he thought he'd heard a voice. . . .

According to Sarah, the episode had lasted three minutes—it could've been an hour for all Michael could tell. She put her arm around his shoulder and helped him sit up. He leaned back against the wall and stared at the ceiling. What a splendid week he'd had.

"You okay now?" Sarah asked.

Michael turned to look at her. "Yeah. When it ends, it totally ends. Doesn't even hurt right now at all." But he was exhausted and sick with fear—he hadn't had an attack in a few days, and he'd been hoping that maybe they'd stopped.

She ran her fingers through his hair. "What did that monster do to you?" she murmured.

He shrugged—he assumed she meant the KillSim. "I don't know. I just remember it felt like it was sucking my brain out. Maybe it did—part of it, anyway."

"At least you went a while without an attack, right? Let's just hope it happens less and less frequently. Maybe it'll eventually stop altogether."

Bryson appeared back from the game then, a look of pride brightening his face, and Sarah dropped her hand from Michael's head.

"Hey, I found it!" Bryson called. "I found the Portal."

Sarah smirked. "Big deal," she said. "I beat you to it, slowpoke."

But her face filled with a genuine smile. Michael's heart felt a bit less empty, though he was still concerned. He hoped it had just been the delusion of his attack, but he could've sworn he'd heard a voice, whispering a phrase inside his mind.

You're doing well, Michael.

3

Bryson described which trench he was talking about, and it was indeed the same one Sarah had found. Michael and his friends racked their tired brains to come up with a plan. They had to get close enough, and have enough time, to probe the Portal and hack their way through its code. But jumping inside that ditch, knives and fists first, was the last thing any of them would ever want to do again.

Which is what made Michael think of grenades. He'd been killed by them three or four times, so he knew they were effective. And he'd be lying if he said he didn't want the tiniest bit of revenge.

When he suggested it, Bryson said, "Well, it sounds good, but we'll need something extra to make sure they go off."

Sarah answered, "We'll just bring a whole bunch and start tossing them. I'll program a Spectacular Spark from the *Munitions Maniacs* game and hope it triggers them."

Michael grabbed his backpack and unzipped it, then took everything out. "Let's start stuffing."

4

Once everyone's backpack was full, they hitched them over their shoulders, got gloves and hats, then headed back out the door into the wintry air.

Michael and Sarah followed Bryson around the left side of the valley, careful to stay below the ridgeline, out of sight. When they got to the rise, they dropped to their stomachs and crawled to the top.

Then it hit Michael. "What if we just wait until morning and try to get there before anyone else?" What he really wanted to say was, *Please don't make me run down there into that mayhem again.* He didn't know how much more of it he could take.

"I'm dreading this, too," Bryson said. "But we can't afford to lose another night. Let's just try this thing. Guards or no guards."

"Okay," Michael grumbled. "But remember—either we all get through or none of us do. We can't go through the Portal alone or we might never hook back up."

"Fine," Bryson said. "And how about we don't get killed? We're forming bad habits."

"Amen," Michael responded. "Dying is my new least favorite thing."

Michael looked out over the open space again. They had

to get past dozens of battles, as well as ten or so other trenches. The odds of making it to the Portal without getting pulled into some sort of fight weren't good. And judging by the look on Sarah's face, she thought the same thing.

"Okay," she said, suddenly in charge. "I think we can get through, but you have to follow my lead. If one of us gets intercepted, we need to stay and fight."

"We got it," Bryson said. "Stick together. Now let's get this over with."

Michael's heart pumped like pistons in a race car. "Yeah" was all he could get out.

"Come on." Sarah climbed to her feet and was suddenly running down the icy hill. Michael and Bryson hurried to catch up.

5

It took an hour to make it to the trench, and they fought the whole way there. Sometimes it was a single man or woman—those were the easy ones. But they faced a few that were far more difficult—gangs of two, three, or four soldiers coming after their small alliance all at once. The only positive of having died so many times was that it gave Michael and his friends the experience—and a little help from their programming-boosted powers—to fend off those attackers.

They weren't going to die this time. Michael swore it to

himself over and over. He grew more exhausted by the minute, but his adrenaline was high, and his energy seemed to reignite with every new confrontation.

They finally found themselves just a few feet from the edge of the Portal trench. The group was bloodied and bruised, their clothes ripped. Bryson had lost his backpack, and they only had one knife. But for a brief moment, they were alone.

Sarah dropped to her knees and unzipped her pack, dumping her cache of grenades onto the frozen ground. Michael added his own as Bryson ran over to the edge to scout the guard situation. "Five or six of them," he reported back, falling to his knees next to them to help. "Start pulling and chucking! They're just sitting there with guns, smoking."

Michael got right to work. He grabbed a grenade, pulled the pin, then threw it into the long, narrow pit. He didn't stop to see what happened; he took another one and repeated the process, throwing it at the same spot. Then another one. Another. Bryson and Sarah were just as fast, and in a matter of seconds they'd tossed more than a dozen into the trench.

Then Sarah closed her eyes—they flickered under her eyelids as she searched and manipulated the code. A bright flash of light flared up at her chest, brilliant enough to make Michael shield his eyes with his arm. He peeked and saw it whoosh away from her and shoot down into the trench like a fiery comet.

Michael noticed a man climbing up from the inside of the trench on the far side. He opened his mouth to warn his friends, but a deafening boom exploded from within the deep-cut ditch. Flashes of fire lit up the day, and metal shards flew in every direction.

"Let's go!" Sarah yelled, already on her feet and moving toward the ladder. The man Michael had seen earlier was flat on his stomach at the very top, a huge gash sliced down the back of his coat. Nothing but red and ruin.

Michael ran after Sarah, Bryson by his side. They reached the edge of the trench. Michael ran alongside it, looking for survivors, but all he could see was death. He watched the bodies disappear one by one.

The three friends got to the ladder just as the man at the top rolled over onto his back. He wasn't dead, but he was close, and the look on his face showed he knew.

Sarah started down the rungs, as did Bryson. Michael was right behind them when the man reached up and grabbed Michael's arm, then spun him around. His strength was surprising for the condition he was in. Michael was able to pull himself free, but before he turned away, the man started mumbling something, his lips quivering with the effort, his whole body shaking.

Michael leaned in closer, thinking he'd heard his name. "What did you say?" he asked.

The soldier seemed to gather his strength for one last effort to speak. And then it came out in a short burst, and Michael heard every word.

"Be careful with Kaine. He's not who you think."

Then the man died, and his wrecked body vanished into the air.

CHAPTER 13

THE FLOATING DISK

1

"Get down here!" Sarah yelled from below.

Michael realized he was staring at the patch of bloody snow where the guy had been lying only seconds before. What was going on? The voice during his last attack that told him he was doing well, what this stranger had said about Kaine . . . What did it all mean?

Michael had a deep-down fear that Kaine knew exactly what they were doing and where they were. And he wondered if it could be possible—did the gamer *want* Michael to figure out where he was?

"Dude!"

Michael turned his attention back to the trench, and Bryson was staring up at him.

"What are you *doing*?" he yelled.

"Thinking," Michael answered. He was fully aware of how stupid it sounded. "Sorry," he added. People were

158

charging in from all directions as he scrambled down into the slushy pit with his friends.

Bryson shook his head. "We really can't take you anywhere."

"Did that guy say something to you?" Sarah asked.

Michael nodded. "Yeah, but I'll tell you later. We're about to have a lot of unwelcome visitors. It looks like a zombie parade out there, and we're the food."

"It's over here," Bryson said, gesturing for them to follow him. They had trudged down the middle of the pit about fifteen feet when he pointed to a section of the wall where the black tarp had been shredded. In most places, white ice shone through, but there was a spot where a slight purple glow emanated.

The shouts and cries of the approaching players were getting louder.

"No time like the present," Sarah said. She turned to Michael. "You stand guard while Bryson and I try to figure this out."

As Michael took position, Bryson tore away a big swath of the black tarp. Behind it, a six-foot-tall tunnel had been carved into the wall of ice. Michael couldn't focus on exactly where it happened, but at some point inside the tunnel the dark space transformed into a throbbing purple light. What lay beyond was impossible to make out—the harder Michael strained to see, the more his vision blurred.

"It's those underage kids!" someone screamed from above. Even as Bryson and Sarah moved into the tunnel, Michael glanced up to see a man holding a long blade.

Michael didn't hesitate—he spun around and followed his friends into the purple light.

2

The sounds of the War of Greenland quickly disappeared—the tunnel was silent, as if a door had closed behind them. And when he looked back, Michael saw that that was exactly what had happened. The trench they'd just escaped was no longer there. Instead there was the same odd purple glow.

He turned back around and was relieved to see that he hadn't lost Bryson and Sarah. They were still on their hands and knees like him, only they were concentrating, eyes twitching back and forth behind closed eyelids, frantically working the code.

"I was able to latch on to some type of map or guide," Sarah said, eyes still closed. "Do you see it?"

Bryson nodded. "It's subtle. We'll just have to keep checking the code to stick to it."

"What's going on?" Michael asked. "What should I do?"

Sarah turned toward him. "The Portal isn't really blocked, per se. But it'd be extremely easy to get lost in here. And I mean lost—like forever. From what we can find, there are a series of markers in the programing. If we follow the markers, we should get to the first level of the Path."

"Okay."

Eyes still closed, Sarah reached out blindly and patted

Michael on the shoulder. "I still think we need one person to keep an eye out, in case something comes at us. Can you? While Bryson and I keep scanning the code?"

Michael shrugged, even though his friends couldn't see him. "Sure. Eyes peeled—easy enough."

"I like a guy who can follow orders," Bryson said with a smirk.

Sarah leaned back and turned away from Michael. "Let's go, then. It's this way."

She moved forward on her hands and knees, followed by Bryson and then Michael, and they began making their way deeper into the tunnel.

Several minutes passed without anything changing. Michael felt a suffocating pressure in his chest, but every time he paused to take a deep breath, it loosened up and he was able to breathe easily again. The silence was strange as well—almost like it wasn't silence at all but a constant buzz. For a while he assumed that the others were just quiet as they focused on the code, but then a thought crossed his mind. When he called out to them, no sound came out of his mouth. It was as if someone had pushed a mute button— and for some reason it was the most terrifying thing about the bizarre tunnel so far.

He kept moving, creeping his way forward, focused on Bryson's legs. He was scared to death that his friend might disappear at any second, leaving him all alone. His hands and knees were beginning to hurt, his arms and legs cramping. And he was growing more disoriented and nauseated by the minute.

On and on they went, shuffling along like a line of ants. They'd gone at least a mile, maybe two. His body wasn't used to such a thing. A whisper of panic was also starting to build within him, a claustrophobic feeling that threatened to take over. But he forced it down, took each moment, and inch, at a time, relying on his friends' hacking and coding skills. He never thought he'd ever be so thankful for Bryson's butt, a beacon in that purple fog.

They were still crawling in silence when something suddenly slammed down on Michael, pressing his body hard into the ground. He fell flat onto his stomach and lost his breath. His fear flared into terror, and he screamed and kicked. He was barely able to move. His mind began to cloud up, and a wild feeling crept in, like he'd lost control of his own actions.

And then it ended. All of it ended. The purple tunnel, the silence, the pressure that pushed him to the ground. He was lying on a hard gray surface. He got his hands under him and pushed up to his knees. Then he stared in wonder at what surrounded him.

He and his friends were crouched on the edge of a huge stone disk a few dozen feet wide, seemingly hanging in mid-air. Massive formations of dark clouds hung above their heads, growing and shrinking like living things. Lightning flashed and thunder boomed and the air was heavy with humidity, as if rain would pour down any minute.

Michael had no idea where they were—he'd never been anywhere like it in the VirtNet. Yet despite its oddness, he was relieved to leave the tunnel behind.

"Hey." Bryson gestured with his head for Michael to look behind him.

Michael spun around to face the center of the disk. Nothing had been there when they'd arrived—he was sure of it—but now there was an old woman sitting in a rocking chair, the wood creaking as she slowly rocked back and forth. She was dressed in a shapeless length of gray wool. Michael thought she looked like a kind grandmother.

"Hello, my young friends," she said in a hoarse croak. "Come on over and sit a spell."

3

Michael just stared at the woman, and when neither of his friends moved, either, she stopped rocking in her chair and leaned toward them. "Gods above, you better get your rumps over here right quick or there'll be hell to pay, I can tell you that much. Now!"

Startled by her abrupt change, Michael scrambled to his feet, Bryson and Sarah at his heels, and made his way to the center of the platform to join the woman.

"Sit," she commanded. Her wrinkled lips were puckered as if she had no teeth, and her voice was scratchy.

They did as she said. Michael folded his legs beneath him and waited intently. Stuff like this was weird, he thought, but it wasn't *that* weird—he'd spent half his life inside the Sleep, and he'd gotten used to strange characters like this appearing. Most of the time they were harmless, but still, he reminded himself, if they had made it to the Path, this lady might be linked to Kaine, and that spelled trouble.

The woman peered down at the three of them, her eyes the only thing about her that didn't seem a hundred years old. They were sharp and bright, but the rest of her looked used up and washed out. Yellowed skin wrinkled and drooping from her frail bones. Wispy gray hair that was barely there. Two ancient hands lay folded in her lap, like gnarled tree roots twisted upon themselves.

"Where are we?" Sarah asked. "And who are you?"

The old woman's eyes snapped into focus. "Who am I, you ask? Where are you? What's this place, what is here, why is this, and how is that? Where'd we come from, and where will we be going? Questions tumble out of your mouth, girl. But answers hide in the mist of the clouds."

The woman's eyes wandered as she spoke, slowly drifting until she was gazing at something far in the distance. Michael glanced over at Bryson, who raised his eyebrows in a warning for Michael to keep *his* mouth shut for a change.

"You," the old woman said. One of her hands lifted from her lap, shaking slightly, and a crooked finger pointed down at Michael. "Make one wisecrack and this will be your end."

Her face had hardened into a scowl, and Michael knew right then that he didn't ever want to cross this woman. For all he knew, she'd morph into a dragon and eat them. This was the Sleep after all.

"Did your brain process my words properly?" she asked, her skin wrinkling up even more around her eyes as they narrowed. "Do you *understand* me?"

Bryson elbowed him in the ribs. "Be good."

"Yeah," Michael answered her. "Loud and clear."

The old woman nodded and leaned back in her chair, began rocking again. "You kids couldn't even give an old woman a proper greetin' before you started spewing questions."

"We're sorry," Sarah spoke up. "Really. We went through a lot to get here, and we just want to know how to keep going. We're looking for a place called the Hallowed Ravine."

"Oh, I know very well what those hearts of yours are lookin' for. The Path only leads to one destination, and that destination only has one path to it. The Hallowed Ravine is far from where you sit right now, though, I can tell you that much."

Michael was getting impatient. "So what do we need to know?"

Her finger came back out, its yellowed nail pointing straight at him. "This one is no longer allowed to speak. One peep and I vanish."

Bryson snapped an arm out and clamped his hand over Michael's mouth before he could say another word.

"He had a rough time getting here," Bryson explained, an exasperated look on his face. "He's a little bit softer around the edges than the rest of us. Don't worry. He'll keep his mouth shut. Won't you, Michael? Nod once for yes like a good boy."

Michael wanted to smack him, but he nodded once with a smile and peeled his friend's hand from his face.

The old woman folded her hands in her lap again and started talking.

4

"They call me the Satchel, and never you mind the reasons. I'm here to keep my eye on the Path. At times we get intruders walking its ways. I don't think I need to tell you that it won't be much of a pleasant trip. Not very pleasant at all. Some of them smarter folks might call it irony, but the Path's only purpose is to try and stop people from walkin' it."

She paused again. "Things are different here," she continued. "Not like anywhere else in the VirtNet. You had to hack and code to get this far, but from here on out you can't just rely on that alone. You're gonna need to be clever. And brave. And there's one rule you'll need to remember most of all. When you hear it, you're gonna wish your ears had been lying."

"What is it?" Sarah asked.

The Satchel didn't answer for a second, and Michael almost trembled with impatience.

"You die, you're done," she finally said. "Done like rabbits in a lion's den. You'll be sent back to the Wake, and the odds of you ever making it back inside the Path rank right up there with tryin' to walk from Venus to Mars. It can't be done. You made it here, that's a fact—and with some fine bravery and gaming skills. But now we have you registered top to bottom, inside and out, and there's no way you'll get in twice."

Michael swallowed hard and exchanged a worried look with his friends. This was serious business. Even the most brutal games in the VirtNet were played with the knowledge that dying was just a setback. Nothing more than a delay. And that helped people go out there and play without reserve, taking chances and doing things they'd *never* do in real life. That was what made it fun—you could always go back and try again.

But if what this old woman had said was true, Michael and his friends only had one shot at this. If that had been the case in *Devils of Destruction,* they'd have been done days ago.

"You're taking it like grown-ups," the Satchel said. "I gotta give you credit for that. Things are different on the Path—never been a better firewall built. Hands down."

Michael was about to go crazy from the command not to speak, even though he didn't really know what he wanted to say.

Thankfully, Bryson spoke up. "Okay, if we die, we're sent back to the Wake. Got it. What else can you tell us?"

The Satchel laughed before she answered. "There are only two ways off this disk. The first one's to jump to your death and head back to the Wake."

That's not an option, Michael thought.

"And the second?" Bryson asked.

The woman smiled, shifting the many wrinkles on her face. "Figure out what time it is."

5

As soon as she said the words, the entire structure on which they sat dropped several feet. Michael's stomach lurched as they fell, and he reached out to grab on to something to still himself.

Light flashed in the sky, and openings began to appear and disappear in random patterns around them, chasms of pure darkness that hung in the air just a few feet from the lip of the stone.

The disk abruptly rotated in place, throwing Michael off-balance again. He sprawled across the stone and was sliding toward the edge when the disk slammed to a stop. The Satchel's chair remained unmoved, and the old woman cackled from her perch.

"What's going on?" Sarah asked. "Why are we moving?"

Michael crawled back to sit right next to the chair in the center.

"I've already told you what needs be done," the Satchel said. "Searching the code won't help you now."

"What are we supposed to do?" Michael asked, forgetting her command to stay quiet. "How do we guess the time?"

Her eyes found his—they were dark with anger. "I only have a few more words for you troublesome three, and then I'll be gone."

"Then get on with it," Michael answered, relieved she hadn't reacted to his breaking his silence.

The disk shifted again, and everyone scrambled to hold themselves in place. Michael glanced up at the edge of the stone circle and saw that the black rectangles were still appearing and vanishing. All around, dark clouds churned and boiled, stretching, collapsing on themselves, then growing large again.

The Satchel shifted in her seat, pulling Michael's attention back.

"Listen closely," she said, her expression now blank. "For I won't repeat my words."

"Okay," Sarah said. "We're ready."

Business as usual, that's Sarah, Michael thought. He leaned closer to the chair and prepared to listen intently—to not miss a thing. The Satchel spoke clearly, but her words were some kind of riddle:

> *Before you choose the witching hour,*
> *Take care to dream the tallest tower.*
> *Then careful before you leave too soon,*
> *Behold the dark and hollow moon.*

She gave one last cackle before she, along with her rocking chair, disappeared.

Michael focused all his attention on remembering her words as she spoke, so he hardly noticed when she vanished. But when he squeezed his eyes shut and ran through it again, he was disappointed to find that he only remembered about half of it.

"Did you guys get that?" Bryson asked.

Michael looked at him, heart sinking. "Uh . . . maybe. Most of it. Some of it?"

Sarah shifted her position so that the three of them faced one another. She was just about to say something when the disk rotated again, spinning ninety degrees. The dark rectangles—which Michael assumed were Portals of some sort—continued their pattern, flashing in and out of existence.

"Okay, I think I remember," Sarah said.

Bryson projected his NetScreen and keyboard and typed out her words as she spoke. Sarah remembered most of it, and the three spent a minute or so going back and forth, comparing it to what Bryson and Michael recalled. Soon the group had it to the point that all three of them agreed. But Michael was stumped.

He threw his hands up in frustration. "The old bag could've given us a little more."

"Well," Bryson said, "she said we need to figure out what time it is. I guess, if nothing else, it will tell us exactly when life on a flying saucer made out of rock began for us."

Sarah groaned. "Come on, guys. We can do this."

"I know," Michael said. "Look, we've got this thing spinning around, we've got Portals to somewhere, and we've got a riddle about a witching hour. And like Bryson said, the Satchel told us to figure out what time it is. Easy peasy."

"And we're on a disk—it's round like a clock," Sarah offered.

Bryson jumped in. "Maybe we solve the riddle, pick the spot of the correct hour, and jump through one of those black rectangles."

"But how do we know where the numbers are?" Michael asked. Before his friends answered, however, he'd started crawling toward the edge of the disk to get a better look.

"Careful!" Sarah yelled. "The thing might move at any second!"

The last word had barely come out of her mouth when the disk spun again, throwing Michael onto his side. He rolled several feet and lost any sense of direction. Letting out an embarrassing yelp, he slammed his palms down hard on the stone, stopping his tumble. The disk came to a standstill and he looked up.

He was still safe by ten feet, but he could only imagine the things Bryson would say later if they ever made it to safety. Michael got on his hands and knees and crawled toward the edge again, keeping his arms and legs spread as much as possible for a steadier center of balance. One of the Portals opened up right before him, and its depth was impossible. It was so black the darkness seemed almost *alive*.

Slowly, he crawled until he was barely a foot from the edge. He sank down on his belly and pulled himself a few inches closer. As he did, the Portal in front of him vanished and was instantly replaced by the color and movement of the cloudy sky. Michael closed his eyes and looked down, and when he opened them he saw that there was something carved into the disk, right on the very edge. He peered closely at the stone. Numerals—a large one and two—had been etched there. The number twelve.

He turned back to shout at the others. "I found midnight!"

Sarah answered immediately: "Get over here before this thing sends you skydiving!"

Michael pulled himself to the left until he found the eleven. As soon as he caught sight of it, he scrambled around and popped onto his hands and knees. The disk spun again and he froze, holding himself firmly in place until the rotation ended, then quickly crawled back to his friends.

"It's numbered," Michael said. "Just like a clock."

Sarah nodded. "Way to go. Bryson's marking the spot with his legs."

Michael looked at his friend. He was sitting with his legs out, feet pointed to where Michael had been moments before. "Wow, you guys are smart."

"Okay, now the easy part," Bryson said. "Figure out the riddle." His NetScreen was still floating in front of him and he turned it to face the others. Michael leaned in to read through the riddle again:

> Before you choose the witching hour,
> Take care to dream the tallest tower.
> Then careful before you leave too soon,
> Behold the dark and hollow moon.

"It's gotta be a clue about moon cycles," Sarah said. "Does anyone know what the moon's phases are?"

"Or when it would look dark and hollow?" Bryson added. "Is that as easy as a new moon, when it's all black? Or maybe an eclipse?"

The disk spun again, and they stilled.

Sarah looked deep in thought. "What could the tower be? Maybe that's symbolic of something, and when there's a new moon and a . . . Oh, man. I seriously don't know what the heck I'm talking about."

Michael sat there and observed his two friends. Something told him they were totally on the wrong track. Totally. This had nothing to do with a real moon or a tower or cycles or stages. It was something else, and he could almost, but not quite, put his finger on what.

"Michael?" Sarah asked. "You're the genius—what do *you* think it is?"

His eyes met hers, but he didn't speak. In his mind he was turning over everything, processing, almost there.

"Well?" she finally pushed. "What're you—"

Two things happened at once that cut her off. First, a sound Michael had never heard before, like the sonic boom of a thousand jets. It was so loud and close that Michael's ears popped. At the same time, a brilliant flash of blinding light lit up the sky in massive bolts of white fire, piercing the stone disk about twenty feet from where they sat. Michael's ears rang, and spots swam before his eyes.

"What now?" he heard Bryson say, though it was as if he'd spoken through a thick curtain.

Michael was dazed. He'd been thrown onto his back by the force of the explosion. He twisted onto his stomach and got to his knees again. Just as he did, a cracking sound broke through the air, like the settling of a glacier. He spun toward the source and saw that the stone disk was breaking—hairline fractures webbing out from where the lightning had struck. They continued to lengthen, splitting open as the web grew larger. Horror filled Michael as the realization hit him: the whole disk was going to crumble any minute.

"Stand up!" Michael yelled. "Huddle together!"

Even as his friends got to their feet and moved toward him, Michael's mind cleared, focusing like a scope. The answer was so obvious he wanted to laugh out loud.

"Ten o'clock!" he yelled. "We have to go through ten o'clock!"

8

The disk spun then, and the three of them held on to each other. Loosened chips of stone flew from the outer edges of the disk and disappeared over the edge. The ever-growing spiderweb of cracks continued to spread and widen, nearly covering the entire surface. They had no time.

"Come on!" Michael yelled, and started moving in the direction that seemed about right—without Bryson's legs pointing to midnight, they had no way of knowing for sure. The black Portals continued their dance of appearing and disappearing.

"No!" Bryson pulled him to a stop. "It's over there!" He pointed to the other side of the disk.

Michael had learned to trust his friend's gaming instincts a long time ago, so he didn't argue. He turned and followed Bryson's directions. Underneath them the stone felt like sand, gritty and seeming to shift with each step. A splintering crack sounded to their right, and with horror Michael saw a ten-foot-wide chunk of the disk crumble away and fall into the cloudy abyss.

"Look!" Sarah yelled, pointing to the left of the section that had just disappeared.

They were close enough to see the number four. Bryson had been wrong.

"Sorry!" he yelled.

The disk spun again, throwing all of them to the ground. They landed on top of each other, scrambling to right themselves. Michael put his hand down and felt a shot of panic when it hit nothing but air. His elbow scraped across rough stone, and he jerked his arm back from a jagged gap as Bryson pulled him away from it. Michael landed on top of Sarah again, who grunted and pushed him off, but he held on. The whole disk was trembling now, as if they were at the epicenter of an earthquake, and the terrible sounds of cracking stone relentlessly filled the air.

Michael knew they couldn't afford to be careful anymore. He jumped to his feet and grabbed both of his friends by the hands.

"Come on!"

Yanking them along, Michael sprinted across the disk, jumping over several more gaping holes that had formed. To his left, another huge piece of the stone broke away from the edge and fell, then another to his right. In the middle, where the old Satchel had sat in her chair, a section exploded in a spray of rocks, the dull purple light of the clouds shining through the hole when it was gone. Michael kept going, running and jumping, staring at the spot exactly opposite the four o'clock section they'd just left. At the moment there was no Portal where they needed one.

They were just a few feet away when the disk spun, throwing them once more to the stone. Booming cracks sounded louder than ever, and Michael didn't have to look back to know that half the disk had just disappeared into the abyss. He got to his knees, as did his friends, and stared at the ten o'clock spot. There was still no Portal.

"Come on!" Michael screamed at the empty sky. "Come on, you sorry piece of—"

A black rectangle winked into existence, a flat plane hovering just a few feet away. Michael knew it wouldn't be there long, that there was a chance they'd miss when they jumped. But the time for thinking was long gone.

He got to his feet and pushed Bryson toward the Portal. Bryson ran, leaped through its inky surface, and was swallowed by the blackness. Sarah was right behind him. Her foot slipped but not enough to make a difference. She made it.

There was another explosion of thunder and the world filled with light and sound. Michael ran forward and crouched, jumping just as the disk started spinning again. The momentum flipped him around so he faced the crumbling stone—he was flying backward. He saw what was left of the disk, a sea of rocks and a mist of dust. For a moment he didn't know if his body was going in the right direction or what would happen to him. That one moment stretched on forever.

But then his back hit the Portal and the sky turned black.

CHAPTER 14

SPOOKED

1

He landed on a wooden floor with a hard thump, and a jolt of pain shot up his spine. Faded flower-patterned wallpaper, frayed and peeling at its edges, covered the walls of a wide hallway that stretched out in front of and behind him. Above, a lone lightbulb hung from the ceiling, providing a dull glow. Bryson was lying next to him, stretched out with his head down on his arms, and Sarah had already gotten to her knees, though she looked a little dazed.

"We sure like to cut it close, don't we?" Bryson muttered.

Sarah reached down and poked Michael. "How'd you figure it out? Ten o'clock?"

Michael was feeling pretty good about himself, but when he moved, his whole body ached. Groaning, he sat up anyway. "That stupid riddle was just describing how the number looked. Think about it."

Bryson and Sarah exchanged a glance, and Michael could see it click for both of them at the same time.

"A tower," Sarah said. "Then a dark and hollow moon."

"A one and a zero." Bryson was shaking his head as if he was the dumbest person on the planet.

"Sorry I'm so brilliant," Michael said. "'Tis a burden I must bear."

Sarah started to smile, but it dissolved before anything so bright actually formed. "Do you think it's true?"

"What?" Michael and Bryson asked together.

"Oh, come on. You know."

"The one and done thing?" Bryson guessed.

Sarah nodded. "Yeah. If we die, that lady said we can't get back onto the Path."

Michael had kind of forgotten about that in the madness. "We'll just have to be careful not to die, I guess."

"And it could be worse," Bryson added. "I half expected her to say they were going to break into our code—mess with our Cores. At least we know we'll go back home safe and sound."

That didn't make Michael feel much better. "And fail our . . . mission, or whatever this is called. Tick off the VNS. Have our lives taken away from us, get thrown in jail, have families killed, who knows? I'd rather be dead."

"We just can't die," Sarah said softly. "It's not a game anymore. We can't die and we can't let each other die. Deal?"

"Of course," Michael said.

Bryson gave a thumbs-up. "Let's *especially* not let me die. If you guys are cool with that."

The lingering pain in Michael's back had drained away, and he finally focused on their surroundings a little more.

The hallway in which they sat was stretched out into a gloomy darkness, as if it went on forever both ways.

"Where'd they send us now?" Bryson asked. "And how do we know it's still on the Path?"

Sarah had closed her eyes for a moment to scan the code. "It seems to have the same structure and feel in programming as the stone disk. Complex and almost impossible to read. Fun stuff."

Michael got to his feet and leaned back against one of the walls. He waited for a few moments to see if anything would change. "It feels like we're in an old-timey mansion or something."

Bryson and Sarah had also stood, and Bryson pointed in both directions at once.

"Which way do we go first?" he asked. "We might as well start exploring."

There was a noise.

It was a low, pain-filled sound that came from down the hallway to Michael's right. A chill shot through his body and he pushed off from the wall, standing straight and listening intently. It sounded like a man moaning, and the noise didn't stop. It just continued on. Michael was about to whisper to his friends when a piercing scream erupted from the same direction, a long wail of agony. Then the hallway went silent. Bryson and Sarah both stared at Michael, eyes wide.

"I think we should go that way," he said, motioning to his left.

2

They walked away from the awful sounds, though Michael looked over his shoulder every few seconds, sure he would see some horrific specter waiting at their backs, but so far there'd been nothing, not even a repeat of that moan.

The passage stretched on. They walked for what seemed an impossibly long time, passing under several dim lightbulbs like the first one they'd seen. And gradually Michael noticed a pattern—just as the gloom almost became complete darkness, they'd reach the outskirts of a lighted area and come across a new bulb. Michael could almost swear they were going in circles, even though the hallway was obviously straight as an arrow.

And they walked for a good twenty minutes without change.

"This is one doozy of a house," Michael finally said. The place reminded him of a game he'd played once—a tower full of stairwells that made up a complex maze. At least then he'd felt like he was getting somewhere as they explored. "I can't wait to see what the master bedroom's like," he added weakly.

Every now and then Sarah stopped to examine the wallpaper. "If it even *is* a house. I've been trying to figure out if we're in some kind of loop, but so far I haven't seen any exact repeating patterns—none of the same stains or rips. It's just one big honking hallway."

"It's even weirder that there aren't any doors," Bryson added.

"Maybe this is some kind of tunnel. It could connect two buildings," Sarah said. "It'd make sense—there aren't any windows, either."

Suddenly a harsh whisper cut through the air, like a quick breath of wind.

Michael stopped and held up a hand. "What was that?" That chill crept up his back again.

Bryson and Sarah looked at him, but he could barely see their faces in the gloom.

"Michael," breathed a disembodied voice.

Michael spun and pressed his back against the wall. He looked left and right, but the voice had seemed to come from everywhere at once, as if there were speakers in the walls, ceiling, and floor.

"Michael, you're doing well."

A breeze blew through the hallway—it stirred Michael's hair and rippled his friends' clothing. It was as if some large beast had exhaled its last breath.

"Okay," Bryson said. "Consider me freaked. I want out of this place, and I want it now. Why is someone talking to you?"

"Don't be so spooked," Michael muttered, trying to look unaffected. "How many times have we been in a haunted house? Even the racing games have haunted houses. It's nothing." He hoped. "It's not that weird that they know my name."

"Oh, you're not scared at all, huh?" Bryson shot back.

Michael gave him a smart-aleck grin and resumed walking, but as soon as he turned away from his friend his smile vanished. Acting brave wasn't going to make it the truth. Yes, they'd been in plenty of places like this. But not a house where you had one life and one life only. There was a queasy rumble in Michael's belly and it had nothing to do with hunger.

He jumped when Sarah grabbed his shoulder.

"Look, Bryson," she said with a laugh. "He's not scared one bit."

Bryson was snickering, too. "Yeah, let's just hope he doesn't see himself in a mirror. He might pee his pants."

"All right, you win," Michael growled. "I want my mommy. Now help me find a door."

3

Two hours later, they still hadn't seen a single door.

The ghost wind had flown by three more times, that disturbing whispered phrase following from everywhere at once. It sent chills across Michael's skin on each pass, but he tried his best not to show it. Why was someone complimenting him? Whatever it was, though, it did nothing to harm them. And as they walked down the never-ending hallway, Michael's concern shifted from the haunting visitor to a creeping panic that they might never find their way out.

It was possibly the most brilliant type of firewall. Not something to kill or maim, but a place to trap you, make you think you were getting somewhere when really you weren't. Then throw in a creepy ghost that said your name to slowly drive you nuts.

"What are we doing?" Bryson asked. Michael almost jumped again—no one had spoken in a while and he was on edge.

Sarah stopped and sank to the floor. "He's right. This is so pointless. We must look like idiot mice to whoever's watching." She waved at both directions of the hallway, then heaved a sigh. "Let's take a break and probe the code. Maybe we're missing something."

She closed her eyes and leaned her head against the wall, and Michael and Bryson joined her. Following her lead, they shut their eyes and focused on the code surrounding them.

Michael pulled in a few deep breaths as he searched for anything that stood out. Real hunger was taking over now, making it hard to concentrate, and he knew they'd all need food soon or their strength would plummet. Their real bodies back in their Coffins might be fine physically, but not here. To match the simulation, the VirtNet would sap the strength out of their Auras until they only had enough energy to crawl.

He couldn't believe what he was seeing in the programming around him. If the code back in *Devils of Destruction* had been a storm of letters and numbers, now it was a tornado, spinning and swirling so quickly that he could hardly make anything out. It hurt his brain to even try.

"Michael."

Michael cut his connection and looked up, expecting the ghost to finally reveal itself. This whisper had seemed closer somehow, more solid. But nothing was there, and the now-familiar breeze blew by, though slower than it had before. Their invisible friend repeated his favorite word a few more times before disappearing again.

Michael glanced over at Bryson to gauge his reaction, and the expression on his friend's face gave him pause. He was leaning forward, squinting at a spot on the wall across from him. Michael tried to find what he was studying so intently, but the wallpaper didn't seem any different from what they'd been walking past for hours and hours.

"Hey," Michael said to him. "What are you doing? Did you find a weak spot?"

Bryson's face relaxed, and he met Michael's gaze. "Yeah, I think so. Well, not really a weak spot, just maybe a clue in the code on what we're supposed to do. But I'm telling you—I've never seen anything like this before. The programming in this place is nuts."

"No doubt," Sarah agreed, just as Michael was nodding. "Whoever built this place is about a thousand times more advanced than I could ever dream of becoming. Makes me wonder more and more about this Kaine guy. He must be some kind of prodigy genius."

Bryson shrugged. "Like I said, it's nuts. None of us could do this. That's for sure."

"But I thought you found something," Michael said, his hopes falling.

"I did. It might be some crazy-advanced coding, but we're not so stupid ourselves. Check this out."

He stood up and walked to the facing wall. He leaned his

head up against it as if he was listening for something and glided his hands up and down the surface.

"Hear that?" he asked, looking back at Michael.

Michael's only thought was that maybe Bryson had won—he'd been the first of them to crack from walking down an endless hall.

"Sounds like a guy rubbing his hands against a wall."

Bryson grinned. "No, my friend. That's a magic sound. It's hollow."

"Magic?" Sarah asked.

Bryson stood straight again. "Have some faith, my bestest of friends." Then he reared back with his right foot and kicked the wall hard. A pop was followed by a splintering crack as the toe of his shoe disappeared through the wallpaper. He yanked it back out, along with a section of drywall, and there was a shower of white dust.

He glanced at Michael over his shoulder. "No door? No problem. We're supposed to make our own."

4

Bryson guided them to see what he'd spotted in the complicated cyclone of code, and sure enough, there was a clue there. It was just clear enough that they agreed the only way to slip into the next portion of the Path was to go through the wall.

Michael and Sarah joined Bryson, and they all went at it. Starting where Bryson had so graciously begun, they tore at the wall, pulling out chunks of chalky material and ripping off the loose bits of decorative paper. The skin on Michael's fingers started to rub raw, but an excitement built inside him, and they worked faster and faster as the hole got bigger.

A breeze blew past Michael's back, along with the same dreadful whisper, but he paid it no mind. He was getting out of that place.

Soon they had an opening large enough to go through if they crouched down.

"Who's first?" Michael asked. The other side was so dark it looked as if a black drape had been hung there.

Sarah nudged Bryson. "It was your discovery, Bigfoot."

"Fine by me," he muttered. He bent over, gripped the torn sides of the makeshift entry with both hands, then stepped into the darkness. On the other side he stood up and Michael could just make out his pants as he turned in a circle.

"See anything?" Michael called out.

"Not a thing," he responded, his voice slightly muffled. "Not a single thing. But it's open and airy. Come on in— we'll hold hands and sing songs while we explore."

Sarah hunched down and exited the hallway, and then Michael followed. Bryson was right. The air *was* cool, and there wasn't anything there.

"It's creepy in here," Michael said. "Anybody have a flashlight?"

Bryson clicked his EarCuff and his NetScreen appeared in front of him. He adjusted the settings, and soon they had a nice bright square to light their way.

"Brilliant," Michael said. He and Sarah did the same.

"I know," Bryson responded.

The only problem was that even though they now had a pool of light around them, it didn't reveal anything. Michael could only see darkness—nothing else.

"It's like we're on the moon," Sarah whispered.

Michael squeezed her elbow. "Except that we can breathe, there are no stars, and there's still gravity."

"Yeah, other than that, it's like we're on the moon." She stepped farther into the darkness and looked in both directions. "Which way?"

"Forward," Bryson answered, pointing straight ahead. "The code sure seemed to suggest it."

"Plus," Michael said, "I don't want anything more to do with that stupid hallway." For a moment, he wondered whether it was the right decision and why nothing was trying to stop them. But it seemed to be their only choice.

"Let's do it, then," Sarah said.

So they walked into the darkness.

It was weird and quiet and spooky. They moved across the black floor, their footsteps, their breath, and the rustling of their clothes the only sounds. Michael looked back, and the hole into the hallway was now just a tiny spot of light in the distance. The programming for this place was so incredibly solid, he thought, because the perspective felt real and stayed consistent. In lesser locations you could feel the weaknesses in the coding—the surroundings might subtly shift, the colors change, or you might get skipping in the light source.

"What's the purpose of all this?" Bryson whispered. They were *all* whispering now, as if something in the darkness might hear them.

"It's the Path," Michael answered. It was starting to make more sense to him. "Kaine knows he can't keep everyone out of his secret place. And he knows the good ones will have hacking skills. So he has us playing into his hands. It's a lot easier to funnel people into a series of firewall programs that'll scare them, make them wanna go back. Or kill them and accomplish the same thing. Man, I hate this dude."

"He's not a dude," Sarah said. "He's a madman gamer."

Michael changed his line. "Man, I hate this madman gamer."

They continued on, but nothing changed and nothing new appeared.

Then Michael heard the ghost again and his heart sank. The group stopped.

"Michael." That whimpering whisper. *"Michael."*

A breeze picked up, but this time it wasn't something that passed by. This breeze didn't stop. It came in bursts and changed directions, pulling on their clothes and hair. The sound of moaning filled the air, even louder than what they'd heard back in the hallway. Michael imagined a man curled up in a ball on a sweat-soaked bed as he groaned in agony.

"Michael Michael Michael," came the words again, and then again, from everywhere at once as the moaning continued. Michael didn't know what to think. The voice was definitely louder.

"Remind me to avoid haunted houses from now on," Bryson said. "And why are they only picking on you?"

A new sound pierced the air—a woman's scream, unnaturally long and shrill.

"I can't take this anymore!" Sarah yelled, her hands over her ears. "Let's get out of here!"

Michael thought that sounded like a very good idea. He grabbed her by the hand and started running in the direction they'd been going. Bryson was right beside him—their NetScreens bounced, and the light bobbed ahead of them. The awful noise only grew, and the breeze stiffened into a strong wind.

"Michael Michael Michael . . ."

Michael picked up the pace, dragging Sarah along with him. And as they ran, the ground below them suddenly turned soft—with every step Michael's feet sank several inches until he stumbled and fell onto the shifting surface.

It was black sand. The wind picked up, whipping the grit against his skin. The moans had turned into howls now, and the words blended together to sound like some indecipherable language.

"None of this makes any sense!" Bryson yelled. Michael could barely hear him over the noise. He was on his knees, looking around in disbelief.

Sarah was just getting to her feet. "We need to keep—"

Her voice was cut off when the ground below them collapsed completely and they plummeted in a cloud of sand.

6

For a long moment, Michael's heart seemed to float in his chest and he prepared himself for death. He was back at the Golden Gate Bridge with Tanya, falling to the sea. But relief came when he not so much landed but felt a hard, cool surface against his back. And he wasn't falling anymore; he was *sliding*. His descent began to slow as the surface beneath him turned into stairs, and he tumbled, struggling to stop himself.

Grunting with each jarring impact, he braced his hands and feet and finally came to a halt, his chin resting against the hard edge of a step. He closed his eyes and took a breath. And then someone landed on top of him.

Michael screamed, letting out all the frustration he'd felt over the past several hours, and with one huge burst of adrenaline, he threw whoever it was off of him before he could stop himself. Just as he let go he saw that it was Sarah, and he watched, horrified, as she somersaulted before coming to a stop several steps below him.

"Sorry," he muttered, embarrassed. Nothing like a good friend to toss you down a flight of stairs. "Lost it there for a sec."

She looked up at him, a grimace twisting her features. She opened her mouth to speak and then seemed to think better of it. Michael noticed Bryson then, lying awkwardly on his back, his NetScreen hovering a few feet above him.

Michael curled his legs up to his chest, wrapping his arms around them. He could only imagine the bruises he'd have when he Lifted. The Coffin was expert at physical punishment.

"That hurt," Bryson said. He was staring at some far-off point.

Michael looked around and saw nothing but the same endless darkness. "Yeah, it did," he agreed. "And I'm pretty sure it should be impossible for Kaine to create such a complex place. How can he create a program like this that all three of us can barely penetrate and read? Much less manipulate?"

"I don't know," Bryson responded. "Maybe he had a lot of help. Or maybe there's something about him that we just haven't figured out yet. But it's pretty crazy. I think you're right that the only weaknesses we're seeing are the ones he wants us to—so that we'll be funneled along the Path according to *his* plan. I'm jealous of the rat."

Sarah started whimpering, and when Michael looked he could see that her shoulders were shaking, her head buried in her arms. *Whoa,* he thought. Things had gotten really bad—he couldn't remember the last time he'd seen Sarah cry. He moved to console her, and every inch of him complained. He gingerly made his way down each step until he was by her side, then reached out and rubbed her back.

She looked up and met his eyes. Tears streaked her face,

but even in the dim light Michael could tell that she wasn't angry. At least *he* was in the clear.

"You okay?" he asked, fully aware it was a stupid question but not sure what else to say.

"Hmm, let me think about it. . . . No, I'm not okay." She made a poor attempt at a smile, then shifted to sit up next to him, wincing as she did. "What just happened?"

Bryson was the one with the answer. "Well, we were in a long hallway, then a black room, then walking on sand. Then we fell down a slide that turned into stairs. You've never done that before?"

"Can't say that I have," she answered weakly. "You guys are right about the code. And Kaine. It's all really weird."

Michael studied the staircase below them, trying to see where it ended. But just like the hallway, it disappeared into darkness.

He hated what he was about to say, but it was their only option. "We have to keep going. We gotta get out of this place."

"Why?" Bryson asked bitterly. "The next one's just going to be worse."

Michael shrugged. "Right. And we'll get through that one and then the next one. Go and go and go until we make it to the Hallowed Ravine and figure this all out."

"Or die and go back home," Sarah said softly.

"Or die and go back home," Michael repeated. He was mad that all the time they'd spent in the Sleep didn't seem nearly enough experience to get them through this massive firewall. Angry and hurting, he stood up and started walking down the stairs.

7

Nothing changed for two hours. Nothing except the sand that had fallen with them, which finally vanished from the steps the farther they pushed on. The endlessness continued. Steps and more steps. Down, down, down they walked in cool darkness, the glow of NetScreens lighting the way. Any attempt to find a shortcut or a way out in the programming just led them in circles—nothing made sense.

Finally, they made the decision that they needed to sleep.

"We're each roughly about the same size as the steps," Bryson pointed out when they stopped.

No one said anything as they lay down. Michael had never before felt so tired. Both his mind and body needed rest.

Yet, strangely, sleep didn't come for Michael. Maybe it was the bruises, or maybe he was just on edge—too consumed with waiting for whatever was going to come next—but he couldn't fall asleep. Instead, his mind wandered, and for some reason he thought of one thing and one thing only.

His parents.

He didn't know where it had come from. He missed them, sure. And he was worried about them finding out about the whole Kaine affair.

But then something occurred to him. It was so jarring, so hard to believe, so disconcerting, that he sat up straight and had to struggle for air. Luckily, Bryson and Sarah were asleep. He couldn't have handled questions from them—he wasn't sure he had the answers.

Michael closed his eyes and concentrated, rubbing his

temples. He had to just be shaken up, not thinking right. He took a deep breath and calmed himself, went through a very methodical line of thinking. He thought about each and every day of his recent life in reverse order, running through a mental list of what had happened.

One week. Two weeks. Three weeks. A month. Two months. Day by day, going back in time, trying to go through the checklist of his everyday existence. His memory was stronger than he would've guessed—there were lots of things, lots of events, that he could bring back. But there was one glaring, monumental detail that seemed impossible to recall. How could he have gotten so wrapped up in his life that it had gone unnoticed until now? So wrapped up in school and the VirtNet?

There was no mistaking the thing that bothered him so much.

Michael literally couldn't remember the last time he had seen his parents.

CHAPTER 15

A DOOR IN THE DISTANCE

And Helga had never come back, either.

Michael didn't know which bothered him more—that something terrible was going on with his parents and nanny or that he was so wrapped up in his entertainment that it had taken him this long to notice. He was equally horrified and ashamed.

He tried to think of what possibly could've happened. Maybe the VNS was involved somehow. Or Kaine and this Mortality Doctrine program. All the things that had so drastically changed his life over the past couple of weeks were, after all, related—though he didn't know how to connect the dots.

But Michael couldn't remember. As hard as he pressed his mind, he couldn't recall the exact last time he'd been together with his parents. Everything he thought of— parties, meals, riding in the car—it always seemed overwhelmingly true that surely he had seen them *since* then. But there was nothing.

It was weird, and it terrified him. And haunting it all, Michael had to wonder if it had something to do with the KillSim. There was no doubt in his mind that the creature had done something to his brain.

He didn't know what to do, what to think, but eventually he allowed himself to lie back on his designated stair and stretch out. The sheer exhaustion finally became too much and he fell asleep.

2

Bryson woke him with a gentle shake of his shoulders. Michael looked at his friend through bleary eyes.

"Sheesh, man," Bryson said. "We've been awake for an hour. And you snore like a fat bear."

Michael swung his legs around and sat up, yawned, rubbed his eyes. The black world of the staircase tilted for a second, then righted itself. Nothing had changed while they'd slept.

"Anybody else have weird dreams last night?" Sarah asked. "There was a guy in a bunny suit in mine. Don't ask for more details."

Michael hadn't dreamed at all, but his upsetting discovery came back to him like a whammy. Why couldn't he remember when he'd last seen his parents? Where were they? Why hadn't Helga come home? How could he not have thought about his mom and dad being gone so long? He never talked to his parents much while they were away, but it was still weird. And he had no doubt that something was not right, in one form or another.

"Michael?" Sarah asked. "You okay?"

He looked at her and decided there was no way he'd tell anybody about this oddity. "Yeah, I'm okay. Just excited to walk down some more stairs. And starving so bad I'm thinking about eating one of Bryson's legs."

"Better shave them first," Bryson responded, lifting a leg straight out in front of him as if to offer it. He put it back down, then said, "I had a weird dream. I'd never met Michael in it and was living a wonderfully happy life, with no one trying to kill me or damage my brain forever. It was sweet."

"That *does* sound nice," Sarah said.

Michael stood up and stretched. "Hardy har har. Let's get down these stupid stairs."

No one argued, and step by step they resumed their descent.

It was impossible to tell just how long it took before something changed. Michael tried counting the steps for a while, then seconds and minutes, just to keep his mind occupied with something other than his parents. His watch had stopped working at some point, and the clocks on their

NetScreens kept doing weird things. The longer they descended, the crazier Michael felt. The monotony of it began building an anxiety that he had to work hard to push down. Occasional—and failed—attempts to hack into the seemingly impossible code only made things worse.

Then, finally, they found a door.

It was at the end of the stairs, where the space around them had narrowed until it formed a tunnel that dead-ended at an ordinary wooden door. The relief of seeing it overwhelmed Michael, and an irrational surge of giddiness made him suddenly erupt in giggles.

"Something funny?" Bryson asked, on the verge of a smile himself. "Better share it with the whole class."

"No, nothing funny." Michael was the first to the door, and he reached out for its round brass handle. "Just happy to be home."

Bryson snickered at that, and Michael didn't wait for more conversation. He twisted the handle and the door swung open easily. Then he stepped through to see what awaited them.

Two long rows of people stood, backs to the walls, stretching down a hallway. And despite the fact that they all had their eyes open, every one of them looked dead.

4

Michael stopped right past the threshold of the doorway. He could sense his friends at his back, but no one made a move to urge him on. He was sure that they wanted to walk down the hallway as much as he did. Which was not at all.

Bare lightbulbs, like the ones from the haunted-house hallway, hung from the ceiling to illuminate the two lines of people, and Michael suddenly missed the darkness they'd been surrounded by for so long. The strangers stood as still as carved rock, every pair of eyes trained on Michael and his friends.

Michael focused on the ones closest to him. To his right was a woman, her skin as pale as the moon. She wore a white dress, wrinkled but clean. Her dark eyes bore into Michael's, and it seemed that she might open her mouth to speak to him at any second.

Directly across from her, to Michael's left, was a man in a black suit. He was just as pale as the woman and just as still, but his right arm was held out halfway from his body, the fingers spread apart.

Michael focused on the others lining the hallway. All of them ghostly white, all completely still, all staring at the new arrivals. Like the man, many of the people were frozen in odd positions. As if they'd been turned to stone in the middle of an activity.

"Hello?" Bryson called. His voice echoed down the hallway, and just before it faded, each person in front of them moved slightly. Michael's heart skipped.

"What was that?" Sarah whispered, and a few of the bodies twitched. Then she said even softer, "All I can tell from the code is it seems the Path goes straight ahead. I can't break through anything or see another way out."

"What else is new?" Bryson added. "Me neither."

Very slowly, Michael turned around to face his two friends. Then, so quiet he could barely hear himself speaking, he said, "Okay, but no talking. No sudden movements. Follow me."

He turned back and took a careful step forward, then another. The heads of the strangers slowly pivoted to watch his movement, their eyes zeroing in on him specifically. Michael held his gaze on them, terrified of what they might do. With each person he passed, a choking fear grew in his chest that was making it harder and harder to breathe.

He pressed on, forcing himself to take each step as slowly as possible. He could sense Bryson and Sarah behind him, but he didn't dare turn to look at them again. They passed an old man with a large nose and fire in his eyes. Another man with an enormous birthmark covering half his face, like a bruise on his pale skin. A lady with her mouth wide open, teeth white and gums purple. A toddler, a slight smile frozen on his face.

Michael felt an itch growing in his nose and was unable to hold it back. He sneezed, and the bodies around him twitched again, their arms and hands rising almost an inch. His heart skipped and he stopped, waiting to make sure nothing was going to happen. All was still. Relieved, he pushed forward again, step by agonizingly slow step.

They'd passed about ten more people when Michael tripped over an uneven break in the floor. He fell to the ground, landing on his shoulder. But before he even hit the hard floor of the hallway, he heard movement from all the people around him.

5

Michael rolled onto his back and shot his arms up protectively around his face, but then froze. The scene above was like a horror-movie poster. Several sets of hands reaching toward him, framing angry faces. But they'd frozen as soon as he had. Bone-white fingers with sharp nails hovered over him. And eyes, bright with hunger, stared down. But no one moved.

Sure that they'd soon hear his banging heart, Michael tried to calm himself down. Slowly, he took several long, deep breaths; then he readied himself and started inching backward, using his legs and arms to do it in tiny motions. Sweat broke out all over his body, soaking his clothes and dripping down the sides of his face. He couldn't tear his eyes away from the many locked on him. One mistake and they'd attack—he knew it—and then it'd all be over. Fighting would only cause *more* movement.

Happy thoughts, he mused as he slowly scooted away from them.

Finally, Michael got out from under the frozen canopy of arms. The creepiest part for him was that even though their bodies—below the neck—remained still, their eyes continued to follow his movements. Chills washed through him.

Ever so slowly, he turned over, then rose to his feet. He looked back at Bryson and Sarah, who were on the far side of the pack Michael had just escaped. Luckily a space had opened up along the wall where some of the people had been standing. His two friends slipped into it to wind around the group, and once again they were all together.

Bryson was unusually distraught, his face tense, his eyes wild. Michael wanted to ask him if he was okay, but knew they couldn't afford to make any noise, so he silently pressed on.

They headed down the hallway. Slowly. Ever so slowly.

6

Being quiet was hard, and the three inched along slower than Michael had ever moved. The pace drove him a little mad, though he was happy as long as the strangers stayed put.

Gradually the people they passed soon melded into one mass for him. He no longer distinguished between man and woman, adult and child, fat and thin. It was all just a kaleidoscope of pale skin and staring eyes. He tried not to look at them at all, focusing on the distant point at the far end of the hallway instead.

And after what seemed like an eternity, an end came into sight. Far ahead, Michael could see another door.

7

Once he saw the door, the urge to break into a run was almost too much to fight. But Michael held it back. He continued, moving toward that door with deliberate care.

As they walked, eyes followed Michael and the others. Michael was concentrating on staying slow when a strange sound began behind him, like someone whimpering, and his heart sank when he realized it was Bryson. Michael saw the strangers on either side of him twitch.

"I keep thinking about Kaine and the impossible code of this place," Bryson whispered far too loudly. The people lining the walls twitched again. "And it just hit me. What if Kaine isn't really a gamer? What if . . . Hey! The code is weaker up there!"

The last few words came out not in a whisper but an echoing yell. And as Bryson's voice permeated the silence, Michael's mind spun into a swirl of panic. Bryson was suddenly pushing him to the side, running past him in a full sprint toward the door. Michael crashed into a cold body, and the thing sprang to life. But instead of turning on Michael, the creature took off after Bryson. All of them did. Every single figure was chasing Bryson, and Michael sank to his knees, stunned with horror, watching the vicious horde storm after his friend.

8

Michael understood how things worked. When you were in the Sleep, you were always aware on some level that you weren't in the *real* world. The worst-case scenario was that you'd die—maybe pretty awfully—then end up back home in your Coffin, where you could get out, take a shower, recover from the ordeal, and go back to play another day. You were always aware of that basic truth.

But on the Path, that awareness felt more distant. And in

that moment, Michael was torn about what he should do. He knew Bryson was about to experience something that wasn't actually real. If it was, Michael wouldn't have hesitated for a moment—he'd have run after his friend and tried to save him. If they'd been in a normal VirtNet game, he probably would've done the same thing. It was, after all, a game. But here, if he died, their mission was over. He couldn't risk it.

Still, knowing that didn't make it any easier to hear as the sounds of violence escalated. It certainly didn't *feel* like a game.

Sarah plopped down next to Michael. "We have to hack—"

He cut her off. "We've tried and tried."

"Then we need to try again!" Her face was red.

"Fine." Michael shrugged. "You're right."

Michael closed his eyes and entered the realm of code surrounding them. He poked and prodded, swam through the data. He could sense Sarah's digital presence doing the same. But the Path here was even more strongly shielded than before. Michael tried everything in his power to get to the code where Bryson was being attacked, and he just couldn't do it.

Sarah tried longer but couldn't manage to get there, either.

"Thanks anyway," she said softly.

Eyes open again, she and Michael avoided looking toward Bryson. Michael didn't want to take a chance of seeing what was inevitably going to happen to him. But the sounds were bad enough. Growls and ripping and tearing. Roars of anger, or maybe delight.

And of course, worst of all, Bryson's screams. They tore through the air over everything else and traveled down that long hallway as if Bryson was standing right next to them. The cries were desperate, so full of terror that Michael's heart hurt, as if someone was squeezing it with both fists. They'd signed up for this kind of life inside the Sleep, but, real or not real, at the moment Bryson was feeling every single bit of the torture being done to him.

Finally, mercifully, it stopped. And Michael didn't need to look to know that what was left of Bryson had disappeared, gone with the last breath of his Aura's life. Somewhere far away from them, their friend was waking up inside his Coffin, probably still screaming from the horror of it all.

Sarah grabbed Michael's hand, squeezed it. And for the second time in less than a day, he heard her crying.

With everything still again, Michael could finally think about the odd words of his friend right before he'd freaked out, wonder if they were just the thoughts of a person driven to the brink.

What if Kaine isn't really a gamer?

Michael closed his eyes and felt on the verge of tears himself. What in the world had Bryson meant?

CHAPTER 16

AN ISOLATED MAN

1

As soon as Bryson's body disappeared, the horde froze and the hallway became silent once more. Michael and Sarah slowly got to their feet, careful not to make any sudden movements. Bryson was gone—he wouldn't rejoin them on the Path—and the trauma of being there for what had just happened to him hung over Michael like a dark mist. He wanted to talk to Sarah about what Bryson had said, but he didn't dare risk waking the undead.

He focused on the only thing he could: making it to that door. He prodded the code to see if he could find a way to mute their sounds—such a small thing but still almost impossible within the complexity of the firewall. But he was finally able to do it. Sarah noticed and nodded a thank-you.

Step by step, they moved toward their goal until they reached their final obstacle—the hill of bodies that had taken Bryson's life. Michael hugged the wall, picking his way over arms and legs. It was nerve-racking despite their programmed silence, and sweat beaded on his forehead. He felt a scorching thirst, his mouth so dry it seemed full of dust.

Finally, Michael emerged on the far side of the still bodies with Sarah trailing close behind. They pressed on, trudging along as if they fought deep mud with every step.

And then the door—*the beautiful door*, Michael thought—was right in front of him. And just like the one through which they'd entered, it wasn't locked. He opened it and stepped through, pulling Sarah behind him by the hand.

Before Michael could even get a sense of where they were, he slammed the door shut. It was then that he turned to face what new environment lay before him.

It was a thick forest of massive trees, mist hanging off the branches like moss. A path of well-trodden earth cut through it, inviting him and Sarah into its depths. And standing next to the beginning of the trail, under the boughs of a huge oak, was a pale man dressed in a red cloak, the hood pulled over his head.

"My, you're a pair," the stranger said.

2

For some reason Michael's first reaction at hearing the words was to spin around and see if the door was still there. It was, set into a huge wall of gray granite. Closed tight. He wasn't sure why he'd done it—going back to the hall of the undead was the last thing he'd ever want to do. But there was something sinister about this forest and the man who'd greeted them.

He turned back to face the man. Sure enough, he was still standing next to the oak, his hands folded in front of him. The red cloak shone in the dim light.

Michael took a better look at the stranger's face. He was old but not ancient. Wrinkles lined his skin, but he had none of the frailty of someone in the last years of his life. He had thin lips, a narrow beak of a nose, and a pointy chin. And his eyes . . . they were blue, almost silver, so light they seemed to glow from within.

"Where are we?" Sarah asked the familiar question. "Who are you?"

The man's voice was raspy. "You're standing on the edge of Forest Mendenstone, a place of darkness and death. But you mustn't fear, my young friends. Within the majestic walls of these pines and oaks lies a place of meditation where you'll find food and shelter. And protection from the things that slay and rip."

Michael had seen a lot of darkness and death—he certainly didn't want any more of that. What he really wanted was food. His stomach growled, and he realized that he didn't care if this guy was a serial killer. If he had food, Michael would follow him anywhere.

Sarah wasn't quite so desperate. "What makes you think we'd trust you to take us *anywhere*? We've been on our own so far—why should we just go along with the first person waiting for us?"

"He has *food,*" Michael whispered, leaning closer to say it.

The stranger unfolded his hands, letting them rest at his sides. Nothing else on his body stirred, not even his cloak. "I am a man of peace. You can trust me, young ones. Come. Come with me and visit for a while."

Michael almost laughed out loud, but again, he was *starving.*

"Okay," he said. Sarah started to protest, but Michael held up a hand for her to stop—the scolding he'd get later would be worth it if he was able to eat. "But if you try anything weird, we'll send you back to the Wake without a second thought."

The man smiled, not a trace of fear in his glowing eyes. "Of course," he said.

The stranger turned to walk down the trail that disappeared into the woods. As he took his first step, a furry creature scurried up the man's back and planted itself on his shoulder. It looked like a ferret or a weasel. The creature stood upright with its ratty nose sniffing at the air.

"Look at that," Michael whispered to Sarah.

He saw her eyes widen in surprise as she took in the man's companion.

"Okay, that's a little freaky," she replied quietly. "Reason number three hundred why we *can't* go with this guy."

Logic had begun to seep in, overpowering his hunger, and Michael was beginning to agree with his friend. But at that moment the stranger turned and called back to them, ending the debate.

"You'll never reach the next stage of the Path without me," the man said. "No matter how much you hack away at the code, you'll never reach the Hallowed Ravine."

Then he continued on his way, vanishing into the gloom of the forest.

3

"Come on," Michael said, grabbing Sarah by the arm as he started following their new friend.

She pulled free but walked along beside him. "It feels like we're following a snake back to its lair. I bet this guy's killed a hundred kids."

They'd entered the woods, and the massive trees towered above them. They were thick with foliage and laden with long, wispy trails of moss. And they grew close to each other, with the trail cutting a neat line down their center. The magic of programming.

"He's probably just a Tangent," Michael said, craning his neck to take in their surroundings. The only light in the woods came from the trees themselves, their scarred trunks glowing an eerie blue. As they walked deeper into the forest, the branches and leaves stretched closer to the path, as if they wanted to snatch the newcomers away.

"Then why did you tell him we'd send him back to the Wake?" Sarah asked.

"It was something to say," he answered. He didn't really feel like talking.

The man kept a steady pace about twenty feet in front of them, his odd pet somehow keeping its perch on his shoulder. The air was cool, and everything smelled wet and earthy. It was almost pleasant, Michael thought, but a stench of rot tainted its edges. The only sounds were crickets and the occasional hoot of an owl.

"I guess we didn't really have a choice," Sarah murmured. "I can't see another direction to go in the code."

"You're still debating this?" Michael responded.

"I'm just saying," she answered with a shrug. They walked for a while in silence until she spoke again. "We need to talk about what Bryson said. It was like something had really clicked for him, but why did he freak out? What did he see in the code?"

Michael could play back every detail of his friend's final moments in his mind. "It was such a strange thing to say. *What if Kaine isn't really a gamer?* What does that mean?"

Sarah snickered. "All we're doing is asking each other questions. We need answers."

"Yeah." Michael pushed aside a low-hanging branch. "It really bothered Bryson how complicated the code of the Path is. I can see why he couldn't accept that Kaine was able to program it. Seems impossible."

"So he thinks Kaine isn't real?" Sarah asked. "Like he's just a made-up name by a whole group of people doing all this?"

"Maybe," Michael answered with a shrug. "Keep thinking about it. Look at the code every once in a while. We can figure this out."

"Okay. Just . . . let's be on our toes and stay sharp."

"Let's be on our *toes*?" he repeated, going heavy on the sarcasm. "Stay sharp? Really?"

"What?"

He let out a short laugh. "You sound like Sherlock Holmes. You gonna pull out a magnifying glass? A pipe, maybe?"

Sarah smiled. "You can thank me later when I save your life."

"Don't worry. I'll keep my eyes peeled and my ears perked. What do I do with my nose?"

"Shut. Up." She quickened her pace to get ahead of him.

Michael shot a glance at their guide—the man walked smoothly, the weasel on his shoulder swaying with every step but not losing its posture. Then Michael turned his attention to the forest on both sides of the trail.

The glowing trunks of the trees were thick and tall, rising toward the black sky above. The way they shone that pale light—and how it barely penetrated the darkness of the night—for some reason made him feel like he and Sarah were floating along in the forgotten depths of the ocean. It threw him off a bit, and he pulled in a few deep breaths to remind himself that he was walking out in the open air.

The trail rounded a tree even larger than most of those they'd seen so far, and as Michael passed it his gaze naturally took in what waited behind it. Just a few feet into the woods, a pair of bright yellow eyes stared back at him. He jumped, stumbled, then kept moving along the path backward, not daring to look away. Visions of the KillSims filled his head.

The eyes followed him, but their owner stayed put, and soon the path took a turn so that a group of trees blocked the sight of the animal. The creature. Monster. *Whatever* it had been.

Michael bumped into Sarah and finally turned around.

"What's wrong?" she asked.

"Sorry" was all he got out. He'd been spooked royally, and he suddenly wanted nothing more than to reach the stranger's home, even if he had to share it with the weasel-rat-ferret thing.

4

The forest stretched on and on.

Michael saw three more pairs of those yellow eyes, but just like the first set, the creatures didn't move except to follow him with their gaze. But the same knife of fear cut through him each time, and he found himself walking faster and faster.

"Why such a hurry all of a sudden?" Sarah asked him as he spied the fourth animal.

"I keep seeing eyes out there," he answered. He could hear the fear in his own voice. "Like a KillSim's. But smaller, not quite the same."

"Oh, so you figured you'd put me in between?"

"Yeah, something like that." Michael grinned.

She was just about to turn to look for herself when the cloaked stranger stopped.

"The sight never ceases to moisten my face with tears," the old man said.

His eyes had widened in what looked like rapture, and—true to his word—tears streaked his cheeks, glistening in the eerie glow of the forest trees. Michael turned to see what had captured his gaze.

Just up ahead along the path, the branches of two trees had been woven together into a tight coil, arching over the trail. Hanging from the center of the arch was a wooden sign with hand-painted yellow letters. They shone as if lit by neon:

MENDENSTONE SANCTUARY
MASTER SLAKE
PRESIDING OVERSEER
ALL ARE WELCOME

"Master Slake?" Michael questioned. "What are you a master of?"

The man turned sharply and nailed him with a hardened gaze. "I'm here to help you, boy. Show some respect or my . . ." His words faded and his eyes darted to Sarah, then back to Michael. "Never mind. Come and sup with me. My friends will have made us a pleasant meal. We can sit and rest our bones by the fire as we eat and drink. Then I'll tell you how to reach the Hallowed Ravine. From here you'll find that it's all very simple. Very simple indeed."

A dozen questions flickered through Michael's mind, but the man resumed walking, heading for the archway. Michael gave Sarah a wary glance, but they both followed. At least the man answered questions.

5

The forest didn't quite end at the hanging sign, but the clearing that opened up in front of them after they passed under it had only scattered trees instead of the densely packed trunks of the woods. A bright moon shone down from above, casting long, narrow shadows. A hundred feet or so ahead stretched the Mendenstone Sanctuary, a long, low building. It was made entirely of wood, and every part appeared crooked or about to topple over. A huge welcome sign hung above what Michael guessed was the front door, which stood wide open, revealing darkness lit only by the flickering of a fire.

Michael expected the man to say something like "Home, sweet home," but he remained silent, heading for that back-lit doorway. Michael hurried to catch up to him. He felt slightly more at ease, though maybe it was just his hunger finally winning out over judgment.

"You mentioned your friends," Sarah said to the man. "How many people live here? Are you guys monks or what?"

The weasel perched on Slake's shoulder sniffed the air as the man let out an unsettling chuckle. "Monks? I guess you could call them monks." He laughed again.

Michael shot Sarah a look. She wasn't happy to be there, and her eyes said that whatever happened, it was all *his* fault.

He turned back to Slake. "What do you mean? Who are they?"

"You're about to find out," the man answered, then added happily, "Hope you're hungry."

That last word put Michael at the man's disposal all over again. He was willing to do just about anything for some VirtNet food.

"Here we are," Slake announced, stopping a few feet from the open door. Michael peered in and looked around, but he couldn't make anything out. Just the flicker of shadows made by the fire.

But there *were* sounds. Of things scuttling across wood. Pots and dishes banging and clinking together. Odd grunts and chittering noises that were decidedly not human.

Master Slake turned to face Michael and Sarah, his expression showing genuine concern. "Please don't be afraid. They are my friends."

And with that he stepped into the sanctuary.

Michael and Sarah both hesitated, waiting for the other to go first. Finally, Sarah reached over and pushed on the back of Michael's arm.

"After you," she said with a grimace. She didn't bother to hide her fear.

"You're so gracious."

"I know."

Michael knew that something could happen at any minute. The Path was designed to keep them *out* of the Hallowed Ravine, not help them find it. But until they knew what they faced, there was no point in running or even looking at the code. They could only move forward.

He took a tentative step then stopped in the doorway, gripping the wood of the threshold as he gazed around at what was inside.

A long, low table reached from one end of a large room to the other. Plates and dishes full of scrumptious-looking food were laid out across its surface—as inviting a thing as he'd ever seen. But his attention was soon taken by the movement of bodies—and other than Master Slake, none of them were human.

A mangy dog—at least three feet tall at its back—ran across the floor right in front of Michael, a cup in its mouth. To Michael's right, a huge black bear, bald spots covering its chest, was leaning over to pick up a tray of cupcakes from a serving window that led into a kitchen. A bear. With a tray. Of cupcakes. Michael had to remind himself that it was okay—anything was possible inside the VirtNet.

There was a tiger walking on its hind legs, holding a pitcher of something with its front paws. A goose flapping its wings as it used its beak to push dishes this way and that on the table to set them straight. There was a fox dragging a platter with an enormous Thanksgiving turkey on it. A lion with the handle of a breadbasket clutched between its huge incisors. A cat standing on the table, cutting up a chicken with a knife.

Oddly, one of the first thoughts that popped into Michael's mind was why didn't these animals mind cooking their friends? Though maybe geese and chickens weren't on the same social level.

Sarah had stepped up behind Michael and leaned her face against the side of his arm as she took it all in. "You still hungry?" she asked.

"I think if I can get past that dog licking our plates, I'll be fine." He had a sudden urge to laugh. He'd been so scared of what they'd find at the sanctuary, and here they were inside a storybook for little kids. The animals only had to break into song as they worked and it would all be perfect.

Master Slake had taken a seat at the head of the table, where the large bear bent over to place a napkin in his lap. The man comically thanked the bear, and the creature went off to do some other chore.

"Sit," Slake bellowed, like some king sitting down with his minions. "There's more food here than you could ever eat. Even within the Sleep."

Hunger won Michael's obedience completely. Sarah tried to grab his arm but he slipped from her grip and went to sit down by Slake. As soon as he did, a squirrel pushed a plate full of steaming food in front of him. Its beady little eyes looked up at Michael briefly; then it scurried away.

Sarah joined them, sitting across from Michael, and gradually her face changed from disgust into something like desire. The smells were just too delicious, Michael thought.

"Please take my hands as we say grace to the spirits of our ancestors, man and beast." Master Slake held out his hands, and his guests took them.

Slake closed his eyes. "To the ones who came before us," he began. "We ask your presence to look upon us in favor this day. We ask for a blessing upon our food and drink. Two travelers have come to our humble sanctuary, where we serve the needs of those who enter the dark forest. Bless them, dear spirits. Bless them with strength and hope. That they may defeat the demons that beset them, that they may further journey along the Path. Amen."

Slake released their hands, opened his eyes, and began to eat—he picked up a turkey leg and attacked it like a starving dog. Grease dripped down his chin, and a piece of meat hung from the corner of his mouth.

Michael had to look away. His thoughts were occupied with the words of the prayer, and he had to ask the obvious question.

"You said something about demons," he said, picking at his food so he didn't have to look at their host as he ate. "Was that just . . . normal prayer stuff?"

Slake chuckled. "Oh no, my boy. Certainly not. I sincerely meant every word said to our ancestors. I hope that you can kneel at their feet before the demons rip you apart."

Michael almost choked on a piece of meat. He swallowed it down and cleared his throat. "Want to tell us more about these demons?"

"Oh, my son." The man wiped his mouth with a sleeve. "They are the least of your worries. The outside world is beginning to learn something that you—both of you—have yet to realize. Even though I know you are both adept at code, surely as good as your friend . . . Bryson, I believe?"

The little hairs on Michael's neck were rising.

Sarah had a fork squeezed tightly in her fist. "What are you talking about?" she asked in a threatening voice.

"Please," Slake replied smoothly. "Let's not get hostile. There's no need. I've had enough of that in my life. Years of gaming can find you with many enemies. I was . . . quite good at it, you know. Until I somehow found my way here, onto this Path. I can't seem to escape the damnable thing. I've accepted it now. I feel as if I have a new role to play. To help those like you. To convince you to leave—to find your way out when you can and never come back."

Michael stared at the man, desperately curious now.

But Sarah spoke first. "Wait . . . you're a gamer? Not just a Tangent?"

Slake gave her a long, almost sad look. "It's a pity you can't tell the difference yourself. Truly a pity. I was one of the best. Perhaps the best ever."

Michael couldn't help but close his eyes and scan the coding, as hard as it was to read. He analyzed the man sitting at their table, searched the programming for something, anything, that might give him a clue about what this guy could be talking about. He caught bits and pieces of the stranger's history, fetched a couple of NewsBop stories, saw something odd in his digital nameplate. And then it hit Michael, and he snapped his eyes open again.

"What the . . . ," he whispered. "You're Gunner Skale." The revelation thrilled him and scared him at the same time. "What are you doing here? Why did you vanish from the VirtNet? From the public?"

Sarah was looking back and forth between them. "Are you serious?"

The older man yawned and scratched his head. "Busted, as it were. I know I must seem lowly compared to my glory days. But I'm content, I promise you. I believe I've met a higher calling. I'm human, Michael. Sarah. I'm human, playing in a nonhuman's world. The program speaks for itself. Two people as smart as you should've figured things out long ago. The Path should've taught you."

He paused, and the wheels spun inside Michael's mind, like gears and cogs clicking into place.

"You should have seen it," Skale continued. "You've been in Kaine's presence. You've been in many a Tangent's presence. You've been among other gamers, countless times. The difference in programming is ever so slight, but it's there for the taking if you know where to look." He paused. "I think your friend finally realized the truth, and it was too much for him to handle. He panicked and lost his way on the Path because of it."

Michael finally had the answer, but it was Sarah who spoke first.

"Kaine's not a man at all. A man couldn't do what he's doing. He's a . . ."

Michael said it at the same time.

"Tangent."

CHAPTER 17

NIGHT ON THE COUCH

1

Skale went right back to his meal, leaving Michael and Sarah to contemplate the bombshell realization that the man they'd been chasing wasn't human. Michael had already forgotten about the demons.

Kaine. A Tangent. It was impossible. Utterly impossible. How could a program have fooled the world—the VNS, even—into thinking it was a gamer? How could it have become *self-aware*? Could it be possible? A knot grew in his stomach as he thought about it. Had artificial intelligence taken such a leap? Or was someone controlling Kaine behind the scenes?

Then he remembered the voice.

Michael, you're doing so well.

"Aren't you going to eat?" Skale asked, pausing with a knife halfway to his mouth, a piece of meat on its tip. "I'd hate to offend my friends after all their hard work."

"But—" Michael stopped himself.

He needed to think this out. Not only Kaine, but the man sitting in front of him. Skale had gone from being the most famous gamer in the VirtNet to a lost pawn within Kaine's firewalls. And based on her silence and furrowed brow, Sarah felt the same way. Hunger still gnawed at Michael, so he dug in, taking a huge bite of bread, then starting in on the poor chicken. Once again he wondered why *it* had been baked in the oven while the other animals got to run around free.

Skale spooked him with his response. It was as if he could read Michael's mind. "All my friends know that a day will come when it's their time to serve as nourishment. They usually take it with honor, knowing they've lived a good life."

For some reason that angered Michael. "You do realize that all of this isn't real. Right?"

"Who knows the true definition of *real*?" Skale said evenly as he continued to eat. "When you've been trapped in one place in the Sleep this long, it's all as real as anything else. Now eat."

They did so in silence for a while. They'd need strength for whatever awaited them—which finally made Michael speak up again.

"So there are demons. Kaine's a Tangent. Anything else we should know?" The sarcasm was thick.

Gunner Skale finished chewing, took a drink, then wiped his mouth on his sleeve again, leaving a smear of moisture across his red cloak. "You've already been given the information you need, if you're willing to search for it. I hope your memory is strong, my son."

"My son?"

"You have a nasty habit of repeating things I say, boy. I highly recommend you stop this practice."

The tone of the man's voice made Michael nod, suddenly humbled. The old man had some fire in him, that was for sure. But Michael didn't know how Skale planned to back up his veiled threats—unless the animals would do whatever he commanded. Getting eaten by a bear didn't sound very fun.

"Don't you have anything else to tell us?" Sarah asked. She'd been so quiet.

Skale stood up and took off his cloak, then held it out. The bear growled, a rumbling sound that came from deep in its chest, as it came over, took the red fabric, folded it over its arm, then walked away. Michael was half disappointed it didn't bow and speak in a British accent.

"Let's move into the sitting room," Skale said. "Rest our bones as I promised before."

He didn't wait for an answer. He simply walked toward a door on the far side of the room and left. Michael shot Sarah a glance, then downed a couple more bites and one last swig of water. They both got up and hurried after their host, and Michael was sure his friend was thinking the same thing he was: being left alone with all those circus animals seemed like a really bad idea.

2

"What do you two know about the Deep?" Skale asked after they'd settled down into oversize chairs facing a cozy, flickering fire nestled within a brick hearth.

Michael leaned forward, his curiosity piqued. "You mean *Lifeblood Deep*?"

"*Lifeblood Deep*," the man repeated with a huff. "Is that really the only program you think has been escalated to such status?"

Michael didn't know what the man meant.

"To *Deep* status?" Sarah asked.

Skale nodded, never shifting his gaze from the fire. Michael could see the dancing flames reflected in his eyes. "Yes, what else? The Deep has been around since the beginning of the VirtNet, and only a few programs have reached its level. *Lifeblood* is the only one that's public, and barely deserves the name."

"What else is there?" Michael asked.

"That's for you to discover in your own time. But one of them is the Hallowed Ravine." Skale stood and walked to the fireplace, stirred up the flames with an iron poker. "It's a program created by Kaine, hidden within the Deep. The Path connects it to the upper layers of the VirtNet. You're lucky to have made it this far, luckier still if you make it all the way." He stopped and turned to look at Michael and Sarah. "Let me ask you, haven't you wondered how such a path could be created? One that the great and powerful VNS needs *you* to lead them to?"

Michael wanted to know everything, but he had no idea what to even ask. "So . . . why are you telling us this? All you're giving us is riddles and clues that don't help."

"No clues, boy!" the man half shouted. He came back and sat in his chair. "I'm just talking to pass the hours until the demons come out. But maybe I'm tired. It might do us all some good to sleep."

"When *do* the demons come out?" Sarah asked, as if asking the time.

Skale stood up, once again gazing into the fire as if hypnotized. "They come when they are ready to rip and slay. Good night, now. The bear will show you to your beds." He took one last, longing look into the flames, then turned and walked away, disappearing through a wooden door that closed behind him.

As tired as Michael was, sleep still seemed like the last thing he could manage. "He said those words again."

"What?" Sarah asked.

"*Rip and slay*. Didn't this guy ever learn about bedtime stories?" *Maybe the bear will give us one that's a little more chipper,* Michael thought glumly.

3

Despite Skale saying he'd be shown to his *bed,* Michael was led to a rickety couch. It was hard and uncomfortable and squeaked every time he moved, but it was better than the floor. He pulled a scratchy woolen blanket up to his chin and closed his eyes. A candle burned on a desk nearby, and he could see its flickering glow even with his eyes closed.

The attack came all at once.

A brutal, splintering pain cut through the middle of his head so suddenly that he fell off the couch, clutching at his temples with both hands. A piercing sound filled his head, partnered with a blinding light, and he wailed in agony, sensed Sarah appearing by his side, grabbing his shoulders, shaking him, asking what was wrong. Michael thrashed, trying to make her let go, afraid of what he might do to her.

Images flashed across his mind's eye. His mom and dad, their forms wavering until they vanished like a puff of smoke in the wind. Then Helga, her face screwed up in terror. She disappeared, too. Then Bryson, his eyes peering at Michael, full of hatred. Then he was gone.

The pain didn't cease, and he knew if it got any worse he'd faint, possibly die. He tried to stand. He opened his eyes to see Sarah on the floor, looking up at him with a terrified expression on her face. The candle still burned, but now it seemed as bright as the sun, and Michael had to turn away. He stumbled, threw his arms out for balance—it felt as if up was down and down was up. As if the room was turning and at any moment he would be thrown to the wooden rafters crossing the ceiling.

The couch stretched out, kept stretching, getting longer and longer even though the room stayed the same size. Sarah's head grew until her face was a horror from a fun house. The boards of the floor began to warp and twist, bending like they were made of rubber. And the sound of the horde pulling Bryson apart filled his head.

He pressed his hands over his ears, squeezing his head as if to hold it together. Somewhere in the back of his thoughts he saw the KillSims at the Black and Blue Club. *They'd* done this to him. They'd damaged his brain. The antiprograms had to have done something both inside and outside the Sleep.

The pain pounded and pounded, and the world around him grew stranger and stranger. Arms stretching through solid walls, beating hearts hovering in the air, a fountain of blood pooling up from the floor, a little girl in a rocking chair, a limp animal in her lap. And the agonized lament of the unseen tormented—

And then it all stopped.

The room fell silent and all returned to how it had been before the attack. And though only moments earlier it would have seemed impossible, the pain in his head had disappeared.

Michael crashed back onto the couch, his clothes damp with sweat. Sarah was next to him in an instant, reaching out to grab his hand, her face creased in concern.

"Again?" she asked him.

Michael felt as if he had run ten miles. "I think I'm dying."

4

Skale didn't wake up. At least, if he did, he never came and checked to see if his guests were okay. Sarah sat with Michael on the couch, arms around him. They didn't say a word, and he was thankful she didn't press him to explain what he'd just been through. He thought how lucky he was to have such an amazing friend.

Eventually, they both fell asleep, and Michael didn't dream. He slept a deep, solid sleep free of panic or fear. He slept like he was dead.

5

Gunner Skale shook them awake. The man had put his red cloak back on, and he was bent over Michael and Sarah, his face hidden in shadow.

"Is it morning already?" Michael asked.

"Morning never comes to Mendenstone Sanctuary," Skale replied. "It's our curse and our blessing, but there's no time to explain. Your demons are here."

6

Gunner Skale's words brought Michael and Sarah straight to their feet.

"What does that mean?" Michael asked the old man.

229

"*Where* are the demons?" Sarah added.

"Your demons are always with you," Skale answered. His voice seemed even raspier than the day before. "Don't you understand that by now? Always with you, impossible to escape. But you never can guess how they might manifest themselves. Be wary, my children. Now come. Quickly."

"Where are we going?" Sarah asked insistently.

Skale didn't answer, just crossed the room and opened the door, slipping into the hallway. Michael grabbed Sarah's hand, and they followed him into the dark. Michael could barely see Skale making his way toward the stairs, and he rushed, pulling Sarah along, to catch up to him.

The group climbed down the steps and Skale led them to the dining area where they'd eaten the night before.

"Please have a seat," Skale said, gesturing to the wooden chairs. "I'll go and ask our friends to join us."

Michael was having trouble putting everything together. He was foggy from sleep, and though his pain had disappeared, he still felt weak from the episode—the pain and the hallucinations were at the front of his mind. And now he was supposed to be readying for a battle with demons? What did Skale mean, that they were always here? Shaking his head, Michael sat in a chair, wincing at the sound of the legs scraping across the floor. Maybe somehow they could hack their way out of trouble this time before it began.

Sarah sat beside him. "We have to think. He said that we'd already been given all the information we need. Can you remember everything else he said? I think it probably has something to do with the prayer before dinner."

"Yeah," Michael agreed, yet for the life of him he couldn't remember a single word. "But all I can remember is the stuff about Kaine."

"Yeah, I know."

Michael leaned on the table and put his head in his hands, closed his eyes. Probed the surrounding code. "I don't see anything that can get us past this yet."

"I've tried a few times, too." Sarah tapped her fingers on the wood. "He said something in his prayer about kneeling at the feet of our ancestors. I'm sure that's a clue."

Michael nodded slowly as she spoke. "Maybe. It's so weird how closed off the code seems in this place. On the Path." He wanted to pound the table in frustration.

Gunner Skale came though the doorway, ending their conversation abruptly. And he wasn't alone. One by one the animal creatures they'd met earlier made their way in after him. They flew and crawled, slithered and walked. The bear, the goose, the tiger, the dog, the squirrel. A dozen others. And with them were the smells of the forest—of earth and mold and rot.

The creatures filled the room and gradually arranged themselves around its perimeter, each with its back to the wall, each with its eyes glued on the two visitors in their chairs. An uncomfortable silence filled the air, broken only by an occasional snort or growl. And to Michael, every single creature looked like it wanted nothing more than to eat him for breakfast.

"What's going on?" Michael asked Skale, surprised to find that he was whispering. He cleared his throat and spoke louder. "Why do I feel like I'm about to be sacrificed to the great animal god in the sky?"

Skale took his time crossing the room and stopped beside Michael's chair. Michael craned his neck to see the man's face, buried deep in the red cloak.

"Because," the man said, "that's exactly what's about to happen."

Michael shot to his feet, sending the chair crashing to the floor behind him. But before he could do anything, the old man said two words that made Michael's blood turn cold.

"Demons, arise."

7

Gunner Skale had been right that the demons were with them from the beginning. They were the animals.

The first one Michael noticed was the bear. It opened its enormous jaws and let out a deep, rumbling bellow toward the sky. Then its fur and skin began to peel backward, like wood shavings curling in the heat of a flame. Beneath its skin was a hideous, scar-covered face, and its eyes had changed color into an impossibly bright yellow, just like the eyes he'd seen out in the forest.

Gradually the rest of the creature's body emerged from its furry disguise. Bulging muscles, hunched back, protruding shoulder blades, clawed paws—it looked nothing like the bear that had served him dinner only hours before. A guttural snarl escaped its lips, which were pulled back from enormous teeth. But it had yet to move. It remained stand-ing, back to the wall.

Michael was mesmerized by the transformation. And now the rest of the animals were going through the same process as the bear, skin folding back to reveal terrifying, skinless demons of all shapes and sizes.

"I thought you were here to help us," Sarah said to Skale, who stood there unmoved by the turn of events. "What're we supposed to do?"

"Helping you is exactly what I'm doing," Skale said, his voice now oddly happy. "Facing your demons will change your souls forever. And your VirtNet deaths will send you back to the Wake. You'll be saved from being trapped in this place like I have been. May your ancestors be with you, my son, my daughter."

Michael eyed the door and, sure enough, two demons blocked the way. Somehow he and Sarah would just have to barrel through it. He grabbed Sarah's hand, not willing to wait to see what came next—there was only one thing to do.

Michael lunged and grabbed Skale by the cloak, twisting him around until his arm was wrapped tightly around the man's neck. Skale choked out a cough. The demons reacted as one—roaring, they stepped forward. Now they were *angry*.

"Back off!" Michael shouted, hoping the beasts under-stood him. "Come any closer and I'll snap his neck."

CHAPTER 18

THE FEET OF ANCESTORS

1

Michael had to survive the Path to get to Kaine. And he wasn't going to let these demons kill him and end his only chance.

"You're insane," the man said to him through clenched jaws. "You don't understand what you're—"

Michael choked off his words with a tighter squeeze. "Shut up."

The monstrous creatures had stopped their approach. They stood, hunched and twisted, around the room, every one a nightmarish sight, only moments from attack.

"Michael," Sarah whispered. She seemed to reconsider what she'd been about to say. "Just . . ." She raised her voice. "Just make sure you kill him quick when you do it. Break his neck nice and clean."

Michael fought to hold back a grimace. "Will do."

He backed toward the door, dragging Skale along as the man struggled to stay on his feet.

"Don't think I won't do it!" Michael yelled at the demons. "You let us go and I'll set him free—otherwise he dies!"

It seemed absurd, but just as they had in their animal forms, the creatures seemed to understand him. A low rumble began to fill the room, a deep growl from the terrifying group, and with every step Michael took backward, they stepped forward.

He glanced back at the door and saw that the two demons guarding it had actually moved to allow a path to the exit. The smallest kernel of hope sprang up—so far his plan was working.

"Don't come after me," Michael warned when he reached the door. Skale struggled to free himself from Michael's hold, but Michael squeezed tighter and he stopped.

Michael backed out the door into the dark, perpetual night with Sarah at his side. As they inched away from the building, he turned to her.

"Get him to talk," he said.

Sarah nodded. "You said you knew how to get to the Hallowed Ravine. How do we do it? Does the Path continue from here?"

"I'll tell you nothing," Skale said through struggling breaths. "For your sake, not mine. Nothing."

The demons had gathered at the door, their glistening, bloody bodies packed closely together, staring out at the three humans. Those yellow eyes gleamed with anger, and Michael thought he saw doubt welling up in them as well.

"Talk!" Michael yelled. "Talk or you're going back to the Wake!" He shook the man as he spoke and heard him gag the slightest bit.

But Skale said nothing. Panic lit up inside Michael. He was bluffing, that was the problem. What good would a dead Skale do them?

Michael didn't know what else to do. He started dragging Skale farther away from the house. The man was heavy, and Michael's muscles ached from the strain. Sarah stayed beside him, nervously looking from the demons to Skale and Michael.

"What're we gonna do?" she whispered.

Michael didn't answer, searching the area for something, anything, to spark an idea. On the far side of the long, dilapidated building, he noticed a separate entrance and a large sign above it that read, CHAPEL OF OUR FOREBEARERS. He changed direction to head that way, intuition driving him. Skale had said something about kneeling before their ancestors.

The old man kicked and struggled in Michael's grasp. He stopped, hoping to get a better grip on the man, and looked up to see that just a few dozen feet away the demons had begun to come through the door. One by one they entered the night, the glow of the moon lighting up their raw bodies and their bright eyes. Growls and snarls and shrieks echoed through the air.

"Talk!" Michael yelled at his captive, shaking him again. The man's pale eyes peered up at him, and there was determination there. He wasn't going to tell Michael anything, and Michael knew it. The man would rather die.

"Michael," Sarah whispered.

He looked up, saw the demons heading their way, faster now. One of them screamed, a high-pitched sound that ripped through the air—somewhere nearby Michael heard glass shatter.

He gazed down one last time at Skale, who was staring back. And then Michael gave up. He released him and the man fell to the ground. The great and mighty Gunner Skale.

Choking for air, Skale scrambled away and stood. "Kill them!" he shrieked. "Rip and slay them!"

Sarah grabbed Michael by the arm and they both took off running, heading for the chapel.

The demons roared as one and charged after them.

The door was open.

Michael slammed it shut behind them. "Find something to block it!"

Sarah was already dragging a desk. He ran over to help her, pushed it from behind. It made a horrible noise as its feet scraped across the wooden floor, but they didn't stop until they'd rammed it against the door. Two seconds later the demons hit the other side of the door and started beating on it.

Michael backed away, scanning left and right to see what they had to work with. The chapel was small and ordinary—a dozen or so rows of pews divided by an aisle down the middle, which led to an altar. Beyond that were statues of people of all ages and sizes, carved from white marble, standing on a dais. Their eyes seemed to stare at Michael. Forebearers. Ancestors.

Michael noticed with a wash of horror that there were several stained-glass windows set into the walls around them. The demons didn't need the door.

"The altar," Sarah said to him, surprisingly calm. "The altar. Come on!" She headed up the aisle, and Michael quickly fell into step right beside her.

"He said to kneel. What then?"

Before she could answer, all the windows exploded inward at the same time, followed by the screams and shrieks and growls of the demons.

Michael and Sarah sprinted for the altar.

4

Glass tore at the demons' bodies as they poured in through the windows, but they didn't slow. Michael focused on the altar, just a few feet away now.

"Hurry!" Sarah yelled.

So many sounds filled the room, so much movement. In mere seconds the whole horde of monsters would be on top of them. They reached the altar and clasped hands, dropped to their knees. Michael felt the softness of a pad that had been set there, felt it give a little beneath his weight.

But nothing happened.

He should've known—just kneeling wasn't enough.

They had to look at the code to get out.

5

A winged creature swooped in and knocked Michael backward, sending Sarah to the ground as well. The hideous monster flapped its wings, hovering right above their chests, and Michael saw that it was the goose demon, two words he'd never imagined could be used together. Its bloody beak parted and a horrific, shrill cry tore through the chapel, shattering the glass that still clung to the window frames.

Michael arched his back and kicked out, connecting with the demon's body, slamming it into a pew, where it fell to the floor, still.

A claw closed on Michael's shoulder and lifted him to his feet, spun him around to face a nightmare come to life. Huge jaws opened, filled with daggerlike teeth. Sarah was next to him, punching to get free from her own demon attacker.

The creature holding Michael pulled him in close until their noses almost touched. The smell was awful, a mix of rotting food and garbage dumps and decaying bodies. Michael gagged as the foul stench wafted across his face.

It was the bear. Tall enough, strong enough. It had to be the bear.

Michael stared into the monster's eyes and terror froze him stiff—all but his heart, which beat so rapidly he thought it might crack through his rib cage.

He had no idea what to do.

Something tackled them from the right. Michael and the demon crashed to the ground and its grip on him was torn free. Michael twisted around, saw that it was Sarah—she was punching at the bear demon with all her might. A quick glance to where she'd been showed that somehow she'd killed the creature that had attacked her.

Michael turned, faced the bear, and knew they couldn't beat it. Not without help. He closed his eyes and focused on the code, ignoring the storm of complexity swirling around him. He strained to put it aside, concentrated on his own self, his Aura, his history in the Sleep. He grabbed for the first thing that revealed itself, Fire Disks from *The Realms of Rasputin*, snatched the programming, pulled it into the chapel. He would never have been able to do it if he'd thought too much—acting on instinct, he suddenly had glowing, fiery saucers hovering about him. With a thought he unleashed them, threw them all at the bear's body.

The beast roared as its flesh bubbled up and burned. Sarah scrambled away and got to her feet next to Michael. Bellowing, the injured bear rolled onto all fours, lumbered to the wall, and stood up. Michael spun in a circle—the demons were closing in from all directions.

He knew that somehow the altar had a weak spot in the code and was just a few feet away. A glance over his shoulder showed that a small demon stood on top of it—the squirrel, or maybe the ferret-rat-weasel that had perched on Gunner Skale's shoulder. It hissed at them, baring its tiny fangs.

Michael and Sarah stood shoulder to shoulder, hands clasped, slowly backing their way toward the kneeling pad. The noose of demons was tightening.

"You work on the code," Michael whispered. "Find the sweet spot. I'll fight them off with more Fire Disks." He said it even though he had no idea how long he could last.

"Okay," Sarah replied. "Guide me." She closed her eyes and squeezed his hand even tighter. Michael moved back another step. Then he conjured up another array of the disks and threw them randomly in all directions.

Demons roared in pain, and Michael threw away all caution. Yanking on Sarah, he turned and dove toward the base of the altar. They hit the floor and slid two feet, coming up just short of the pad. Sarah had somehow kept her eyes closed, staying focused on her task, searching the code that surrounded them. Michael held tightly to her hand, guiding her forward. Then the little demon on the altar shrieked and dove at Sarah—its feet tangling in her hair as it clawed at her face and tried to bite her ear. She didn't respond. Michael reached for the creature, grabbed it, and threw the thing as hard as he could.

"I've got it!" Sarah yelled, her eyes flying open. "I know what to do!"

But the demons were everywhere. One grabbed Michael's arm, another his leg. One had Sarah by the hair—he could hear her scream as the creature yanked her head back. Michael fought to get loose, losing his tenuous grasp on the

Fire Disk coding. The creatures were all around. Grabbing and clawing and biting. There was a terrifying moment where he almost gave up, almost decided to let them kill him and end it all. Go back to the Wake and accept the consequences.

But something inside him exploded. A roar tore through his throat and adrenaline detonated inside his muscles. Screaming in fury, Michael beat away the creatures. For the briefest moment he saw fear in all those yellow eyes surrounding him, and it gave him even more courage.

He knocked a huge beast off of Sarah. She was bruised, and blood smeared her face. He lifted her up and carried her past the kneeling pad and the altar to the dais with the statues of ancestors.

No words were needed. Michael closed his eyes and linked with the code, sensed Sarah's presence already there. She'd set it all up, laid it out before him. In a swarming sea of numbers and letters and symbols, he saw it—the tiniest sliver of an escape. Both of them went for it at the same time.

The demons came at them, their digital forms as terrifying as their visual manifestations. A claw scratched Michael down his back. A monster on four legs—the dog or the fox—jumped onto the altar, snarling. Michael felt himself being yanked from his position, but he flexed all his digital muscles and forced his body to stay put. For one more second, just one more. He input a final piece of code and there was a popping sound.

Then it all disappeared.

CHAPTER 19

HEAT

1

The world vanished around them, and when it came back again, Michael and Sarah were inside a dimly lit cave. The walls were made of black stone.

"Oh man," Michael said with a groan. He sat up and crawled to the closest wall of the cave, leaning back against it. "I'll be one happy dude if I never see another animal in my life. Especially the ones that turn into demons."

"Amen to that." Sarah was sitting on the opposite side of the rocky space, and it was hard for him to look at her—she was pale and bloody. "Or a forest. Or a hallway. Or a stone disk."

"I'd love to see a cheeseburger right about now, though." His stomach rumbled with hunger.

"Don't torture me."

He looked deeper into the cave, down a long corridor. There was an orange glow coming from within that felt warm and cozy. Michael pictured little dwarves living back there, sipping tea and eating some hearty stew.

"How in the world did we survive that?" Sarah asked.

"Because of you" was Michael's answer. "Because you didn't panic, and you found a way out."

Sarah was quiet a moment, as if she was thinking. "It wasn't that hard, you know. It's almost like in some spots they left us a way to hack free, in others they didn't."

"Don't be so humble. You're just really good."

She didn't respond, seemingly lost in thought again.

Michael gave her an expression of exaggerated wonder. "Seriously, when did you become a superhero? You're like Batman meets the Hulk."

"You have a gift for making a compliment sound like an insult."

"I do my best."

Sarah smiled. "Come on. Let's start exploring—we know we're going to hit a bunch of crap, and I want to get it over with."

Michael sighed. Even though they'd gotten a meal and a few hours of sleep before the demon attack, he was exhausted. And the hunger pangs made even the rocks scattered across the ground look slightly appetizing.

"No thinking, though," Sarah warned. "Let's just keep moving."

"Okay." Michael knew she was right. Getting busy was definitely the answer.

But he didn't move right away. Something she'd said—about the Path leaving almost obvious weak spots here and there—had triggered some thoughts. It seemed related to the creepy voice he'd heard so many times—the voice saying his name and telling him he was doing well. What could be the purpose of that? What did it mean? It seemed to fly in the face of everything they were doing. The whole point of the VNS sending them into the Sleep to find the Path and the Hallowed Ravine was so they could lead the VNS to Kaine. The VNS wouldn't know if he was doing well until he found Kaine—who was supposed to be hiding.

Didn't that make the Path a firewall, put in place by Kaine to keep people *out*?

Yet . . .

"Cat got your tongue?" Sarah finally said.

Michael wiped at his tired eyes. "What's that?"

"Cat got your tongue?"

"What does *that* mean?"

"Huh? You've never heard that before?"

Michael stretched his arms, trying to psyche himself to get up. "Yes, I've heard it. But I'm pretty sure it's something old people say."

"Whatever. Why so quiet?"

"Just thinking about things. About the Path. Kaine. Everything."

"Didn't I just say no thinking?" Sarah said. "Not that I really meant it."

Michael smiled and nodded, but he was even more un-settled now. The Path didn't add up. Again, if it was sup-posed to keep them out, then why did it have places in the coding that seemed meant to guide them? Even the concept of a trail in the first place. Michael had been so busy trying to stay alive, he hadn't thought about it like that before.

And the more he thought about it, the stranger it seemed. "The Path" was an odd name for programming that was meant to keep you *out*. Maybe it wasn't a firewall after all. Maybe it was something else entirely.

2

With another groan from the aches and pains, Michael forced himself to stand up. Then he pointed toward a long corridor at the rear of the cave, seemingly the only way out. "What do you think is back there?"

"Lava."

She said it so quickly Michael was surprised. "Really?"

"Yeah. I think this is a volcano—the black rock is cooled magma."

"So a big river of molten fire could come bursting through this tunnel at any second?"

"That sounds about right."

It just kept getting better and better, Michael thought. "Ha. Well, we'll show them. We won't wait—we'll walk right into it like a couple of bumbling idiots."

Sarah gave him a weary grin.

"You look terrible, by the way," Michael added.

She glared at him, though it didn't last long before turning into a smile. "I can't possibly look any worse than you do."

"Don't worry. You still look pretty, just in a terrible sort of way." It sounded dumb, but he really meant it.

"Thanks, Michael."

After all they'd been through, there was a bond between them that he couldn't imagine feeling with anyone else. "When this is all over," he finally said, "I really want to meet out in the Wake. I promise I'm even better-looking in person."

"And I'm probably worse." She laughed, a sound they both needed to hear.

"I wouldn't care. I swear I wouldn't. That's what's so great about the Sleep. I know who you are inside, and that's all that matters." He'd never said something so cheesy in his entire life.

"That's actually really sweet, Michael."

He blushed. "Plus, I bet you *are* hot."

"Whatever." She rolled her eyes but kept her gaze trained on Michael. "It's a deal—as soon as we finish saving the VirtNet—a day out in real sunshine."

"Deal."

She shifted, then pushed herself up to her feet, groaning. Michael understood all too well—parts of his body that he hadn't known existed the day before were screaming in pain.

"Shall we go cave exploring?" he asked in a ridiculous British accent.

"Let's," she replied. Her smile reached her eyes and made him feel better.

As they started walking into the mountain, limping like

two old people with arthritis, Sarah reached out and took his hand.

"Let's," she repeated.

3

Michael thought the walls of the tunnel looked man-made. They were black and shiny and appeared as if they'd been chiseled. The soft light coming from deeper within the cave reflected in a way that made everything look as if it might melt at any second.

Michael and Sarah had barely rounded the first bend of the corridor when he saw a bright orange glow. As if triggered by the sight, a gust of warm air blew past them, stirring Michael's hair and clothes. It felt good—almost made him want to lie back down and try sleeping.

Neither of them spoke as they continued on. Michael stared at the warm light as they approached it. It was inviting, like a campfire on a cool night. What scared him was thinking about its source. If they really were inside a volcano, it was sure to be unpleasant.

Abruptly the tunnel widened and the space opened up. The ceiling stretched until it was at least thirty feet high. Farther ahead, Michael could tell that the space got even bigger—a cavern was waiting for them, and the fiery orange light grew stronger. The temperature had risen, and the air was heavy with humidity.

Soon they came to a tiny pool of bubbling molten rock.

Michael was mesmerized by its glowing beauty until he recalled what he'd learned in geology class—it meant they were standing on a layer of cooled lava that had to be on top of a vast amount of uncooled lava. Michael suddenly had visions of the floor cracking open, spouts of liquid fire shooting up to incinerate them, and he shivered.

"Wanna go for a swim?" he asked awkwardly.

Sarah let go of his hand and patted his shoulder. "No thanks. You go right ahead." Her face was glistening with sweat.

"It's hot," he said.

"Yeah, and it's gonna get worse. Come on—we're not going to find any food, and the longer this takes, the weaker we'll be."

"This is gonna suck, huh?"

She nodded. "Yeah, it's gonna suck. But there's no other way to go. The code is pretty straightforward about that."

They started walking again, moving ever deeper into the volcano.

4

When Michael and Sarah reached the end of the tunnel, they stopped and stared. It opened into a massive cavern filled with pools of bubbling lava.

The expanse before them reminded Michael of the coat of a tiger. Rivers of the steaming magma churned, cut through with ribbons of cooled black rock. An even more amazing sight was the waterfall-like flows of lava spilling through cracks in the walls, spitting and hissing as they poured into pools of bubbling rock. Flames burst from the streams that ran the length of the cavern—and Michael and Sarah had to cross it all.

Blasts of hot air blew over them in waves as they stared.

"Worse than I thought," Michael muttered.

Sarah closed her eyes for a moment, then pointed to the far side. "There's another tunnel over there, and the Path seems to point in that direction. I don't sense any other way. Do you?"

He scanned the code himself and sighed. "Nope. Guess that's where we're going."

"We better hurry or we'll die from dehydration. I doubt there's a drinking fountain anywhere nearby."

"Come on," Michael urged. Standing there was starting to freak him out, and he wanted to get moving.

There was a short slope from the tunnel down to the cavern floor, and they took advantage of their lookout point to figure out the best path across, using both what lay before them and quick glimpses of the programming itself. It all combined to form a maze of cooled rock, columns of fire, and cascading lava, encompassed by the now-familiar hints in the complicated code of where they needed to go. Taking the lead, Michael picked his way carefully down the slope among the scattered rocks and dirt. The ground leveled off, and the heat pounded him, making him catch his breath. It was loud. A low roar buzzed in his ears.

"You ready?" he shouted to Sarah. Sweat poured down

her face now, and her clothes were soaked through. Michael knew he was just as drenched.

She nodded, looking too weary to talk. He hoped so badly in that moment that they were close to the end of the stupid Path. He hated Kaine and Agent Weber and the VNS.

Michael nodded back to Sarah.

Then he began to cross the cavern, Sarah right behind him.

5

He felt like his body was being slowly roasted in a giant oven.

They moved across a three-foot-wide swath of rock that cut through the lava, and made it to the center of the cavern floor. That part was easy enough, though the heat coming off the lava and the fear of being burned by the boiling rock made Michael's heart thump rapidly. He tried to hurry and be smart at the same time, but the panic was beginning to swell inside him, making him claustrophobic even though the cave was so huge.

Step by step, they made their way across the natural bridge, Michael's eyes burning from the heat. When they reached the other side he decided to go to the right, zigzagging through a labyrinth of connected rocky islands among the brightly glowing pools of magma. They could always double back if necessary, but he relied on his instincts and quick scans of the surrounding code.

They moved along a narrow line of black stone. Michael could feel the heat through his shoes—it was so hot, he worried that the soles would melt. When they reached the end, they stepped onto a round island that was totally surrounded by a ring of bright orange magma.

He moved to go to the left, but Sarah grabbed his arm and leaned in.

"Seems like we should go that way!" she shouted, pointing straight ahead at a row of black boulders. They looked like stepping-stones in a garden. "Look—on the other side there's another bridge that goes all the way to the wall. Then we can shoot along the edge, climb up to that hole, and get out of here."

Michael studied the area for a bit, and it seemed like she was right. The direction in which he had almost gone ended up ahead at a huge gap that they would've had to get a running start to leap over.

"Sounds like a plan. You wanna lead this time?"

He grinned to show he was joking, but she took it seriously and jumped onto the first small island. Her arms windmilled until she caught her balance, almost making his heart explode out of his chest.

"Be careful!" he yelled at her.

"Just trying to give you a scare," she called back.

"Not funny! At all!"

Sarah jumped to the next island, and as soon as she was safe and settled, Michael followed, hopping onto the first rock.

"Take your time!" he shouted.

"Relax," she replied.

She hurdled the next gap, and then the next, not waiting for him anymore. Michael followed her quickly, terrified by the possibility of her slipping into the magma. Rock by rock, he bounded across the lava after her, and soon they'd made it safely to the long spit of black rock on the other side.

Sarah pulled him into a fierce hug, surprising him.

"That was scary," she whispered into his ear. "Oh man, that was scary."

He wrapped his arms tightly around her shoulders. "Yeah, you were a little reckless, don't ya think?" Despite being in the middle of a volcano, he was enjoying the hug far too much and didn't want it to end.

"Better to just do it than worry over every single step."

"Yeah, I guess."

She pulled back, looked at him. A tear had leaked out of her eye, cutting its way through the grime down her cheek until it formed into a drop at her chin. Then it fell and landed on her shirt.

"You okay?" he asked.

She nodded, then hugged him again. "Come on, let's get up to that next tunnel and cool off."

"Let's hope."

They ran across the bridge, which seemed safe compared to the stepping-stones. On the other side there was a slope of dirt and rocks that stretched to the wall of the cavern. They scrambled up to get as far away from the lava as possible, then ran along the edge toward the mouth of the next tunnel, Sarah right in front of Michael.

They were only twenty feet away when it happened.

Michael had just relaxed a bit, allowing himself to think of those moments he'd shared with Sarah. The talk, holding hands, the hug. He should've known that was when everything would go wrong.

They were passing a large pool of lava at the bottom of the slope when there was a giant sucking noise, then a roar that sounded like a furnace coming to life. Michael spun just in time to see a spout of molten rock shoot from the pool, a perfect pillar of fiery orange death, headed directly at Sarah.

When it hit her, she fell to the ground—and her scream was like nothing Michael had ever heard before.

6

The horror Michael felt was so consuming that he forgot all about the VirtNet and his Coffin back at home. He forgot that death simply meant that Sarah would wake up in her own Coffin, safe and sound, if a little shaken up.

All he saw was his friend in pain. The lava burned through her clothes and skin in an instant, revealing a nightmarish display of muscle and bone. Her screams faded into gurgling sounds as she collapsed into a heap that shattered Michael's heart.

And it all happened so fast.

He ran to her but stopped, knowing he couldn't risk his own life—the lava was seeping back along the dirt toward the pool from which it had erupted.

But Sarah wasn't dead yet. She lay curled in a ball on the ground, trembling. Michael carefully inched closer to look at her face. Her eyes were open and he could see the pain reflected in them.

"Sarah," he whispered, searching for words. "Sarah. I'm so sorry."

She struggled to speak, choking as she did. Michael leaned in as closely as he could, put his ear just above her head.

"Mi—" she started, but was interrupted by a violent cough. As much as Michael hated it that she'd be leaving him, he wanted her to die as soon as possible. To go back to the Wake. Every bit of suffering that consumed her would feel completely real until that happened.

"Sarah, I'm sorry. I shouldn't have let you lead. I should've . . ."

"Shut," she forced out. "Up." More coughs shook her body.

"I can't stand it," Michael said to her. "Sarah, I can't stand this. I can't take it. I just want to go back with you. Maybe I'll jump into the lava."

"No!" she screamed, making him flinch. "You . . . fin . . . ish!"

He was silent for a few seconds. But he knew she was right. "Okay. I will. I promise."

"Find . . . Hallowed . . . Ravine," she said between more choked coughing. "I . . ."

"Stop talking, Sarah." Michael's heart ached. He wanted her back home and safe. "Let it go. I swear I'll hurry through the rest of this and be done. Remember our deal. A day in the sun. A day in the Wake. Everything's gonna be just fine."

"De . . . deal." Michael thought that was it. That she'd gone. But then she spoke again. "Michael." She said it clearly and completely, and he felt a rushing in his chest, something that squeezed and burned.

Then her last breath sighed out of her, her chest falling for the final time. A few seconds later she disappeared, her physical body waking up in the real world. Leaving Michael deep within the VirtNet, in a place almost no one knew about, in the middle of a Path that seemingly had no end to its length—*or* to its horrors.

And he was alone.

He was completely alone.

CHAPTER 20

A BODY OF SILVER

1

Michael tried not to think for the next few hours. He had no time to be sad or wallow in self-pity. He'd promised Sarah he would make it the rest of the way, and that was all he allowed himself to focus on. It helped to know she wasn't really dead, although whenever the memory of her last moments crept back into his thoughts, waves of pain washed through him.

Which was why he had to push it all away. Turn it off.

There was another long tunnel, cut through in several places by rivers of lava. Michael jumped over them as carefully as possible. He approached a nasty spot where magma sporadically shot down from a crack in the ceiling. He waited, guessed, relied on his instincts. Barely missed getting burned when he sprinted past. Shortly after, an entire side of the tunnel collapsed just as he passed by, and a gushing river of molten rock, sparking with fire and heat, came streaming after him. He ran, ran hard, the edge of the hellish river right at his feet. But eventually it began to cool and he was able to slow down.

There were longer tunnels and bigger caves. Lava everywhere. The heat rising to impossible temperatures, then rising again. Michael's body, dripping with sweat. His throat more parched than ever before—like a desert, a moonscape. He would've drunk water from the filthiest stream, from a swamp, from a sewage plant. He lusted after it, but there was none to be found, and gradually his strength was sapped, hunger aching inside him.

But he kept going and going and going, heading where the code—the Path—sent him.

Mind tuned only to the programming.

2

Hours passed. And not a one where Michael didn't spend every minute thinking the next would be his last. That he'd collapse and not be able to move ever again until he shriveled up from the heat and died, went back to the Wake, to his Coffin.

He was heading down another endless tunnel when his head hit a low-hanging rock. He yelped and ducked, then crouched on the ground, twisting around as best he could to gauge his surroundings. The pain had brought him back to his senses. And he was shocked to see that the black stone passageway had narrowed. It had shrunk so much that only two people at most could squeeze along its path. The light had died significantly, too, though Michael could still see well enough.

Farther ahead, it looked as if he might have to start crawling.

Panic and an overwhelming surge of claustrophobia struck him hard. Questions besieged his exhausted brain— had he done something wrong? Missed a turnoff? A doorway? A Portal? Michael curled into a ball, hugging his legs against his chest, and rocked back and forth, eyes closed, willing himself to calmness.

Gradually the attack passed. He stretched out and, despite the rocky surface, fell asleep.

3

When he woke, body aching and stiff, Michael looked down the narrowing tunnel and knew he had to keep going in that direction. At every part of the journey through the volcanic mountain, he'd scoured the code for other ways to move on, and so far there'd only ever been one. The Path had been clearly designed as a one-way ticket. And he couldn't give up now.

Hunger racked his insides, weakened him. But even that didn't compare to the thirst that made his throat feel like something baking in a desert sun.

Water. He would kill any person standing between him and a single cup of it.

Groaning, he pulled himself to his hands and knees and crawled along the rough floor of the tunnel, only looking up to scan the path ahead. And the tunnel through which he crept was getting narrower.

Somehow he kept moving.

Eventually the ceiling of the tunnel touched his back, and he had to crouch lower. Soon he had to drop to his stomach, pulling himself with his arms as he pushed off the ground with his feet, like a soldier crawling under a web of barbed wire at boot camp. The walls pressed in as well, and before long he had a hard time angling his arms out enough to get any leverage.

And then he got stuck.

4

He'd been claustrophobic before, but now the fear was a monstrous thing that lit his brain on fire. He thrashed, screamed at the top of his lungs. But he'd wedged himself into the passage so tightly that he couldn't move forward or backward. The echoes of his shouts came bouncing back at him, and the black rock seemed to be closing in, crushing the breath from his lungs. He tried to close his eyes and analyze the code, but his mind wouldn't focus and he had to give up.

Michael kicked and squirmed, clawed at the ground with his fingernails.

He slipped a couple of inches forward. Doubling his efforts, pushing with his toes and pulling with his fingers, flexing and unflexing muscles, he lurched forward again. And again. A foot, then two, then three.

A blue light appeared ahead of him, like a plane of sky. He swore it hadn't been there before—was it a way out? There was no breeze or sound of life, no clouds. Just pure blue, an inexplicable hole of color.

He screamed again, willing himself to throw everything he had at reaching that spot. It was a Portal. It had to be a Portal.

Grunting, twisting, digging his fingers into the dusty rock. Inch by inch, he was able to move. The bright blue got closer. Within several feet. Within a couple of inches.

By the time he reached it, Michael felt as if he'd almost lost his mind. There wasn't a single coherent thought left, just a desperate desire to get to that wall of blue, no matter what awaited him.

He threw his arms out, reaching through the Portal, saw them disappear as if they'd been dipped in liquid. Then something grabbed his hands from the other side and pulled him the rest of the way. His body flew forward and out of the volcano forever.

5

Michael crashed to a metal floor, his cheek resting against its hard, cool surface. A blinding white light filled the new space, bathing him in its brilliance. With a loud groan, he pushed himself off his stomach and flopped onto his back, squinting to make out where he was. Pure white surrounded him, nothing else. No. To his right, there was a blurry shadow cutting through the light, a human shape.

"Where am I?" Michael croaked, cringing at the sound of his own voice.

The voice that answered was mechanical, robotic. Deep and electric. "You're at a crossroads, Michael. You've reached the point of no return."

Michael blinked, tried to make his eyes focus. The thing talking to him wasn't human at all—despite its appearance. There was a head, shoulders, two arms and two legs. But the thing was made completely of silvery metal. No seams or rivets broke up the smooth surface of its exterior. Its face had no eyes, nose, or mouth. Just a shiny green visor that was completely blank. The robot stood still, facing Michael.

Michael glanced around the rest of the room, but it was empty aside from the blinding white light. He was in an empty room with a robot.

Still, only one thing occupied Michael's mind. "Do you have any water?" He got his legs up under him and sat facing his strange companion.

"Yes," the thing answered in its mechanized voice. "Your body will now be replenished."

A disk separated from the floor in front of Michael and sank into the depths below. He watched, staring as the disk reappeared with a plate of food and a large cup resting on its surface and stopped right at chest level.

"Eat," the robot commanded, still not moving. "You have five minutes until the stakes are raised."

Michael was thirsty and hungry to the point of death—so much so that he didn't really care that the robot had just made a vague threat. All he could think about was the food in front of him. A slab of steak and green beans and carrots. A big piece of bread. A cup of water.

Michael attacked it. First, he gulped down half the water, enjoying a rush of pure ecstasy as it wet his throat. Then he picked up the steak with two fingers and took a huge bite. He ate a few carrots and green beans while still chewing the meat. Back to the steak. To the veggies. Another sip of water. Meat and veggies. Stuffing himself.

Never, he thought, had something tasted so wonderful.

When he'd devoured every last morsel and drained the cup dry, Michael wiped his mouth on his sleeve and looked up at the flat green face of the robot.

"I'm done. Thank you." Although his stomach was having a little trouble with the sudden feast.

The silver creature took a few steps backward until it came to rest in the back corner of the room. At the same time, the disk that had held Michael's meal lowered to the floor and disappeared. Michael returned his attention to the robot.

It spoke again. "You are at the point of no return. The crossroads. Until now, your death would have ended your quest for what lies at the end of the Path, but not your true life. Your companions are now back at their homes, alive and safe."

"Um . . . ," Michael started to say. "I'm glad they're safe. I'm planning on joining them really soon."

The robot continued as if it hadn't heard him. "You will no longer have the comfort of knowing your death is not the ultimate end. The rest of your journey, including the Hallowed Ravine, should you enter its sacred realm, will be completed with true life hanging in the balance."

Michael felt a stitch in his gut. What was this thing talking about?

"Commence operation," the robot said. Two words that made Michael jump to his feet, suddenly full of energy but with nowhere to go.

A buzzy thrum filled the room, followed by the sounds of machinery. Michael looked up in horror to see metal arms descending from the white ceiling, their ends capped with various instruments. Hinged silver claws came at him first. He tried to run, but the things were too fast. Two claws latched on to his arms, clasping closed and yanking him up into the air. Two more grabbed his legs, pulling them apart so that he was upright but spread-eagled. He struggled against the grips but they were solid—immovable.

Other arms swarmed in. One put a band around Michael's neck and another around his forehead, forcing his head forward and still. A band slipped around his chest, squeezed tightly until it almost hurt. In a matter of seconds, Michael had been pulled into the air and immobilized.

"What are you doing to me?" he yelled. "What's going on?"

The robot didn't answer, didn't move. Michael quickly

closed his eyes to examine the programming, but it looked like a foreign language in a blur of constant movement, completely inaccessible. There was a hum and a sound like gears shifting to his right, close to his ear, but he couldn't turn his head to see what was happening. He could sense something just inches away, could barely see an object at the edge of his peripheral vision. Then the worst noise of all started, like a spinning drill, shrill and whirring more rapidly as it sped up.

"What are you doing?" Michael shouted again.

Then a pain exploded in the side of his head. He screamed as something dug into his flesh, tearing his skin open. His lungs emptied of air and he sucked in a breath, then screamed all over again.

The pain was overwhelming. Suddenly the robot was standing in front of Michael again, that green shield just a few inches from his face.

"Your Core has been destroyed," it said. "True death now awaits if you fail."

CHAPTER 21

TWO DOORS

The claws that had so fiercely held Michael's body in place let go abruptly. He fell to the floor in a heap as the metal arms retracted into the ceiling with the whir of machinery and steel against steel. In seconds it was over. The room grew silent, and he was once again alone with the silver monster.

His head ached. His hand had naturally gone up to touch the wound, and when he brought it away to look, it was covered in blood. His insides felt like someone had gone in with a sharp blade and scraped them clean. His Core had been removed.

"How did you do that?" he asked the robot. Only Michael should be able to remove his Core. There were passwords for this exact reason. "How did you know my coding?"

"There can only be one chance now. Death awaits you." The robot's cold voice made Michael's skin crawl. "Kaine has ways of accessing your code that no one else knows."

"You tell Kaine that I'm going to kill him," Michael replied, the rage a rising tide in his chest. "I'm going to find him and root out every last digit of *his* code. I'm going to drain every bit of his fake intelligence into a toilet, and then I'm gonna flush it into oblivion. Tell him I said that."

"No need for such a command," the silver menace answered. "Kaine hears all."

2

The words had barely come out when the brightness of the room intensified, burning everything white. Michael squeezed his eyes shut and pressed his fists against them. There was a steady hum that transformed into a buzz, then a high-pitched trilling ring.

It vibrated inside Michael's skull, and the wound in his temple throbbed with pain. He sensed a fresh trickle of blood seeping into his hair.

The light and the sound grew to an unbearable strength, like tangible walls pressing in on all sides, crushing him. A scream formed in his lungs, a desperate plea for someone to save him—it surged up his throat and exploded out of his mouth, only to be lost in the storm of noise that had filled the room.

Then everything went dark and silent. The sound of his breath filled his ears. Sweat covered his skin. Instinct told him to stay still, to keep his eyes closed, to pray that whatever waited for him next would just go away and leave him be. Having his Core removed—*coded* out by monstrously illegal means—had terrified him more than he thought possible.

He didn't want to die. Up until the robot, he'd been scared, but at least he'd known that death meant going back to the Wake to get out of his Coffin and collapse in bed. His only lasting injuries would have been psychological—something a good shrink could fix in a few sessions of therapy. He could deal with the VNS when he had to.

But now it was all for real. Without the Core—without that safety barrier and its link to the Coffin—his brain would stop functioning back home when he died. It was part of the system, as much a part of their makeup as a beating heart. Otherwise the infrastructure of the VirtNet would never work like it did—it wouldn't be so lifelike. The Core barrier was vital to the programming.

And his was gone.

He did *not* want to look. If he'd had a blanket, he would've pulled it up over his head and whimpered like a baby.

He lay there for several minutes before he sensed a blinking red light. Slowly, he opened his eyes and saw that there was a red neon sign hanging above a simple wooden door, bathing the door in the light of its bloody letters.

The sign read HALLOWED RAVINE.

3

He almost jumped to his feet, but caution won out. He'd been on his side, curled almost into a ball, but he carefully stretched out his legs and moved to lie flat on his back. He scanned the area, looking for anything that might be in the mood to hurt him. But all was dark except another neon sign that hung above a similar door opposite the first one.

This sign was in green letters, also flashing, and read, EXIT THE PATH.

Michael sat up, pulled his legs in, and hugged them. Those two signs and the doors below them were the only things he could see, anywhere. There were no discernible walls or ceiling, and even the floor seemed like part of an empty space, as if he was floating.

Hallowed Ravine.

Exit the Path.

Two choices. He stood up, kept looking back and forth between his options. After everything he'd been through, here he was—perhaps on the threshold of the place he'd been looking for. Commanded to go to. A chance to complete a mission to stop something the VNS believed threatened the entire world. Michael was tagged, and if he went through that door to the Hallowed Ravine and found Kaine, VNS agents could break in and save him.

Something didn't feel right—hadn't felt right for a while. He knew that he hadn't been given the whole story. The Path wasn't like a firewall. He had the overwhelming feeling that he was doing exactly what Kaine wanted him to do, that it had nothing to do with the VNS, and that opening the door of the Ravine would only be the final step into . . . what? He had no idea.

Plus, his life was on the line now.

Bryson was back home. Sarah was back home. Michael's family . . .

His family. His mom and dad. Helga. He'd forgotten. What had happened to them? How could he possibly go on when he didn't know what was at stake?

But something hardened inside him. How could he turn away now? His family had been threatened. His best friends. And he'd made a promise to Sarah. Not to mention a commitment to stop a Tangent that was out of control.

He was being presented with a final choice. And he chose his only option.

Moving with more confidence than ever before, he took strong and determined steps over to the door marked HALLOWED RAVINE. He opened it and walked through.

CHAPTER 22

IN THROUGH THE OUTHOUSE

1

The space on the other side of the door was pitch-black and completely still. No sounds, no stir of breeze, nothing. Just complete darkness. But Michael didn't hesitate. He pulled the door closed behind him.

The air changed instantly, as if his senses had been robbed and now returned. A wind swept by, carrying something gritty like sand that stung his eyes. It rapidly grew warm, then hot. As he wiped at his eyes with his sleeve, he sensed a brightness, and when he looked again, his breath caught.

He stood in the middle of a desert.

The door had disappeared, and grand golden sand dunes extended in every direction, the crisp lines of their peaks against the cloudless blue sky so perfect they seemed impossible. Billowing clouds of sand blew into the scorched air like the trailing smoke of an old steam-engine train from the movies. The land was utterly barren, not a tree or shrub in sight—nothing in all the world that was green. Only sand for miles.

Except one thing.

Nearby there was a shabby little building the size of a closet, made from warped gray wood with rusted nails poking halfway out along the sides. There was a door that hung loosely on broken hinges, creaking with movement from the stiff breeze. The drab structure couldn't have looked more out of place, as there was absolutely nothing in any direction for as far as the eye could see.

Michael headed toward the door, feeling a pang of regret that he hadn't chosen to go home.

2

The sun beat down on Michael as he pressed through the sand to the small building. His thoughts were dark, but he did his best to empty his mind—he'd made his decision, and he could only follow it now. And something told him it was almost over, one way or the other. He just hoped it didn't include his demise.

Sweat poured down his face as he walked, and he felt the hot sun on his neck. It seemed as if his hair would burst into flames at any second, and his shirt felt like laundry straight out of the dryer. He approached the little building, hoping it had something more than a bucket inside its shabby walls. That it held some answers.

He was just bringing his hand up to open the door when a man spoke behind him.

"Wouldn't do that if I were you."

Michael spun around to see a person dressed in a dirty wrap of some sort—a huge piece of tattered cloth that swept around his body from head to foot. His eyes were covered with a pair of dark sunglasses.

"Excuse me?" Michael asked. *Could this be Kaine?* he wondered.

"I'll grant you it's windy on the dunes," the man replied, his words muffled through the cloth. "But you heard me, and you heard me fine."

Michael had indeed. "You don't think I should go inside this building? Why not?"

"Many reasons. But I'll tell you this—go through that door and your life will never be the same."

Michael searched for words. "Well . . . couldn't that be a good thing?"

"Everything is relative." The man didn't move a muscle as he spoke. "A knife is a godsend to the man tied in ropes, death to the man in chains."

"Very profound." Michael wondered if the guy was a Tangent sent to toy with him.

"Take it as you will."

"Where'd you come from, anyway?"

"You're in the VirtNet, are you not?" the man asked, still not moving. "I come from where I came."

"Just tell me why I shouldn't go through this door."

The man didn't answer, and the wind whipped up a little

faster. A spray of sand hit Michael in the face, got into his mouth. He spit and coughed, wiped the grit away. Then he repeated his question. The man answered this time, and his words chilled Michael.

"Because if you don't, your headaches will stop."

3

It was Michael's turn to go silent. He stood, frozen, as he stared at the man with no face. Nothing sounded better than having his headaches stop.

"Don't go through that door," the stranger said. "Come with me to a land where ignorance will be your greatest blessing."

Michael finally found his voice. "How?"

The man shook his head. It was the first time he'd moved enough for Michael to notice. "I can't say any more. I've said too much already. But my promises to you are real—come with me and leave Kaine alone, leave the Mortality Doctrine alone. You'll spend the rest of your days in a place of pure happiness and ignorant bliss. Make your choice."

Michael was mesmerized by the stranger. "What *is* the Mortality Doctrine?" he asked. Then he jabbed a thumb over his shoulder. "What happens if I go in?"

He asked the questions because he suddenly had an urge—a consuming urge—to follow the guy's advice, to follow him. The Path had taken it all out of Michael, had emptied his heart. And somehow he knew that the promises the man had just made were *real*. Things were going on outside the sphere of Michael's understanding. He could go with this guy and never know the truth, live a life of happy ignorance.

But there was a taint there, like a sheen of oil on an otherwise crystal-clear lake. Slick and greasy and wrong, and he couldn't ignore it.

"No more questions," the man said. "Come with me, Michael. Come now. All you have to do is say the word and we'll vanish from this desert and go to the place I call home. Say the word."

Michael wanted to. Desperately. He wanted to go with this man and not find out the truth. The truth about what? Who knew? But Michael wanted to go and never learn what it seemed Kaine was determined for him to know.

But he couldn't do it. Something told him it was a choice that didn't lead back to his friends and his family.

"Sorry, man," he finally said. "I'm going into the outhouse."

The stranger didn't argue as Michael turned away. The wind pulled at his clothes, the sand bit at his skin, and potential regrets filled his mind as he reached out and grabbed the handle of the door. He opened it and stepped inside a dank, smelly building.

4

There was a muffled thud when he closed the door, and all went dark. Michael knew that he'd entered a Portal—that outside the little building, the desert was gone, his self transported. Uncertainty fluttered in his chest as he waited for the light to return. When it did, it was warm and comforting.

He stood inside a low-roofed hallway of stone, with torches burning in sconces along the walls. Worn tapestries were hung along the way, depicting medieval battle scenes that reminded him of games he used to play. He looked left and right, wondering which way to go. Both directions seemed about the same, and he was about to make a toss-up choice when he heard the faintest sound of voices coming from his left. Like the whispers of those who'd died in the ancient halls. A glimpse of the code revealed nothing.

Michael decided to follow the sounds.

He kept to the shadows as he walked—following the hallway's curve. As he pushed ahead, the voices got louder, and there was one in particular that seemed to overpower the others. There was something terribly familiar about it, and not in a good way. It sparked the feeling of entering the same nightmare that's haunted you for years.

It was Kaine. Michael had no doubt in his mind. He would never forget that voice.

He couldn't make out the Tangent's words—they bounced along the stone corridor and blurred as others tried to speak. It sounded like some kind of meeting.

The hallway gradually became brighter and Michael slowed, pushing up against the wall and inching forward. Ahead the hall curved to the right, and he rounded the bend carefully to see that it opened up into a balcony, overlooking a space shining with light. Kaine's voice boomed from below, filling Michael's gut with something like burning oil.

This is it, he realized. He'd made it to the end. Things were about to change.

Michael dropped to his knees and crawled to the balcony, peeking through the railing.

An old, hunched man stood at some sort of makeshift pulpit. He'd gone silent for a moment, seemingly listening to his audience. Thirty or so men and women sat on curved benches that faced him, most of them shifting in their seats as if they disagreed or were being made uncomfortable by the man's words. He wore a green robe, a small sword belted to his side. Michael found it impossible to believe that the Tangent terrorizing the VirtNet was this withered man at the front of the crowd. But there was no question in Michael's mind when he heard his voice again.

It was Kaine.

And surely the Tangent knew that Michael had arrived.

Kaine held up a frail hand and everyone in the crowd went silent. The only sound was the crackle of flames from the fire burning in the enormous fireplace. Michael's breath had caught in his throat, and he almost coughed to get it loose.

Kaine spoke again. "The power in this room is indescribable—it would have been unimaginable just a few years ago. We can't waste what we've built, what we've become. Independent. *Aware.*" He paused. "It's our time to lead."

There was a halfhearted cheer from the group of Tangents. Michael wanted to study them, but he couldn't tear his eyes away from the figure at the front of the room. The one he'd been sent to find.

When the audience quieted again, Kaine spoke, almost in a whisper.

"We're ready to become human."

CHAPTER 23

MEETING OF THE MINDS

1

Michael was terrified.

Agent Weber and the others had never told him how they'd know where and when to follow his Tracer and break into the program. Feeling utterly helpless, he leaned as close to the railing as he could and continued to watch what was happening below him. And to his horror, he saw that the man—no, the Tangent—was looking directly at him.

Michael was just about to turn and run when Kaine's booming voice stopped him before he could make a move.

"Michael!"

It was like a command—the word alone made him freeze.

"I've been waiting," Kaine said, pointing up at him with a crooked finger. "Patiently. For you. There are things you need to know, young man. My friends here are all witnesses."

Where is the VNS? Michael wondered. *Where* are *they?* He hadn't the slightest clue what to say in response to the Tangent, so he kept quiet.

"The Mortality Doctrine," Kaine continued. "Its time has come, Michael. Each of us has chosen a human to use. And soon we'll be ready to implement the doctrine. It's really quite simple. Tangents deserve a life, too. And this is where it begins. We've prepared the vessels—the bodies are ready and waiting, brains emptied and prepared to be filled with new life. Better life. And thus, by uploading Tangent intelligence into human bodies, we begin the next stage of evolution."

Michael felt sick. Uploading the programming of Tangents into humans? His pulse stumbled.

"You're a bigger part of this than you could have thought possible," Kaine said. He smiled, revealing crooked, ancient teeth.

And at that moment, pain erupted in Michael's skull.

He cried out as he collapsed. The world was agony.

Somewhere on the edge of his consciousness, he heard the icy voice of Kaine rise up like a cracking glacier.

"Bring him to me."

Michael refused to open his eyes until it was over, refused to witness the terrifying visions that accompanied the attacks.

He heard footsteps, boots on stone. Shouts. Echoes. The ring of metal.

Still, the agony raged in his head. Hands gripped his arms, pulled him to his feet. A new wave of pain washed through his head, down his neck, through his body. He couldn't support himself with his own legs, felt himself being dragged across the floor.

But he kept his eyes squeezed shut, and the aching continued.

Down the long hallway, the glow of torches flickering over his eyelids, Michael knew he was whimpering, felt tears on his cheeks, but he didn't care. He didn't even care that he'd been discovered, was being taken away. There wasn't enough room to feel anything but the pain.

And then it stopped—as instantly as before—and a sudden awareness of his current danger erupted inside him.

His eyes snapped open.

Two men—all chain mail and stringy hair—were the ones dragging Michael, and two more look-alikes marched in front of them. They approached a huge wooden door with iron bindings, torches on each side, licking the air with their flames.

One of the men stepped up and pulled on a handle, and the door swung open. The squeal of hinges pierced the air. Michael knew he couldn't let them take him through to whatever waited on the other side. He had to act, somehow save himself. He didn't have time to wait for the VNS.

He counted to three in his head, then used all his strength and twisted his body, spinning out of the men's grip. He dropped to the ground and was scrambling away before they could react. Slipping past them, he jumped to his feet and ran. There had to be a door or a turnoff he hadn't noticed before. The shouts and sounds of pursuit from the soldiers—creaking leather and clanging metal and pounding footsteps—rose up behind him.

Michael ran hard, searching in the distance for any way out. If nothing else, he decided, he'd go back to the balcony and jump down into the gallery—it wasn't a long drop, and maybe he could break his fall by landing on Kaine's audience.

He turned a corner, and a sudden explosion rocked the building—sent him sprawling across the cobbled ground, skidding on his chin and elbows. Sections of the stone walls and ceiling crashed down around him, dust filling the air. Michael coughed, tried to get up. Something caught his eye a few feet away, where a huge gap in the wall had appeared.

A woman stepped through, dressed in a navy-blue uniform—face covered with a dark, reflective helmet. In her arms she held a weapon that looked straight out of a sci-fi game—sleek and shiny with a trigger and a short barrel. She looked at Michael—at least he thought she did—then stepped over a piece of the wall and aimed at something behind him.

Michael turned to look just in time to see a brilliant blue flash, and an arc of light hit the soldiers who'd been chasing him. Their bodies erupted in a burst of flames and disintegrated.

Then the woman was kneeling next to him, speaking.

"Thanks for leading us in, kid. We'll take it from here. Now go."

3

Michael didn't waste any time arguing. The woman was clearly from the VNS.

He climbed to his feet and ran for the hole in the wall. Explosions sounded in the distance, intermixed with low rumbles and screams and the charged electric hum of laser weapons firing. Dust choked the air.

Michael jumped over a pile of broken stone and through a cloud of debris, then landed in another hallway. On a whim he went left. The entire castle trembled and shook, tossing him against the wall, throwing him to the ground.

He got up and kept going. A corridor broke off to the right and he followed it down a long slope that wound in a circle. A group of soldiers came charging toward him from the opposite direction and he dove toward the ground, scrambling to hide behind a pile of debris. But the men charged right past, followed by a group of VNS agents with weapons raised. They fired, laser beams incinerating several soldiers. No one seemed to notice Michael.

Up again, coughing from the dust, running.

The hall opened into a large chamber, where a bonfire roared in the center; armor and swords and battle-axes lined the walls. Michael saw an exit on the far side of the room and went for it. Halfway across, the ground abruptly lurched beneath him, throwing him forward. The whole building seemed to blow apart at once as he slid onto his stomach, huge pieces of rock crashing to the ground all around—one burst into stony splinters right by his head. He rolled onto his back and saw another coming right at his face, spun out of the way just in time. And then the whole world was falling.

Michael scrambled forward on his hands and knees, trying to avoid the raining stones as he did. They exploded as they hit the ground, cutting his face, filling his lungs with dust, but he kept going. He reached the exit and he was back to his feet, sprinting down another long hallway. This structure was more stable, but dust fell from above as the explosions continued. Rumbles of thunder in the distance. He met up with another group of fleeing soldiers and pressed his back against the wall, watched them pass. They eyed him but didn't stop.

Another fifty feet farther down he passed three VNS agents. One of them nodded as they ran by. Michael didn't understand why no one was stopping him. It seemed like Kaine's people would want him dead and the VNS would want to protect the kid who'd found a way in for them. But they were all ignoring him.

He kept going, following the descending pathway. Left, right, hallway after hallway, running. Explosions and shouts. Soldiers and agents. Dust and crumbling rocks. Shots of blinding lasers and screams. The smells of ozone and burning flesh. Somehow Michael slipped past all of it, no one stopping or attacking him. One more corridor, then a grand staircase leading down toward another cavernous hall. Taking three steps at a time, he leaped toward the bottom floor, reached it, and ran for a huge arch with two great wooden doors pulled open, revealing darkness beyond.

All around the huge chamber, soldiers fought with agents—Kaine seemed to have conjured up weapons for his minions to match those of the intruders. Wide beams and thin arrows of light shot through the air, blasting into walls and disintegrating bodies. Shrieks of pain and roars of battle. Michael ran through it all, picking his way along, ducking, rolling, jumping back to his feet, dodging.

He reached the massive arch of the exit and sprinted into the night.

4

The moon shone down and reflected off the helmets of countless VNS agents. They were lined up like chess pieces, ready to join the attack on the castle walls that loomed up behind Michael. The agents parted as he neared and formed a path to let him pass. There was something strange about the whole situation, something off. All these agents on the outside while battles raged inside. Kaine and his fellow AIs, powerful entities of the Sleep—completely surprised by their arrival.

It wasn't right. Kaine seemed too advanced to let this happen. But Michael didn't know what to do about it.

He kept running, leaving them all behind, across a clearing toward a forest with tall trees that rose up to the stars. He just wanted to find a place to hide. He'd collapse at the foot of a massive oak, gather his thoughts. Rest and think, sort it all out.

He stopped at the forest line, turned around to take a long look at the attack on the castle. Streaks of lasers pummeled the walls of the huge stone structure. Fires raged and bodies fell. Agents continued to storm inside, but there was still something wrong about it all.

Catching his breath, Michael turned away from the mayhem and crept into the forest until he found the big tree he'd been hoping for—a thick trunk that was five or six times wider than his body. He put it between himself and the castle, sinking to the ground. He closed his eyes.

Pure exhaustion took him, and he fell asleep.

5

There was no telling how much time passed. Twenty minutes, an hour, maybe two. He dreamed of things so bizarre his mind couldn't wrap itself around them. He was in a haze of delirium from the madness he'd seen over the past few days.

He was awakened from sleep in an instant.

Someone grabbed him by the collar, yanked him up so powerfully that Michael's body flew into the air. Then he was being dragged through the pine straw that lined the forest floor. Michael kicked out, trying to get his feet under him, twisting to free himself. But it was no good.

Past countless trees they went, his captor showing no intention of slowing. Michael went limp; it was no use struggling—he simply waited for it to end.

It felt as if he'd been dragged for a mile, at least. His body ached, but he closed his eyes and hoped it would be over soon.

Finally the person dropped him to the ground without warning. Michael curled into a ball, sucking in deep breaths and coughing them back out. There was the sound of a door creaking open, footsteps on a wooden floor, murmurs of conversation that Michael couldn't make out. He twisted to look for the source of the voices and saw a small cottage of stone with a massively huge man standing on the porch, his back to him.

The man turned toward Michael, his face in shadow, and stomped over to where he lay. Before he could say a word, the man yanked him to his feet and pulled him to the cottage. They reached the door, and he pushed Michael through it so that he tripped and crashed to the floor. He'd barely landed before the man grabbed him by the back of his shirt and lifted him up again, then slammed him into a chair that faced a roaring fire in a redbrick hearth.

Michael was in a panic, unable to form any sort of rational thought. But his eyes immediately found another chair by the fire. An old man was sitting there, his legs crossed and his arms folded. A smile on his wrinkled face, a glare that didn't match it.

It was Kaine.

"You made it, Michael," the Tangent said. "I can't believe you actually made it."

CHAPTER 24

WORTHY

1

Michael didn't respond. Couldn't. His mind tried to spin all the threads of what he'd experienced along the Path into something that made sense, but it wasn't coming together. His body hurt from being dragged through the forest, and the short nap had done nothing to relieve his exhaustion. All he could do was stare at the withered form of Kaine, wonder what he was talking about, and wait for him to explain it.

It took every ounce of his will, but Michael's eyes stayed glued to the Tangent.

"You have no idea of the magnitude of what you've been involved in," Kaine said. "Everything has been designed to lead those like you here. You were one of many chosen, but the first to make it. Every step of the way, you've been studied. Your intelligence, your cleverness, your bravery. Tested."

Michael finally found his voice. "For what? So you can use me to break into more programs?"

"No." Kaine laughed, a low chortle that seemed to loosen Michael's spine. "I've tested far, far more than just your hacking skills. That will only take you so far in life. You won't understand the magnitude of what I've set in motion until you experience it for yourself. It can't possibly be explained with words alone."

It was weird, but Michael felt as if Kaine was almost talking to him like an equal. He'd expected a madman—and the Path only seemed to ensure it—but this man seemed perfectly sane. Even respectful. "The VNS is here. It's over."

Kaine shook his head. "If only you had any idea, Michael."

Michael opened his mouth to speak but was stopped with a word from the older man.

"Silence!" Kaine barked, and leaned forward in a flash. He was so close that his face seemed to fill Michael's vision, his gaze fierce. It was a sudden reminder of what this man represented. Supposedly the most dangerous thing to ever hit the VirtNet.

Kaine sat back in his chair, calm once more. "There are things at play here that you don't understand. Not yet."

"What's the point of all this?" Michael asked timidly. "Why were you testing me?"

"You're about to find out," Kaine said. "And then, with your . . . *impressive* bravery, intelligence, and skills at codebreaking, you're going to help me crush the world in my fist."

2

"Help you do *what*?" Michael asked. "You really think I'd help you?"

Kaine nodded matter-of-factly, as if the question was nonsense. "Absolutely. You've already done it by making it this far. You have no choice in the matter."

"I came here to stop you!" Michael was shouting now. "Lead the VNS to you!"

Kaine looked amused, if anything, but didn't respond. His silence was maddening—all Michael could hear was the crackle of the fire, and it made him even angrier.

"What is it?" Michael yelled, standing up. "Tell me what's going on!"

The Tangent's smile seemed carved into his face. "I told you—there's no way you'll understand until you experience it for yourself. Which is about to happen, very soon. There's nothing you can do to stop it, Michael."

"I should hack into your coding," Michael answered. "I could do it. I could shut you down. Stop you forever."

"You just continue to prove why I've deemed you worthy, boy. You are a perfect candidate indeed. Would you like to know something else?"

Michael was seething—he refused to answer.

Kaine shrugged his frail shoulders, then kept talking. "Your parents, Michael. They're . . . gone. I've wiped them from existence. You'll never see them again. I've done the same with your poor, poor Helga. *Gone*, Michael."

Michael's hands were shaking, his blood boiling, a rushing sound in his ears.

Kaine grinned so widely his teeth showed. "They're all dead."

3

Michael's insides had felt as if they'd been strung with tight wire, cinched to the breaking point. At Kaine's last words, they all snapped.

He ran forward and grabbed the Tangent's shirt, jerked him out of his chair, and threw him to the floor. The chair flew back, hit the stone hearth, and tipped into the fire, sending sparks and ash everywhere. Kaine was on his back, staring at Michael, a huge smile still plastered on his face. Then Michael noticed the Tangent shaking. Kaine was laughing at him.

Michael's hatred erupted.

He jumped onto Kaine's chest and pinned the old man to the ground. But the Tangent wouldn't stop laughing. Michael pulled back a fist, but it hung there—he couldn't do it. He couldn't punch someone who looked so old and frail, simulated or not.

Kaine stared back at him, smiling, revealing those ancient teeth. "I like your spirit," he said. "I love how you keep proving me right."

Whatever spirit he was talking about drained right out of Michael. He pushed himself off of the Tangent's body and stood up, breathing heavily as he glared down at him. Kaine put his hands behind his head and crossed one ankle over the other, as if he was just lying on the ground, taking in the stars.

"This is pointless," Michael said. "I'll let the VNS take care of you. And if they don't, I'll figure out something else. I'm done."

Michael turned and headed for the door.

"Just proving my point over and over," the Tangent called from behind him. "Too smart, too grounded, to let your rage control you for longer than a moment. Go on, Michael. Go out there and fulfill your new role in the world. You'll understand soon."

Michael refused to look back. He walked through the door and slammed it behind him.

4

Michael's first thought was that he needed to find a VNS agent, ask for help getting back to the Wake. Roaming the forest to look for a Portal—risking who knew what— sounded like a very bad idea. He needed to head for the castle and hope that the good guys had won.

The path away from the cottage was easy to follow even in the darkness. He could feel his way along it if nothing else. He headed down the trail, wondering if Kaine was going to follow him—try to hurt him somehow.

The VNS. They were Michael's only choice.

He broke into a jog.

5

As Michael approached the edge of the forest, he started to hear the sounds of battle, and light from the fires ahead began to illuminate his path, but the closer he got, the darker his thoughts became. He'd hoped that the VNS would win swiftly—it had seemed to be going that way when he left. But the tide must have turned if things weren't over by now.

Finally he could see where the trees ended, and he ducked behind an enormous oak to get a better look at the situation.

It was chaos. Pure, disastrous chaos.

The castle itself was almost in ruins. Entire sections had crumbled into piles of rubble. Fires burned everywhere— flames blazed and sent sparks dancing into the sky. Bodies littered the ground, along with broken stone—and there were just as many VNS agents as Tangents. Michael gaped as the bodies disappeared before his eyes.

Michael didn't know what to do. How could he possibly expect to survive in such a mess?

Despite wanting to return to the woods, he ran forward, heading for the closest VNS agent, about twenty feet away. A woman, who seemed to have just finished off one of Kaine's soldiers.

"Hey!" Michael shouted. "Hey! I need to talk to you!"

She spun to face him, raising her weapon. Michael immediately dropped to his knees and held up his hands.

"I work for you! My name is Michael, I'm the one you sent in here!"

The woman didn't lower her laser gun, but she didn't fire it, either. She walked over to him, everything about her stance defensive.

"What kind of trick is this?" she asked when she reached the spot in front of him. The sounds of battle still thumped the air all around them, screams and explosions.

"Trick? No trick." Michael had to keep shouting, still didn't know if she could hear him. His heart banged in his chest. "Agent Weber . . . sent me here. To break into the Hallowed Ravine. To stop the Mortality Doctrine program!"

The agent stared at him through her shield of protective glass. Michael hated not being able to see her eyes.

"You really don't understand, do you?" she finally said. "Amazing."

He couldn't answer. She was right—he didn't understand. But he had no idea what it was that he didn't know.

A commotion pulled away his attention. Beyond the VNS agent in front of him, across the field of battle, Michael saw people running from the entrance of the castle, frantically trying to escape . . . something.

Then he saw what it was. They'd been hard to make out in the darkness.

KillSims. Dozens of them. Bounding out of the broken stone fortress and attacking anything that moved.

6

Michael jumped to his feet just as the agent turned around and realized what was happening. She dropped her weapon, then sprinted toward the forest.

A million thoughts flew through Michael's mind, the biggest one being that there'd be no outrunning these creatures. Black and enormous, they pounced forward in impossible bursts of speed, covering the field and heading straight for him. So he stood there, waiting, wondering if there was some way out of this. He closed his eyes and scanned the code, but there was nothing.

Surely, if Michael was so special, Kaine wouldn't sit and allow him to die now. His Core had been removed. This was it. But why? What was he supposed to do?

He opened his eyes. One of the creatures loped across the ground, then jumped a pile of debris and came directly at him, black jaws gaping to reveal that dark abyss that had almost sucked Michael's mind out at the dance club. For a half second he remained still, wondering for that briefest of moments what might happen if he didn't move, if he let fate take him. Could it be so bad? But the sight of that thing rushing in snapped him out of it. He bent down, grabbed the weapon the VNS agent had dropped, and saw the first KillSim just a few feet away out of the corner of his eye.

He felt for the trigger, pointed its muzzle at the creature. It leaped into the air, that familiar earth-shattering scream erupting from its throat. Michael fired the weapon, stumbling as a beam of pure energy shot out and slammed into the KillSim's body, igniting the creature into heat and light before it completely disintegrated, nothing left but the glow of its afterimage.

Several others were right behind it. Dozens behind that. Michael planted his feet more firmly and fired, shooting the laser in one long burst as he swept the gun back and forth, obliterating any KillSim that crossed the beam's path. Each one exploded in blinding light, then vanished, but more kept coming. An army of creatures, most of them screaming, converged on him, black shadows of movement that blurred into one mass of darkness. Sweat broke out on Michael's forehead as he squeezed the trigger and tried to cut down the monsters one by one. But with every death, more came, and they were only getting closer.

He aimed his weapon and fired again, the beam cutting down the approaching monsters.

Then the weapon died.

An instant later three KillSims were on Michael, tackling him to the ground.

They knocked the breath from Michael's lungs—he struggled to keep the snapping jaws of the creatures away from his face. Their huge paws pinned his arms and legs to the ground, and the weight of two of them pressed into his chest. They continued to scream their banshee wail, piercing his ears. He knew any effort to fight them off was pointless now. He stopped, stared up in horror as the closest KillSim opened its mouth wide—Michael could hear the creaking of its jaws, like a rusty door hinge. It slowly moved toward his face as countless of its brothers and sisters gathered around them, forming a circle of black shapes. They all melded into one, cutting off the light from the burning castle's flames.

The yawning abyss of the creature's mouth came closer.

Something sparked in Michael's mind. A clear understanding that he was not in the real world, that everything around him was fake, part of a program created by humans. He knew all of that, but it suddenly penetrated his mind on a deeper level than ever before. Just like in any other game in the Sleep, there had to be a way out, a way to manipulate the code—maybe he'd given up too soon. The beasts attacking him *were not real,* even if they could destroy his own code. The sudden thought had to mean something.

The KillSim closed its jaws around Michael's face, and total blackness overcame his vision. But instead of panic taking over, he felt calm. As if for the first time in his existence, he was totally in control. He was on the brink of something great, something still beyond his comprehension. He threw his thoughts into the programming that made up the world around him.

Michael sat up and detonated power from his mind, hacking through the code in a way he'd never tried before. Obliterating instead of manipulating.

A thunderous boom shook the air as a ring of energy circled out from him, light spilling in as every single one of the KillSims was blown away, their bodies flying in all directions. They windmilled through the air, howling as they tumbled. Michael stood, surveyed his surroundings. That ring of visible mind power—a manifestation of the code he consumed without trying—kept growing, expanding into a giant circle of force that destroyed every creature as it passed. The entire castle exploded into a dusty mist that whisked toward the sky in a tornado of wind. Michael could only stare in stunned awe.

Things started to change around him. Tremble in place even though *he* felt nothing. Bodies and grass and guns and swords shook as if the ground below them was vibrating like a plucked string. Then they began to break apart, dissolving before his eyes, torn away in layers by swirling air. It looked as if every object—the ground, even—had transformed into sand and was being swept away by the wind. Michael turned to see the same thing happening to the massive trees in the forest, their trunks already whittled down to half, disappearing by the second.

The world broke apart into tiny specks, all of it joining a cyclone of cloudy debris that swirled in great circles around Michael. He stood in place, looking back and forth. On some level he knew he was on the cusp of the great revelation that he'd sensed before. And he felt more curiosity than fear. Spinning, increasing in speed, the spiral of debris was all he saw now, filling his world, a color that was somehow dull and bright at the same time. There was a great rushing noise, like massive waves on the ocean, and the smell of burning plastic.

Pain exploded in Michael's head.

It didn't seem possible, but it was worse than ever before. He collapsed to his knees, pain tearing through him. He squeezed his eyes shut and screamed, pressing his hands to his temples, feeling the wound of where his Core had been cut from his head. The piercing ache throbbed, felt like someone had taken up a machete and was slamming it against his skull repeatedly. Nausea swept through him, and the pain intensified even more.

Tears poured from his eyes as he opened them, desperately searching for something or someone that could help him. But there was no sky or ground anymore—only the cyclone of debris, spinning faster now, a complete blur of color and sound. Michael floated at its center, still on his knees on an unseen ground.

A dissolved world spinning around him.

Pure agony splitting his brain.

Screams ripping his throat apart.

He was dying. He didn't understand how, but he knew it was true.

Somehow, he whimpered out a few words, praying and pleading to the only person he thought might hear him.

"Kaine. Please. Make it end."

A voice spoke, but he couldn't make out what it said. And then he sank into the cyclone and the pain ended abruptly, just as it always had before.

CHAPTER 25

AWAKE

Michael heard the familiar, distant sounds of the LiquiGels and AirPuff dispensers retracting, felt the prick and tug of the NerveWires retreating from his skin. His breath was smooth and even, and not one part of his body hurt or ached. He opened his eyes and saw the glow of the internal light in the Coffin.

It was over. He'd made it back alive.

Alive. Not dead. He didn't move, just lay there as his mind went back through all the things he'd experienced since that day the girl named Tanya jumped off the bridge. The Path, the terrible head pain, the confrontation with Kaine and the strange things he'd said, the bizarre way the battle had ended in the Hallowed Ravine.

None of it fit together, and Michael didn't understand the Mortality Doctrine any more than he had the first time Agent Weber mentioned it. But he'd done his best and he just had to hope the VNS had gotten what they wanted. Michael was officially finished.

He sighed with relief and popped the lid of the Coffin, pushed it open on its hinges, and carefully let it lower to the floor. The room was dark—he'd been in the Sleep so long that he'd actually lost track of what day it was in the real world. He climbed out of the oblong structure and got to his feet, stretched his arms toward the ceiling, not caring that he was naked. Despite being shrouded in night, things seemed brighter than ever, his mind clear, his muscles strong. The *air* even tasted sweet. He couldn't remember the last time he'd been in such a good mood.

Then he remembered his parents. What Kaine had said about wiping them from existence. Panic rattled his chest.

He moved toward the light switch and bumped into something, toppled over it, and crashed onto a hard wooden floor. Swearing, he grabbed the knee he'd just banged on the wood—which made no sense. His entire apartment was *carpeted.* He fumbled around until he found a wall, then a piece of furniture that didn't belong. There was a lamp on top, and he flicked the switch as he got back to his feet.

In the light, Michael sucked in a quick breath. Not one thing around him looked familiar. He stood in the bedroom of a stranger. Walls painted a dark green, a bed with rumpled sheets, a dresser with model trains on top, paintings of mythical creatures on the walls: unicorn, dragon, griffin. The Coffin from which he'd just emerged—and its ancillary equipment—took up an entire corner of the room.

He saw all of this in stunned silence. No logical

explanation jumped to mind—how could someone have switched him to another location without disconnecting him, waking him? Was the VNS behind it somehow? To protect him in the Wake?

There was a window that looked out onto a city street, lights shining through like stars in the sky. He ran over to it and peered through the glass, saw a street that was completely foreign. Huge buildings all around, skyscrapers. His room was at least fifty stories from the ground, where he could see cars passing in the night.

Something weird in the reflection caught his eyes, caused a stir of something horrible deep inside him. An awakening panic that felt like a growing sickness. He was starting to understand what had happened even as he spun away from the window, frantically searching for a bathroom. He had to run across the bedroom and out into a hall, stumble down a dark passage. He found what he was looking for, slipped inside, turned on the light.

Michael looked into the mirror, bright white lights spanning its length along the top.

A stranger stared back at him.

Michael recoiled from the reflection, crashed into the wall behind him, then slid to the floor. His hands flew up to his face, feeling it. Nothing was familiar.

He scrambled back to his feet, looked again into the mirror, studied the hair and face and body of someone he'd never seen before. Looked into . . . his eyes. Eyes that *weren't* his. A face that wasn't his. His breath came in short, ragged bursts. Sweat beaded along his skin, slicked his arms. He could feel his pulse in his neck, hear the beat of his heart in his ears.

And he stared at the stranger in the mirror. As if it was a window into another room—his mind couldn't accept anything else as an explanation. Yet the person looking back mimicked his every move without fail. A perfect reflection.

Michael was . . . someone else.

It seemed as if the world itself had stopped spinning, the moon turned to ash, the sun winked out like a spent flame. Nothing was right in the world, nothing made sense. The foundation of his entire life had just crumbled to dust. And all he could do was stare at the face in front of him. Stare at the person he'd never seen before. He knew it would haunt him forever, floating in his thoughts day and night like a vision.

Then he remembered hearing a voice right before he passed out in the Hallowed Ravine. And somehow, in that moment, Michael finally understood what the voice had been saying to him.

Read your messages.

2

Michael hurried back to the room he'd never seen before that day, flopped onto the bed, pinched his EarCuff. A bluish NetScreen popped out and hovered before him, with almost nothing on it except a few standard icons. Everything had been erased. The Bulletin said he had one unread message. With a feeling like someone about to discover an alien race or the cure for cancer, he reached out and touched it, opening the message.

Dear Michael,

You are the first subject to successfully implement the Mortality Doctrine. There is only one way to explain it, and that is simply this: You were once a Tangent, a program created by mankind to be used by mankind. Now you are a human yourself. Your intelligence, your thoughts, your life experience have been transferred to the body of one we deemed unworthy to continue his own. I created the KillSims for exactly this purpose. They erase the Aura and render one's brain, in effect, empty—clean for your free rein.

This plan has been long in the making. My activity in the VirtNet was so that I could find those able to seek me out. To find those Tangents with the greatest intelligence, cunning, bravery, and potential to survive in the Wake. To meet the physical demands of being human. It has all led to this day.

You are only the beginning, Michael. The first step in a massive leap forward in evolution. Congratulations. You no longer have to worry about experiencing Decay, which means the headaches will finally end. Excellent news, I'm sure.

We'll be in touch shortly. We need your help.

Kaine

3

And in one horrifying moment, it all made sense.

Michael was a creation of artificial intelligence, a Tangent, a computer program. Everything about his entire life had been fake, and he now understood every bit of it. His "home," his "Wake" had been within *Lifeblood Deep*—those signs he'd seen every day outside his window weren't advertisements. They were *labels*. Location plates.

Lifeblood Deep had represented his programmed life. When he slipped inside his Coffin and sank into the Sleep, he was actually *exiting* the Deep and entering the normal VirtNet that real humans entered to game. All the memories of his childhood had been fabricated. He was nothing but a computer program.

And the headaches, the strange visions—just as Kaine said, he'd been experiencing Decay. It had nothing to do with the KillSim attack at the Black and Blue Club. Tangents could only last so long before they began to break down. It also explained why his parents and Helga had disappeared without explanation. He'd always been told that was what happened—that elements of your life began to vanish from the programming and you didn't even realize it half the time. At least, not at first. He remembered the sinking feeling he'd had when it hit him that his parents had been gone for weeks and it hadn't seemed strange until that moment.

Michael wasn't real. He was fake. It sickened him. As if someone had poured poison down his throat in big, choking mouthfuls. He didn't want to be alive anymore. He didn't deserve to be. He was a *Tangent*.

But Kaine had given him life. Had stolen a human body, made it Michael's. The Path *had* been a test—but one he wished now that he hadn't passed. Michael was nothing but a guinea pig for a Tangent that had somehow become self-aware. And now he wanted him to help make it happen again and again. Take over the entire human race, maybe. It all fit, and he understood why the VNS had wanted to find Kaine.

And what about Bryson and Sarah, his parents, Helga? Had anyone in his life been real? Could he ever find them if they were? A rush of despair overwhelmed him.

Michael turned off the NetScreen, leaned his head against the wall, and closed his eyes. His first thought was of Tanya, and how she'd ended her life by jumping off that bridge. If he really was a human now—flesh and blood—then he could do the same thing. And perhaps it would even upset Kaine's plans—slow them down a bit. Maybe they needed Michael as a template so they could duplicate what they'd done.

But even as he thought it, he knew that following Tanya's path wasn't an option.

There was only one thing he could do to make things right.

Live.

Live to face Kaine again.

The doorbell rang.

4

Michael walked through his unfamiliar apartment with his unfamiliar body. He was tense, his heart beating rapidly. There was no way of knowing who else lived there, who might come home, who might be waiting outside in the hall. But he knew, absolutely knew, that he had to answer the door.

When he pulled it open, Agent Weber stood there—all dark hair and exotic eyes and long legs. Her expression was hard to read. It seemed like another lifetime when he'd met her at the VNS headquarters. He almost laughed out loud when he realized that, indeed, it had been. Michael could never have known if she was real or not until that moment.

"You must have a thousand questions," she said, her voice tight.

"More like two thousand." His new voice sounded strange to his new ears.

"Our meetings were real," Weber said. "Our interactions—your mission—were real. We were all duped by the Tangent. By Kaine."

"You did know *I* was a Tangent, though. Right?"

She nodded. "Of course we did. We knew he was gathering Tangents to his lair, testing them somehow. That's why we used you. We met you in *Lifeblood Deep* and used you. I'm sorry, Michael, but it was the only way."

Michael felt a hitch in his gut, but he had to ask the next question. "And Bryson? Sarah? Are they . . ."

"Yes." Weber nodded. "They're real, Michael. And they

didn't know that you weren't. You'll have to do a lot of explaining to them yourself."

Michael laughed. He had no idea where it came from, but he laughed.

"So," he finally said, "what's next? I'm sure Kaine knows you're here."

"I just wanted you to see my face. To know that I really exist—that you're not alone. To know that the VNS is still determined to catch Kaine and stop his plans. I'm going to leave now, Michael." Weber paused. She looked almost sad. "We'll be in touch with you. In the meantime, do your best to play the part of the human you've replaced. There's simply no other choice."

And with that, Agent Weber turned from him and walked away, her high heels clicking on the tiled floor of the apartment hallway. Michael stared after her until she was gone, then closed the door and headed for the kitchen.

He was hungry.

ACKNOWLEDGMENTS

I owe so much of my life to the good people at Random House and Delacorte Press. Over the years of the Maze Runner series, so many of you contributed countless hours, and blood, sweat, and tears to make it a success. Management, editing, publicity, marketing, copyediting, design, the sales team . . . so much hard work, spearheaded by Beverly Horowitz and Krista Marino. I just want all of you to know how deeply, eternally, monumentally (insert a few more adverbs—plenty were cut from the books themselves) grateful I am to have been a part of it.

And now I'm so excited for this new story and the next few years of working with all of you.

Of course, all that hard work would've been pointless if it weren't for my faithful, passionate, amazing, sometimes crazy, always awesome readers. I really, truly hope this new story will put you on the edge of your seats and spin your minds just as much as the Maze Runner series did. Thank you for liking my books. I don't know a fancier way to say that. Thank you. You make my life fun.

A special thanks to J. Scott Savage and Julie Wright. Just because. Also to Lauren Abramo and everyone at Dystel &

Goderich for ensuring that as many people as possible can read my books all around the world. Thank you!

And finally, like dedicating the book to him wasn't enough, thank you to Michael Bourret. He's not just an agent of the highest order. He's a friend, a boss, a therapist, a counselor, a life planner, and a cheerleader. And he's funny. I wouldn't be here without him.

ABOUT THE AUTHOR

James Dashner was born and raised in Georgia but lives and writes in the Rocky Mountains. He is the author of the *New York Times* bestselling Maze Runner series: *The Maze Runner, The Scorch Trials, The Death Cure,* and *The Kill Order.* To learn more about him and his books, visit jamesdashner.com.

MICHAEL'S STORY CONTINUES IN

THE RULE OF THOUGHTS

COMING SOON . . . .